T0082734

GENETIC
IMPERATIVE

GENETIC
IMPERATIVE

JIM MILLER

GENETIC IMPERATIVE

Copyright © 2021 Jim Miller.

All rights reserved. No part of this book may be used or reproduced by any means, graphic, electronic, or mechanical, including photocopying, recording, taping or by any information storage retrieval system without the written permission of the author except in the case of brief quotations embodied in critical articles and reviews.

iUniverse books may be ordered through booksellers or by contacting:

iUniverse
1663 Liberty Drive
Bloomington, IN 47403
www.iuniverse.com
844-349-9409

Because of the dynamic nature of the Internet, any web addresses or links contained in this book may have changed since publication and may no longer be valid. The views expressed in this work are solely those of the author and do not necessarily reflect the views of the publisher, and the publisher hereby disclaims any responsibility for them.

Any people depicted in stock imagery provided by Getty Images are models, and such images are being used for illustrative purposes only.
Certain stock imagery © Getty Images.

ISBN: 978-1-6632-2080-6 (sc)
ISBN: 978-1-6632-2081-3 (e)

Print information available on the last page.

iUniverse rev. date: 03/31/2021

FOREWORD

The history of humankind is a rising graph of productivity. The first real humans were certainly nomadic hunter-gatherers barely sustaining life. After many millenniums they developed weapons and basic tools, began hunting game, tanning hides and making bone implements. Then came agriculture, and with it, better tools that greatly increased productivity, yielding more abundant food and that led to stable communities. Gradually, the manufacture of tools became even more sophisticated leading to powerful machines that made more and better products. But human power, particularly slave labor, remained the most important factor for centuries.

As the machinery got better and better, more complex machines took over more and more duties. The industrial age grew into the information age. Now machines were making decisions, amassing huge memory storage and handling complex algorithms. The Information age saw the merging of all the previous improvements into the developing age of automation. Now machines could do almost anything a human could and do it faster, better without human error.

So now the critical question: *Who* will make the decisions; who will benefit; and who…or what…will rule the world?

If men were angels, no government would be necessary.
If angels were to govern men, neither external nor
internal controls on government would be necessary.

James Madison Federalist Papers

CHAPTER ONE

Thirty Eight Thousand Feet Over Winslow, Arizona

Captain Mat McCoy was nobody's idea of a hero. A quiet, overly conscientious pilot, he tended to obsess over details, and he did *not* like turbulence in his flying or in his life. Tonight, he had both. As he threaded his way through storm clouds in a broken-down Boeing 747 freighter, the last thing he expected was that he was about to be propelled by events that would force him to first to save his plane, and then his country and then, maybe even the world.

He had been called out for an unscheduled flight just as he was climbing into bed. Even worse, he was flying with a bickering copilot and flight engineer who just could not get along. Mat sat back in his seat, sighed and used an alcohol wipe on his hands. He did that when he was nervous.

A jolt rattled the forty-year-old airplane. Mat had just reached for his coffee cup as the plane bounced and sent the liquid splashing. "Damn it. This is a fresh shirt." He flicked a hand to disperse coffee from his chest. It would stain - no doubt about it. *He didn't need this aggravation.* Still, he was making double pay for this no-notice midnight trip and his airline, Silver Streak, was notoriously stingy with their cash. For that much money he could put up with a lot.

Sharon, the flight engineer, breathed out hard as the plane pitched. "Man, I hope this rust bucket holds together. These old gas-guzzling legacy planes should have been retired years ago."

Copilot John Cook slouched in the right seat. His accent was thick, and it wasn't the solicitous, sweet drawl of a southern politician. It was hard-edged, self-righteous redneck. "Listen, Sweetie, the only reason you got a job is 'cause Silver Streak is still flying these old junkyard dogs. In newer airplanes the flight engineer's job, your job, is handled by a computer chip no bigger'n the one in my watch." He held up his wrist in the dark cockpit.

Sharon was a new hire. Fresh and eager to move up the airline hierarchy, she was eager and young and pretty. "Wow," she feigned amazement. "That's a really big wristwatch. You must be even older than I thought. How come you're still a copilot?"

John spoke through clenched teeth. "Because this damned industry thrives on failure. Every time the economy dips, they declare bankruptcy and reorganize, firing everyone, defaulting on debts and contracts. I've worked for TWA, Continental and Delta. All of them took my pension and kicked me to the street to start over at the bottom. You don't know how lucky you are to get hired here. I'm for sure you don't have the experience or flying hours to get on with a major airline. But then, hiring you probably met a whole bunch of quotas."

"You mean because I'm black?"

He shrugged. "And female and young and probably low income…"

"Hey," Mat interrupted, "you can't accuse Silver Streak of rational thinking in their hiring practices. With the pilot shortage, they were probably thrilled to find someone as motivated as Sharon to be a flight engineer."

She thought for a moment and asked, "So, just how many other airlines do still have flight engineers?"

Mat tore open another alcohol wipe. "Well, not many; just us, some third world airlines…and the Air Force."

She seemed interested. "The Air Force?"

"Yes, they have several 747's that use engineers including Air Force One, the President's plane. It's a two hundred model, just like ours."

"How cool. I could be working on Air Force One."

Copilot John came back. "Well, yah not. Yah on this flying garbage truck. Now how 'bout you get me a cup of coffee." He held up a paper cup."

Sharon sighed. "How do you take it?"

"Like my women." He snickered.

She reached up between the pilots and took his cup. "You mean hot and black? How clever. Say, do you still pay your Klan dues?"

Mat had enough. "All right, you two, cut it out. We have work to do and the radar display is really lighting up, so tighten your seat belts and pay attention. I see some pretty big storm cells on both sides. We may have to deviate…" He was cut short by a wind shear that rattled the plane and made the airspeed jump ten knots.

Now, coffee forgotten, the three of them hunkered in seats close enough to touch one another, Mat on the left, John Cook on the right and Sharon sideways behind him facing her elaborate panel of gauges.

A distant flash of lightning lit the cockpit for just an instant. It was as cramped and dingy as a broom closet, but this closet was jammed with banks of warning lights, switches and circuit breakers, all fronted by enormous three-inch-thick, sharply-angled windows.

Despite the high-tech look, it smelled from decades of close human occupation. Generations of pilots sat in the same fabric-covered seats to litter, sweat and spill food. If the cockpit had ever been cleaned it didn't show. Crevices held moldering bits of tissue, dental floss and alcohol wipes. Bored pilots had, over the years, unscrewed blank metal panels to draw dirty pictures and sayings on them so other bored pilots could take them apart and have a laugh at the dusty graffiti.

John, the copilot, made an offhand comment. "She is right. This tub is pretty damned old to be banging around in this turbulence. Might come apart any time."

3

Mat used the alcohol wipe on his hands. "This old bird has lasted through worse."

Another jolt that made oxygen mask hoses flap and papers float in the air. It was a particularly hard smack that compressed Mat's spine. He recovered and leaned over his brightly colored radar scan. "I don't see anything real close. There are thunderstorm cells on both sides of us. I'm continuing straight ahead."

John moaned. He was an accomplished moaner. "Yeah, but we're in and out of clouds. Maybe we should climb and slow down."

They were interrupted by a chime like an elevator door and an automated woman's voice that announced, "Cargo smoke detected." The voice had no more emotion than that elevator announcing "third floor."

Mat pulled himself upright and commanded, "Main deck cargo smoke checklist."

John too lurched to sit up straight and Sharon started reciting the memorized items as she opened her laminated checklist. Her voice was clipped and professional.

"Oxygen masks and regulators- On, one hundred percent."

Mat replied, "Not required, continue."

"Smoke goggles - on."

"Not required, continue."

"Inspect main cargo deck through viewing port." She put down her checklist. "I'm going back now."

Mat turned in his seat to face her. "Okay, yell back to me."

She shot him a look as if to say, *I know what I'm doing.* Then she took off her seatbelts and walked unsteadily through the dark, vacant space that had once been the first-class cabin back when this battered old plane was a passenger liner. This was the hump on the 747's back. Now, it was empty except for a couple of seats for extra crewmembers and some spare parts. Insulation had been removed to save weight, so it sounded like a wailing wind tunnel. She steadied herself and fought to keep her balance as the plane burbled.

Mat saw her bend to look through the viewing port on the cabin's back wall. It was just a six-inch Plexiglas square, yellowed with age around the edge. She had to move her head left and right to scan the whole area below. He knew she wouldn't see much, just twin rows of ten-foot-square plastic shipping containers packed together like bricks without mortar. Plain white plastic under brilliant lights, they always looked stark, sterile.

She yelled back to Mat with all her might. "I don't see anything unusual, certainly no smoke."

He turned forward in his seat, checked the radar again and grimaced before shouting, "Okay, don the PBE, take a crash axe and Halon fire extinguisher and inspect the main deck."

John sat up straight now. "You want me to go, boss? She's awful inexperienced."

"No." Mat tried to sound confident. "It's her job. I need to let her do it."

"Yeh, but that's an awfully big area and it's full 'a stuff that could hurt a girl like her. Just the cargo restraint system on the floor alone could rip her up if she fell. Nobody'd ever know if I went instead of her."

"She would know, and she would think I didn't trust her."

John threw up his hands. "Okay boss, she's your flight engineer. I was just making an offer is all."

Sharon returned to the cockpit and began attaching equipment. The fire extinguisher had a shoulder strap. The oxygen bottle had a strap, a hose, a facemask and a belt. The axe was a miniature fireman's tool with a hatchet blade on the front and a bent spike on the rear. She put on gloves and headset and stood for inspection before climbing down the precarious folding ladder to the main cargo deck.

Mat nodded approval. She looked small and vulnerable with all those cords, straps and hoses dangling but her smile seemed confident.

"Okay now. Be careful. There's only about two feet of space between the containers and the fuselage walls and they're full of protruding supports and hangers and other stuff to snag you. If you get hung up, don't panic. Just take your time and disconnect any caught strap or whatever. There are old flight attendant call stations from the plane's passenger days. Use those to check in at mid-plane and from the aft bulkhead so we know you're all right. Got it?"

"Yes, daddy, and I'll be in before curfew." She smiled with perfect teeth that shone even in the darkened cockpit.

So young. Mat wondered what his daughter would look like at that age. "Don't be a smart ass. Just be careful. Okay?"

Sharon turned away and lifted a trap door in the cockpit floor that led down to a cavernous cargo deck. Banks of lights from below glared up into the upper deck like a searchlight beam. The folding aluminum ladder-stair leading down was rickety even on the ground. In a heaving airplane it would be more challenging, particularly encumbered by her mask, hoses, oxygen bottle and other equipment.

Both pilots watched her go. After she disappeared, John turned and said, "I gotta say she's got a cute ass on her but then, they tend to have…"

Mat glowered in the faint light of cockpit instruments. "Back to the checklist, John."

Now it was the copilot who read dutifully, reviewing a series of challenge and response items. That done, they sat in silence. Behind them, that shaft of light from the open trap door silently reminded both that Sharon was down there all alone.

Mat keyed his radio button, "Albuquerque Center, this is Silver Streak 822, we're investigating a possible cargo smoke indication. We'll keep you advised. Also, the turbulence here at flight level three-eight-zero is much worse than forecast. Do you have any ride reports from other altitudes?"

The radio crackled back. "Copy that Silver Streak 822. Keep us advised. As for ride reports, I don't have much traffic at this time of night. FEDEX reported moderate chop at three-five-oh. He was ten south of your flight path about fifteen minutes ago. And, uh wait, I'm just getting an update that the National Weather Service. There was a slight pause. "Okay, they're upgrading their prediction for your flight path to severe turbulence at all altitudes above two nine zero for the next eighty miles. Are you requesting descent?"

Without a moment's hesitation, Mat shot back. "Affirmative. Silver Streak 822 requests immediate descent to flight level two-eight-zero or lower."

"Roger. Stand by."

Mat turned to his copilot. "Good, maybe we can get out of this."

His words were cut short. The airplane lurched as though it had hit a wall, the jolt so violent it threw Mat forward into the control yoke and ripped off his headset. Then the plane rolled into a steep turn and the nose pitched down making everything, including humans weightless. Papers, books, and debris floated in air. The copilot's tablet computer bounced off a window and shattered. Only their seatbelts, loosened to relax during cruise flight, kept the two men from doing the same.

Bright overhead emergency lights snapped on and a pleasant "bing-dong" chime was followed by an equally pleasant automated voice announcing, "Autopilot disconnected." It was like someone saying "Have a nice day" in the midst of an artillery barrage. The overspeed warning horn shrieked an insistent "beep-beep-beep."

Mat grabbed the control yoke just as the weightlessness reversed into a roller coaster bottoming out. He sagged against the G-force but righted the plane. They were still being slammed by one shock after another. He clawed for his headset but couldn't find it. Now the control yoke vibrated as a stick shaker warned of *low-speed* stall. His airspeed indicator was unreadable with the needle bouncing up and down.

There was a corded microphone by his left leg. Mat grabbed it with one hand while keeping a death grip on the flight controls to fight the bucking-bronco of an airplane. "Mayday, mayday, Silver Streak 822 experiencing extreme turbulence, departing three-eight-zero in emergency descent. Request you clear all traffic."

An overhead speaker crackled. "Roger your emergency, Silver Streak. You're cleared unrestricted descent. Be advised minimum safe altitude in your area is thirteen thousand three hundred feet. You have no traffic. Advise your altitude when level."

Mat fought as the yoke jerked in his hands. "Speed brakes to flight position," he shouted. John moved the lever. Their airspeed indicator was still unreadable, bouncing wildly as the plane pitched and wobbled with stomach-turning gyrations like a lifeboat in a hurricane. For long minutes they heaved and lurched and then…it all stopped. Everything smoothed out and Mat brought the airplane to level flight.

In the chaos, neither pilot noticed the red warning light on their overhead panel but now they saw it – "Cargo Fire Warning."

"We've gone from cargo smoke to cargo fire warning," John blurted, almost in disbelief.

"Damn it, John. Go back there and find Sharon."

"Mat, you know I can't do that. It's against Federal Air Regulations for a primary pilot to be alone in the cockpit especially during…"

Normally reticent Captain Mat McCoy reached over, grabbed the thick copilot's shoulder and hissed, "Go now." Then without breaking eye contact, he picked up the mic and nearly shouted, "Center, Silver Streak 822 is declaring additional emergency. We are level two-two-zero with a cargo fire warning. Request diversion to the nearest airport that can handle a seven four."

The controller came back crisp and precise. "Silver Streak 822, copy your emergency. You are cleared left turn heading two zero zero and then direct Phoenix for either west runway. Descend to eight thousand feet on altimeter two niner eight eight. Expect lower in twenty-five miles. When able, say number of souls on board and fuel remaining"

John threw off his shoulder harness and slammed his seat back to climb out. He gave Mat an angry scowl and muttered. "Not right. It's her responsibility. I shouldn't be leaving you alone."

"Just go."

John stomped to the hatch and down the stairs like a two-year-old on the verge of a tantrum. Mat, now alone in the cockpit, returned to a nervous scan of his instrument panel. There were no other warning lights of significance. He continued a controlled descent toward Phoenix, tuned in the weather info and set up for an approach. But his mind was on the cargo fire and what could happen. *Where was Sharon and why hadn't she checked in?*

It seemed forever until John lumbered back up the stairs, huffing and out of breath. He plopped into the copilot's seat and exhaled. "She's hurt, badly burned. A container right under the center wing fuel tank exploded. The fire is out. It may have burned itself out or been snuffed when we partially depressurized. Anyway, it's no longer a factor."

"What about Sharon? Where is she?"

John grimaced and looked away as though embarrassed. "I...I couldn't carry her up the stairs. I put her in the luggage bin."

"You did what?"

"Well...she's safe there. I strapped her in."

Mat stared in disgust but there was no more time for conversation. As they neared Phoenix the workload got too busy. Radio calls, text messages, navigation displays, checklists, and just flying the airplane required total attention. And they had no flight engineer to control pressurization or properly set up the fuel panel.

After they landed and turned off the runway, Mat could see fire trucks, an ambulance, cargo loaders and an armada of other vehicles assembled and waiting. Two of those flashing fire trucks pulled out onto the runway and followed the plane as it taxied to the parking spot. There, Mat set the brake and cut the engines.

Beneath the cockpit he saw a pair of Silver Streak management men in white shirts and ties standing with arms folded, waiting. *Where did they come from at this hour of the morning?*

He shook his head. There was going to be a lot of explaining to be done. The stair truck was the first to pull up, even before the ten-foot-wide jet engines had finished winding down. As soon as Mat saw the "wheel chocks" sign from a ground crewman, he released the brakes, jumped out of his seat and clambered down the flimsy stair to the cargo deck.

John was already there, swinging the big passenger entrance door open. Instantly, the pleasant hum of the airplane's internal machinery gave way to a cacophony of sirens, engines, horns and the constant beeping noises of the Phoenix airport flight line. Lights flashed everywhere beneath the two-story-high door

Sharon lay small and huddled on a metal baggage rack. Her breathing was shallow and slow. Mat released the nylon tie-down strap around her waist and carefully turned her shoulders. Her tailored, neatly pressed uniform shirt was black with soot and partially burned. Raw flesh peeked from under charred cloth from her neck to her ribs. The stench of burnt skin and blood made his eyes water. He wanted to gather her in his arms and comfort her but that wouldn't help. He stood helpless, hovering.

In seconds, an EMT team charged up the stairs and pushed him out of the way. They were fast, efficient and careful as they lifted her unconscious body onto a narrow stretcher designed for use on airplanes. The four-man team carried her down the stairs to an ambulance waiting with open doors. Halfway down, the two white-shirts pushed past them to climb up.

Mat blocked the two men and motioned to go back down. He didn't want to contaminate the scene for accident investigators. Once down on the ground, the adrenalin rush faded, and he felt all energy drain from his body. He tried to stay sharp, in control, but a nagging doubt lurked.

There were a few absolute rules in aviation and first among them was that the captain takes care of his airplane and his crew. *Could he have prevented this tragedy?*

The white-shirts both wore laminated ID badges with a copper-colored background. They had the same question as soon as they got in his face. "Captain Mathew McCoy? What happened here? How was the girl burned? How much cargo was damaged? Is the plane flyable?" They had notepads and cell phones set to record. They pressed close, almost pushing him back against the truck-mounted stair rail. Two more white-shirts arrived. They, too, had copper badges. He felt mobbed.

Mat held up his hands. "Okay, slow down. I'll get the copilot down here and we'll…" He cocked his head. "Wait, I hear the main cargo door opening. I have to stop that. The aircraft is quarantined until the NTSB investigators arrive." He tried to push through the group of interrogators and head toward the rear of the plane, but someone shoved him. He felt a smack on the back of his head and the world went dark.

The Hospital

Mat McCoy woke in a pale green world of matching sheets and walls. Tubes and wires connected him to blinking gauges on a pole beside his bed. He was in a hospital, in a hospital bed. Mat tried to sit up and immediately felt a jackhammer in his brain. The electric shot of pain took his breath away. He fell back and tried to lie still until the throbbing above his eyes slowed.

What happened? Why was he here? What hit him? Slowly, the night's events came back. The image of Sharon burned and helpless on the luggage rack. He had to help her, but he didn't even know where he was, let alone how to find and help her. Still, he had to try. Had… to…try. Mat closed his eyes and drifted, consciousness slipping away.

Sometime later he woke with a jerk. A nurse or orderly stood with a clipboard. Her green scrubs blended nicely with the décor.

He turned his head left and right. It still hurt but it was better. Everything seemed slightly remote, as though viewing the world from inside a fish tank.

The clipboard lady gave him a perfunctory smile. "Mister McCoy, glad to see you're back among the living. We have a whole lot of people out in the lobby who just can't wait to meet you, but first I need to get the doctor,"

"Wait. Where am I? What happened?"

She smiled again. "You're in Phoenix Methodist Hospital. You've been here about two hours. That's all I know. The doctor will be able tell you more. So, you just wait right here, okay?"

As if he were going somewhere with all these lines attached. His blood pressure cuff inflated, and the array of machines made their cheerful, beeping noises. The doctor, or resident judging from his youthful appearance, breezed in with a clipboard - *all this technology and still clipboards*. He used a pen light to look in his eyes, turned Mat's head, inspected the wound and hummed a song Mat didn't recognize but then, they were from different generations.

"Well, okay then. Your vitals are all good. You took a real crack to your skull, almost twenty stitches. I think they said you backed up into a forklift or something like that. Anyway, your wound is not draining. You may have a mild concussion. We'll get an X-ray and keep you under observation for twenty-four hours and then you'll probably be released. I'll send Cynthia up to get your insurance information.... you do have insurance, don't you?"

Mat started to answer but his throat was too dry. He coughed, winced and nodded.

"Good, then I'll tell your visitors it's all right to speak to you."

And the boy-doctor was gone, clipboard under his arm, still humming the unknown song.

The NTSB Arrives

First out of the starting gate was a thin man with thin hair, thin eyes and a thin smile. He had a clipboard. "I'm Sanders, National Transportation and Safety Board Accident Investigation Team Investigator-in-Charge." Pleasantries over, he set up shop, turned on a small pocket recorder, opened his briefcase, retrieved a spiral-bound checklist and settled into a chair with his clipboard before him.

"I am required to inform you that this is a formal inquiry and that anything you say may later be used in evidence. Civil and Federal charges may be brought. Do you understand these warnings?"

Mat was sitting up propped by pillows. He nodded and the movement brought a dull pain. Sanders did an imitation of a smile. "Please describe, in your own words, the events of this morning's incident which is currently being investigated as a Class Three Accident because, though physical damage was slight, there was significant personnel injury." He sat back, ready to write.

Mat cleared his dry throat and spoke, surprised by how quiet his voice seemed. "We were in moderate to severe turbulence when a cargo smoke light came on. I notified Albuquerque Center. We followed checklist procedures and I sent the engineer to investigate. The turbulence became extreme and I initiated an emergency descent. During the descent, a cargo fire light illuminated. We landed successfully at Phoenix Sky Harbor Airport."

Sanders didn't look pleased. "Which came first, the warning light or the turbulence?"

"They happened in the order I described." Mat answered, choosing his words carefully. This was, after all, a legal interrogation. He would offer no more information than necessary.

"So, your flight engineer was not on the flight deck at the time of the incident?"

"That's correct."

"You requested an ambulance to meet the aircraft. When did you discover she had been injured?"

Mat paused for a long time. "You know what? I shouldn't be talking to you without my union attorney present. I think we're going to have to put this interview on hold until he arrives."

Mister Sanders stiffened like an indignant parson and put his clipboard down. Mat knew investigators weren't allowed to pressure witnesses. Sanders gathered his briefcase, sniffed and slammed it closed.

"Please notify me as soon as you feel up to continuing. It is vital to gather information as soon as possible. The human memory decays rapidly." He placed a business card on Mat's tray.

"Uh huh. Say, do you know how my flight engineer is doing?"

"Yes, second officer Sharon Prentiss is here in ICU, listed as stable with first and second-degree burns. She is conscious but they won't let me near her. No one here seems to care a damn about my investigation, but I *will* find out what happened. You can bet on it. Good day, Captain McCoy."

Prentiss? Mat had forgotten her last name. He tried to stay focused. He needed to find Sharon. He was her captain, and he needed to take care of her...as soon as his head stopped spinning.

Silver Streak Headquarters

The MidAmerica Saint Louis airport, actually located across the Mississippi River in rural Illinois, was a joint use facility shared by Silver Streak Airlines on the East and Scott Air Force Base on the west. The airline's offices were old renovated military buildings, but it was obvious Silver Streak had not wasted too much money on the renovations. A flat-roofed single-story gray building held the austere offices of Jerome Halstead, Director of Airline Operations. Nothing about the place gave any hint of the man's real power.

In a darkened conference room, a briefer's face was illuminated behind a lighted podium. "We believe the Flight 822 accident has been contained. The NTSB will hit us with a $10,000 fine for disturbing the accident scene by unloading the cargo but all evidence of the damaged container has been destroyed. In its place we have substituted a conventional container with a burned a case of lithium batteries inside to explain the explosion. None of the crewmembers have raised any flags."

Halstead leaned back. "Where is the special cargo?"

"Destroyed. Incinerated. I handled it personally. Only six people know of the cargo and they are all Gold Badge members. In fact, they are all sitting around this table. I anticipate no fallout." The briefer sounded both serious and confident.

Halstead pondered. "The crew you mentioned - who was the captain?"

The briefer was ready. He sorted through papers and read, "Captain Mathew McCoy, eight years with the company, no incidents, no problems, good pilot with a reputation for competence and on-time performance."

"What did he tell the NTSB?"

The briefer smirked for an instant. "Almost nothing. He's not feeling well. Seems he received a bump on the head after the accident and has a concussion. We think he may have backed into a forklift tine."

Halstead nodded without emotion. "Keep an eye on him in case he remembers things we want forgotten. I don't trust pilots. They have big egos and sometimes let themselves believe they are heroes. There will be no heroes to complicate this mess. Any questions?"

There was a murmured chorus of "No sir's" and the meeting was over. Halstead stayed in his seat as the other men filed out. As the briefer passed, Halstead reached out to grab the man's arm. "This girl flight engineer, will she recover?"

"Yes. It looks like she'll have some extensive reconstructive…"

Halstead's voice was hard, direct. "No Jack…she won't. See to it."

There was a long silent pause. The briefer's answer was almost a whisper. "Yes sir, I'll take care of it."

CHAPTER TWO

Bourassa Somalia

The warden was tall with close cropped hair, dark skin and steady, if tired-looking, eyes. His forehead was dry despite the furnace-like desert heat. He looked up and made a world-weary sigh. "Yes Hamid, what do you seek?"

The skeleton of a man held his traditional koofiyad cap in trembling hands. "Sir, I know I should not be coming to you directly but, as a moral man, I must. So many are dying in the eastern cell block. Sir, it is horrible. They have gone mad, screaming and ranting and killing each other in the most awful ways. I beg of you, sir, to do something for them."

The warden put down his pen and sighed. "Hamid, I know you are a good man with a good heart - and I share your concern, but we must be reasonable. This terrible disease has no cure and any who come near an infected man will also be infected. We must keep these men isolated and keep our guards away until it has run its course."

He looked hard at Hamid, sighed and forced a paternal smile. "Insha Allah. It is the will of God. We must not interfere. Do you understand? We must *not* interfere."

Hamid's head bobbed as he wrung his hands and pleaded, "Oh please sir. It is so awful. The men are screaming like maniacs, killing each other, killing themselves. It is madness. There are rotting bodies on the ground."

Now the warden sniffed and drew himself up. "And if I allow other men to go in there, men like you, they will be infected and go mad also. You mean well, but you have overstepped yourself, Hamid. Go and tell your supervisor you're to be punished for insubordination. He will decide the penalty. And know this; I shall protect my guards and the remaining uninfected prisoners. I will burn down the east cell block to destroy any trace of this terrible disease. I will *not* allow this thing to spread, do you hear me?"

He banged a fist on the desk and glared directly into Hamid's face as he shouted. "I *will* protect my men. Go…now!" The warden pointed a stiff arm toward the door. Hamid bowed and backed away, still shaking visibly, still making anguished little sobs.

The warden sat back down but now with clenched fists and bare teeth. He tried to control his breathing. Once composed, he raised one hand, palm down and said aloud, "As it is above…" He lowered that palm and turned it face up. "So, shall it be below."

Despite his professed belief in Islam, he was actually a follower of a much more ancient religion, one that predated either Jesus or Mohammed. He was an Archon, a warrior in service to the old way.

Russell Building, Washington D.C.

"Senator Rutledge," the page was polite, even timid. "I'm sorry to have bypassed your secretary but I was asked to deliver this directly to you and no one else."

Rutledge took off his reading glasses and crossed his arms to let the glasses dangle. He reclined and puckered with irritation. "Is it important?"

"I don't know, sir. A Mister Halstead sent it with a note that directed it to be delivered directly to you and no one else - and quickly."

Rutledge sighed and sat forward, flipping his glasses open and locating them on his nose. The boy page extended a straight arm as though feeding a lion through cage bars and handed two pieces of paper. Rutledge snatched them and read. His body language changed, and his voice took on a hint of urgency. "How long ago was this sent?"

"I believe it just arrived. I was tasked just minutes ago."

"Thank you. That is all."

The page left, pausing at the outer door to breathe.

Rutledge read the printout of an article posted on the Diplomat News Network. It described an outbreak of rabies in a remote Somali prison. Officials were at a loss to explain how the disease was transmitted. An entire cell block, more than four hundred inmates, had died within a week of the first symptom appearing. The entire prison was now quarantined but two other cell blocks were so far uncontaminated.

On the second page a note read, "All guards and the residents of two buildings had received flu shots. No illness reported among them." It was unsigned.

Senator Rutledge spun his leather desk chair to face a document shredder and ran the message and note. He turned back and sat staring into space for a long time. Then he intertwined his fingers, stretched his hands on the desk before him, bowed his head and prayed.

"Oh Lord Jesus, tell me we are acting according to your wishes." He paused and added, "As it is above, so shall it be below." Then he sat erect and took a deep, deep breath.

It had begun.

Phoenix Methodist Hospital

Mat groaned as he sat up in his hospital bed and gathered his thoughts. He needed to find Sharon and see for himself how badly she was hurt. Somehow, he didn't trust the hospital staff - or anyone else. Maybe it was just paranoia. After all, he had a head injury and probably shouldn't trust his own judgment. Didn't matter, this was something he had to do - captain's responsibility and all.

He had been in the hospital since early morning and had the routine down. His IV needle had now been removed, but he still had a tangle of blood pressure and EKG sensors attached. No matter; he had watched the staff remove all the wires when they changed his bandages and gave him a sponge bath. He was sure he could turn off the machines without alerting the nurses' station. But, how to get around the hospital unnoticed?

The short, open-back, show-off-your-butt hospital gown wouldn't work. He needed clothes. He found his uniform hanging in his room's tiny closet. Good.

He waited until after the evening feeding. He suspected activity on his floor would slow as everyone attended to paperwork in preparation for shift change. With things quieted down, he disconnected his sensors and prepared to make his move. First, he put on pants, shoes and the shirt with a coffee stain - minus the tie and captain's epaulets. Now, except for the matted hair where they stitched his injury, he looked pretty much like a regular human.

Mat took a breath and walked purposefully to the locker room sign. *Always look like you belong. If questioned, act as though you're the one who should be asking.* Nothing worked better than a good bluff.

But no one challenged him. No one even noticed him. The locker room door had a cypher-lock just like every airport gateway crew access door. He tried a 1-2-3-4 combination. That worked on 90% of locks around the world - and it worked here. A quiet buzz and he was in. Now to find a badge.

There were people in the back of the room. He heard their voices behind rows of lockers and tried to stay away from that area. Most lockers had padlocks but a few did not. He tried them one after another until he found one with a uniform hanging, but it had no badge. He kept looking, daring to get closer to the talkers.

There was a break area in the back where four men sat around a table. They laughed and told stories. One of them showed an image on his cell phone and the others stood to lean over and look.

"Oh, my goodness, look at them titties," one of them exclaimed. They pressed closer.

"Yes, sir. That little student nurse had probably never been to the big city of Phoenix. She was a farm girl from one of the ranches up on the Rim, all wide eyed and excited. I don't know if she had ever seen a real black man up close and she wanted to check me out."

They were all huddled, concentrating on the phone. Mat saw a coat on an abandoned chair with a laminated hospital badge clipped on its lapel. He eased his way out of hiding, bent low, and snatched the badge without being detected. After pausing to once again breathe, he made his escape, picking up a coat and cap as he passed an unlatched locker.

Out in the hall, he found a cart full of mops and brooms and buckets, put on his new coat and badge and headed for the Intensive Care Unit. It was easy to find, but its door required a card scan. He tried the laminated badge – no luck. So, he puttered and milled and waited. It didn't take long. A couple of laughing orderlies wheeled an empty gurney down the hall. They used their card to open the door and entered, still laughing about something. Mat pushed his cart and yelled, "Hold the door." They obliged.

Once inside, he knew he had to be more careful. No one would tolerate foolishness there, particularly the scowling nurse at a central desk backed by a wall of monitors. Mat pretended to mop even though he had no water. He whistled softly and shot scans at monitors, one for each patient's room. He couldn't be sure, but he did see a bed with what appeared to be a smaller woman. That could be her. He guessed that the order of the monitors matched the arrangement of rooms and went down the left hallway. The staff had been kind enough to put patient name tags on the doors. He found "Sharon Prentiss" and cracked it open.

Inside, the dark room had an antiseptic hospital smell as well as the distinct odor of ozone. In an airplane, ozone meant the pressurization system was not recycling air fast enough. Here, he didn't know what it meant. He approached her bed warily while staying just outside the camera's field of view.

It was Sharon, still the same young, attractive girl even under the tangle of tubes and wires attached to monitors, dangling IV bags and an oxygen mask. She was breathing deep and shifting uncomfortably.

He whispered, "Do you hear me?" There was no sound but the monotonous rise and fall of an air pump. He dared to move closer. "Sharon, do you hear me?"

Her eyes blinked. She looked at the ceiling and then turned with some discomfort. Her dry lips formed a numb smile distorted through the plastic mask. She was able to speak but her voice was strained. "Captain Mat, you came to see me. You're such a sweetie, I knew you were a sweetie." She sounded drunk – must be drugs.

"Sharon, are you going to be all right?"

Her voice had a little girl's tone. "I don't know. I guess so." Then she scowled. "Mat, know what? I got all burned up. All my front got burned up." She shifted again and sighed but in the pleasant, slightly distant way of someone under anesthesia. "Little Sharon got all burned up. No more bikini for Sharon."

Mat asked, "What happened in the airplane? What caused the explosion?"

Serious now, she answered, "Oh yeah, I remember…the head."

"The head?"

"Yeah. There was a cargo container with a little bit of smoke coming out, kind of white and a little bit blue, like those pretend cigarettes. I couldn't get to the lock, so I used my axe to cut a hole in the plastic side." She sounded serious. "You know, those things are really, really hard. That plastic they use is so-o-o strong." Then she settled back into her story. "Inside the container was this box made of clear glass or plastic or something and it had a little motor. The motor was smoking."

"Was it an electric motor?"

"I don't know." She was drifting a little. "Smoking, that's all I know. But guess what was in the box? It was a head."

"A head? What kind of head?"

"A black man's head, all cut off and nasty." She licked dry, cracked lips under the plastic mask. "It was really, really nasty– stringy with guts and stuff. I tried to move it, but the airplane started to bounce all around and then - 'Boom'- little Sharon got all burned up."

Mat was confused. "What blew up? Sharon, what exploded?" But she was gone, drifted back into her drug fog. Mat stepped back and bumped something. He was still a little unsteady on his feet. A metal bowl fell from a stand and resonated like a bell on the tiled floor. He had to get out of there.

He grabbed his janitor's cart and tried to look nonchalant as he wheeled by the evil-looking charge nurse. Her eyes tracked him like radar. Once outside the ICU he dropped the badge on a hallway floor, threw the stolen clothes in a garbage can, went to his room and undressed. He was back to being hospital inmate number 612, or whatever.

In the morning, after what seemed hundreds of pages of paperwork, he was released. He called a taxi and sat waiting in his mandatory wheelchair by the downstairs reception desk.

A well-dressed black couple, obviously in distress, came in the front door accompanied by two close-clipped white men in suits. The woman wore church clothes and tear-streaked cheeks. The man was gray haired, formal and lock-jaw stern. A doctor with a long white coat and clipboard met them and spoke quietly.

"Mister and Mrs. Prentiss? I'm Gordon Fletcher, Director of Emergency Services. I am so sorry for your loss. Please, come with me."

"*Prentiss?*" These were Sharon's parents. "*Your loss?*" Sharon had died? Mat stood up from his wheelchair and marched to block them.

"Sharon Prentiss? Are you her parents?" Then, without thinking, he blurted, "What happened to her? She was okay last night. I saw her. I spoke to her."

The father gritted his teeth. The woman reached out and touched Mat's arm. She shook an anguished head. "We've just learned that she passed. Did you know her?"

He collected himself and said, "Yes, I'm Matthew McCoy. I was the pilot on the plane. I didn't think her injuries were that severe."

The father spoke through clenched teeth. "Tell me, could it have been prevented?"

Mat ignored the question and turned to the doctor. "What happened to Sharon? Why did she die?"

White coat sniffed, cradled his clipboard and said, "I'm sorry. We can't divulge that information beyond the immediate family." He extended an arm and led the Prentiss family away to an elevator. The father shot an accusing look back at Mat.

Mat McCoy stood for a long time with his mouth open. *Could he have prevented her death?* He wasn't sure. He could have sent copilot John Cook to check out the smoke. How would that have helped? Well, John was more experienced. Maybe he wouldn't have used the crash axe to chop open the container. Maybe that's what caused the explosion. *But why?*

Mat felt a heavy weight of guilt, a weight that he knew would not soon lift. More than that, his gut told him there was more going on than he knew. The explosion, a box with a human head, his own unexplained injury—he had to figure out what happened. For Sharon's sake, he had to find the truth.

He was distracted by a cabbie with a cardboard sign that read "McCoy."

"Over here. I'm McCoy. Take me to Sky Harbor Airport south cargo entrance. There's a flight back to MidAmerica St. Louis. I'll get a jumpseat ride. Oh, and you did get an authorization from Silver Streak to pay for this trip?"

The cab driver sighed. Mat knew he was thinking, "Another cheapskate pilot.

Back Home in St. Louis

The ring tone from the phone on his nightstand sounded like a jet passing low overhead. Mat fumbled and fought against the tangle of his thousand-thread-count Egyptian cotton sheets to find the offending instrument. "Yeh, hello. Who's this?" He sounded bleary.

"It's Chandler, damn it." Her voice was shrill, just short of a scream.

He ran a hand over his face, still coming out of a deep sleep. "It's seven o'clock in the morning Central Time. You know I don't get up that…"

"What the hell is wrong with you?" Now the screaming was unrestrained.

He worked a crink out of his neck and sat up in bed. "Well, uh…" He took a breath and sounded fairly alert. "Well, I guess I would have to blame it mostly on my Irish Catholic upbringing. You know that involves a lot of alcoholism and abuse. On top of that…"

"What the hell are you talking about?"

"Whoa now, slow down pretty lady. That is no way for a high-priced lawyer to be talking. It's just that kind of overbearing attitude that will make it hard for some kindly old gentleman to make you his bride and, let's be honest, you're not getting any…"

"I just heard on the news that you were the pilot of that Silver Streak airplane accident in Phoenix."

"Oh that. Yeah, I thought you were asking why I turned out the way I did. I was just trying to explain."

"Mat, be serious for once. For some reason that defies any rational explanation I care about you. And now I find out on television that you were on that airplane where an in-flight explosion killed a crewmember. Why didn't you call me?" She was calmer but still upset.

Mat grimaced, blew out a long breath and tried to come up with the words. "You're right. I should have called. To be honest, I didn't know what to say. Truth is, I'm still pretty shaken by the whole thing. My flight engineer was young, just a kid really. She was doing her job inspecting a cargo fire warning when the explosion burned her very badly."

"Are you okay?"

"Yeah, I got a mild concussion and they threatened to ground me for a year, but I have a friend who is an Aeromedical Examiner. I'm sure he can convince the FAA that I wasn't really unconscious, just dazed. So I'll be back on flying status in less than a month."

He sat for a long minute of silence. "I'm sorry about the smart-ass response. You caught me off guard. I intended to call you as soon as I had my head on straight. I shouldn't have waited. You've always been the one who kept my head level."

"That's just another load of your bullshit isn't it?"

"Well…maybe just a little bit."

"Oh Mat, you're going to make an old woman of me."

"Well, take some comfort in knowing that you'll be the most beautiful and smartest old woman in the western world and I will always be your greatest admirer, even when I'm old and gray."

"You're already getting gray." She allowed a hint of a laugh. "Please, don't ever do that again. At least call me when something bad happens. I mean it. I do care about you, oddball that you are. I have to go now, but take care of yourself and don't make me age any faster, okay?"

And she was gone. Mat leaned back on his pillows and smiled a little. He was lucky to have Chandler. He sure as hell didn't deserve her and he didn't understand why she tolerated him, but he was glad. His first marriage—he stopped himself. He didn't like to think about his first marriage. *Wipe that thought or it will ruin the whole day.* Instead, he thought of his daughter, so young, so bright and so pretty. And so much like Sharon, who now lay dead and almost forgotten. But he would never forget her…not ever.

He threw off his sheets and stood in the middle of his private little palace and saw himself in a full-length mirror wearing only his jockey shorts. He was thin but fairly well-muscled thanks to his workout schedule and healthy regimen. He stretched and surveyed his personal kingdom, the upper floor of a hundred-year-old brick storefront with a view of the Mississippi and Gateway Arch. The neighborhood was a little run down, mostly black, but friendly and safe. He had designed and supervised construction of every detail of the renovation that created his magnificent man cave.

The single open room had black marble floors and an odd mix of furnishings. A stainless steel professional kitchen stood behind a massive island of matching marble. Black leather couches faced an oversized television suspended against gray linen wallpaper. One wall was floor to ceiling glass with a multi-station weight machine and elliptical walker that looked out over the Mississippi River where today passing barges were covered in thin January ice.

Overhead plantation fans gave it all a tropical feeling despite the freezing weather outside. Everything was oversized: his raised bed, a fake stone grotto hot tub, an open three-person shower, a chrome and glass computer work station and a billiard table. The only enclosure was a small toilet.

This was Mat's hideaway. Here, he could relax and put aside the stresses and conflicts of the world. Here, he worked out, read, watched the History Channel and cooked gourmet meals, to be eaten alone. Except for Chandler, he was always alone. But here, he could forget all the pain of being human. Here, he bathed in classical music, soft light and panoramic views of a world he found interesting but indifferent. Here, he was master of every detail.

At least, he was master until Ruby arrived. She didn't knock, didn't care if he was awake or – as it was - standing in his underwear, or even splashing in the hot tub. Ruby blew in like a sudden storm, swirling and overpowering everything in her path. She was a black lady of formidable proportion and volume. If she was in a room, she was in charge of the room, and Mat's little kingdom was no exception. She slammed the door.

"And what the hell is this I hear on the television? You have been in a damned accident and your young lady pilot has been killed. What the hell? And why don't you call nobody to let them know your skinny white ass is still alive and able to pay me…which, by the way, is due?"

"Good morning, Ruby. It's good to see you on this lovely morning. I have just been awakened by Chandler and she has already given me a load of shit. So, how about you relax and make us some coffee, okay?"

"Coffee? You want me to make you some coffee? How about you show some respect by puttin' on your damned pants and *you* go make the coffee. I am your damned housekeeper not your house nigger."

"Hey, watch your language. You know I don't like that word. Never have." She glared at him and he cleared his throat before asking, "So Ruby, what do you take in your coffee?"

Headhunters

Two worlds lay juxtaposed across from St. Louis. There was the all-white town of Belleville, Illinois with its wholesome mid-western atmosphere and right next door, the urban wasteland of East St. Louis, black and poor and violent. Whole city blocks had been bulldozed and the few buildings that remained were crumbling ghetto relics. There were no stores, no industries and few legal sources of employment. Crime was the business of East St. Louis and it had had the highest murder rate in the entire western hemisphere outside of Central America.

Once there had been a chain link fence to separate the two communities with a gate that was closed every night at sundown. The gate was gone but the separation remained. There was still a barrier, invisible but just as solid as the old gate.

Two men parked their rental car by a city block of old house foundations and brick piles. The lone building still standing had a neon sign that once read "Kelsey's Bar," but only the "K" and "r" still lit. Large black men with conservative suits, short haircuts and serious expressions they looked up at the sign as though confirming their destination. One of them had decorative scars cut in his cheeks, thin horizontal stripes long since healed. Their breath steamed in the cold.

They entered the bar and all conversation stopped. There wasn't that much conversation to begin with. The bartender sized them up and gave a gold-toothed smile. "Well just a looky here. What you fellows want? You DEA or something?"

The man with scars replied. "Oh, no sir. We are looking for a gentleman. His name is Deray Lewis. Do you know of such a man?"

The bartender wiped a glass. "And if I did, who should I say has come calling?"

"Ah yes. You should say two businessmen have come to discuss a profitable venture and he has been recommended to us as a possible partner. Could you be so kind as to inform him we are here?"

From a dark corner of the barroom a voice called out. "Mister Johnson, why don't you send these gentlemen back so I can meet them?" The bartender returned to wiping glasses and indicated the direction with a nod. Scarface thanked him.

Deray sat with his back to a fire exit surrounded by three women, probably hookers judging by their clothes and heavily made up faces. He, on the other hand, was young, handsome, physically fit and dashing in a suit coat and brilliant orange silk shirt.

He held a drink in his left hand. Long pianist fingers were heavy with gold and gemstone rings. His right hand remained beneath the table. Deray flashed a wide smile. "You're not Americans, are you? Well just how can I help you fine gentlemen on this fine afternoon?"

The larger stranger spoke for the first time. "Sir, I am Chala and this my friend Mudi. We are Nigerian and we are looking for partners to establish a business here in America, You have been highly recommended for your connections and your, shall we say, aggressive attitude. We would like to do some business with you."

Deray's grin broadened. "Business, you say? If it's business you want, you in the right place 'cause Deray Lewis is the business man. Yes sir. Now, just what kind of business is you wanting to start?"

"Heroin. We can supply great quantity at much lower price than you pay now. Would you like to try a sample? It is very good quality. We guarantee it."

Deray leaned back and let his smile fade. He was obviously considering his options. As though not wanting to trust strangers, he looked hard into their eyes before answering. "Sure, why not? Let's see what you got."

Chala, the larger man, reached into his shirt pocket and produced two zip lock baggies of white powder and tossed them in the center of the table where Deray would have to reach, but the man in an orange shirt didn't move. He kept his hand under the table and turned to the woman beside him. "Yolanda, you like this stuff. Check it out. Tell me what you think."

Deray sat back with a suspicious grin and bit his lower lip.

Chala grinned. He had big piano keyboard teeth in a square jaw and looked like a boxer who had gone one too many rounds. "Yes Ma'am, try it. It is very good. Here, I have a little spoon for you to use." He pretended to be clumsy and dropped the spoon in her lap. Deray and all the women followed the spoon with their eyes. It was an involuntary action, a momentary but fateful distraction.

Scarface Mudi drew and fired his pistol with little more than a flick of his arm. Deray's forehead exploded. Chala drew his gun and turned to the bartender who already had a shotgun halfway out from under the bar. Two shots and he fell.

Screams and shouts, panicked pushing and shoving—the half dozen other patrons surged toward the door. The two Nigerians calmly and systematically executed them one at a time.

Their work done, the two men walked out into the sunlight and hunched against the chill. The street was empty. No one would report the shots. No police would be coming anytime soon. Later, it would hardly make the evening news - just another East St. Louis shooting.

As they reached the rental car, Scarface Mudi asked, "So Chala, how shall we claim this in our report?"

The bigger man replied thoughtfully. "We will claim one assigned target and nine additional hits. Ten thousand for the target and one thousand for each additional for a total of nineteen thousand American dollars."

"Oh, this is very good. I shall use this money to start my new 401K."

Big man Chala laughed. "Where did you learn about 401K plans?"

"The other day, I was filling out paperwork for the company for tax withholding and the lady explained that I could start a retirement plan."

"My friend, this is a very noble idea but we must be honest. Neither of us will live to see retirement. All these hits we do are just a beginning and eventually, it will be our time. We are killers of black criminals, but we are ourselves black criminals and therefore targets for other men just like us."

"Men like us? There are others?"

"Yes, I'm sure of it. So, send your money home to your family and enjoy the day. It will not last forever."

Cave Hill Cemetery

Mat didn't like funerals. Never had. He remembered his father's, a noisy Irish wake. An endless stream of men he barely knew had slapped him on the back and told him how great his wife-beating, beer-guzzling, belt-wielding bully of a father had been. There had been crying and singing and hugging, but mostly, there had been fighting, both verbal and bare-knuckle. Fingers waved. Punches were thrown. Beer bottles smashed. His brothers were younger versions of their bellicose father. He was not.

It had been an easy five-hour drive from Mat's St. Louis home to Sharon's funeral in Kentucky. The Old Louisville neighborhood of elegant turn-of-the-century homes now dowdy with age. The downtown church was old and elaborate, its statues and stone walls darkened by the soot of time.

The attendees were overwhelmingly black but a contingent of white Silver Streak executives stood out as they sat together in a single row. Mat took a seat in the last pew trying to be inconspicuous. He could see Sharon's parents in the front. They sat stiff and intense without tears or visible weakness. The funeral was solemn and respectful and thankfully brief.

The preacher asked if anyone cared to speak and several relatives stood to say what a sweet girl Sharon had been. He hated mushy, meaningless words. Despite his usual dislike for public attention, Mat rose and walked down the aisle. He didn't know what he was going to say but it wasn't going to be some generic bullshit read off a 3" by 5" card.

The preacher looked slightly apprehensive as Mat stood before the open casket and looked at Sharon's face, almost serene under heavy makeup. He cleared his throat and was surprised by his own volume and steadiness.

"I am Mat McCoy, captain of the 747 flight that took the life of Sharon Prentiss. I did not know her as well as many of you but I saw her in a time of duress and I must tell you how proud I am, and how proud you should be, of this lady. She was a damned fine crewmember and a damned fine person." *Shit. Was it okay to say damned in a church?*

"Our aircraft was nearly out of control and we had a warning of a fire that could have destroyed the plane and all of us in it. Sharon went down to the cargo deck alone, in severe turbulence, to fight the fire. She died as a result."

He took a deep breath but felt he had to say more. "Did she save the plane and my life and the other pilot's life? Probably. In any event, she was courageous and she was competent. I am proud to have known her and I will never forget what she did. I spoke to her just before she passed away. Even then she was still confident, upbeat, and brave, despite her terrible injuries. I am humbled by her courage and I sincerely thank her for her sacrifice."

His voice ran out. He went back to his seat as all eyes followed him. He wasn't sure that had been the right thing to do or whether his words were right, but he felt better just by saying something.

He drove behind the rest of the funeral procession to the Cave Hill Cemetery. It was a well-manicured old Victorian burial ground crowded with obelisks, marble mausoleums and elaborate statues commemorating Louisville's deceased gentry. The day had turned bitter cold and gray with a wind that whipped fallen leaves along the ground and destroyed women's hairdos.

The crowd was huge and television cameras, banned from the church, were everywhere. Cherry-picker satellite dish trucks competed for prime locations. A helicopter hovered overhead. Overly made-up reporters straightened their clothes, put on phony faces and babbled about the accident and the funeral. Mat heard one anchorman say that no one could remember a black person being buried at Cave Hill since Muhammad Ali.

Mat took a position near the back of the crowd but on a small rise that allowed him to see the pallbearers struggling with an ornate casket that must have cost a fortune. But then, Silver Streak was probably paying. He was intent on watching the procession when several white men approached from behind. Mat was aware of their steaming breath and turned to face them. It seemed strange that they chose to join him so far apart from the rest of the crowd. One of them wore a mohair coat with a cashmere scarf. He spoke softly and with a bit of hesitation.

"So, you actually talked to Sharon Prentiss before she died?"

Mat nodded. "Just briefly. She was heavily sedated. It wasn't a coherent conversation."

"I see. What, exactly, did she say?"

Who were these guys? What did they want? He chose his words. "She said she chopped a hole in the side of the smoking container and it exploded. That was actually a pretty dumb thing to do but she was inexperienced."

"I see. Did she report seeing anything unusual in the container?"

"Well, yes. She said she saw a head but I don't know what that meant. Do you?"

"No. Did she say anything else?"

"No. She dozed off and I left her. I wasn't supposed to be there anyway."

The two men turned to leave but one of them leaned close to whisper to Mohair. The wind seemed to blow his words back to Mat's ear. "Do you think he's telling the truth?"

Mohair coat shrugged and responded. "I don't know. Just make sure he doesn't become another Merriweather. I'll report back to the D.O."

Who were these guys? Who was Merriweather? But really, what did he care? Sharon was dead. That was all that mattered.

Maston and Severed Heads

Mat was having trouble filling his day. Time off with pay but on short-notice call by the accident investigation team left him pacing and exercising and watching daytime TV. It was a little like prison. He was almost pleased when he got the phone call telling him to report to John Maston's office at Silver Streak.

Now, Mat and John had known each for more than two decades. They had once been friends. But that was before Maston became a scab, a union pilot who crossed the picket line to fly during a strike. Breaking strike ranks was considered fratricide by the other pilots. Turning against your brothers, in their eyes, was a sin that could never be atoned. He was to be shunned forever.

John Maston was on the Scab List carried by union captains. They would not allow him to travel in a cockpit jump seat. Flight attendants acted as though he was invisible and didn't serve him. He didn't check bags because they were likely to get lost. He was still a pilot, but he was a management pilot, and when he flew with a union crew, there was no conversation except mandatory checklist calls. John Maston was a pariah.

As a reward for abandoning the union, the company appointed him Silver Streak's Chief of Safety, a position where he would serve out his time until retirement - in solitude.

Mat stood outside Maston's small office at MidAmerica Airport and collected himself. He would try to be civil, just for old times' sake. John was waiting inside with a stack of documents on his desk. There was no handshake.

"Thank you for coming. I just want to keep you up to date on the investigation and share some confidential information." Mat sat and leaned forward to scan the documents.

"The accident investigators have a long way to go before releasing even a preliminary report but here's what we believe they will say." He paused to get his wording straight. "The batteries shipped by Milburn Industries were actually made by an Indonesian firm with a bad track record of safety violations. The packaging and documentation all looks proper but the lithium batteries themselves were defective. During turbulence, the batteries rubbed and ignited. That caused the explosion that burned your flight engineer."

Mat sifted through a dozen printout photos of the container inside and out. The container was a ten-foot square plastic box with black streaks on the side and a melted section of the roof. The burn pattern was clear. It all looked reasonable. But then Mat hesitated and shuffled back through the pictures.

"I don't see any marks where the container was chopped open by my flight engineer's axe." He looked up at Maston.

"I would guess they were in the section that melted."

"I would guess they weren't. These containers are almost six feet tall. My engineer was barely five five. The melt is all on the top. She couldn't have reached that high. What's going on here?"

Maston turned a pen in his hand tapping it a little too hard on the desk. His face tightened as he concentrated on the pen and tapped harder and harder. Then he slapped his pen down and eyeballed Mat.

"I didn't think you'd buy that story but I had to try. That's what we're telling the NTSB." His voice quivered. "Did you understand what I just said? We are lying to the National Transportation and Safety Board, lying under oath. We can all go to Federal prison."

He rocked back in his chair and ran his hands over his face. "And now, I'm going to tell you the truth and give you the power to destroy this company and put me and many others away for years. I'm doing this despite orders."

His stare was direct, but his eyes were wide, almost pleading. "I'm doing this because I think you have a right to know what happened on your plane, what happened to your crewmember. I'm betting my whole future on your discretion, Mat. I have always respected you and I feel I owe you that."

Mat responded slowly. "O-o-kay."

John Maston looked at the wall as he spoke. "We, Silver Streak, support a group doing very important brain research but that work requires carefully preserved human brain tissue in fairly large quantities. To that end, we have developed special shipping containers that provide a supply of fluids and an oxygen-rich environment to keep the tissue viable. Several participating doctors provide heads of deceased indigents which we ship to the lab in San Jose, California."

"Heads?"

"Yes, human heads. We ship the preserved cadaver heads of accident victims in a container of compressed oxygen. When your engineer chopped open the container she must have created a spark that, along with leaking oxygen, caused the explosion."

There was a long pause before Maston continued. "We do this in complete secrecy. There are some crackpot fundamentalists - a group called NORMAL - who think this is just a government plot to enslave the population through mind control - or something like that. They have waged a war of threats and actual sabotage against the lab. They actually killed one of the scientists involved just as he was on the verge of announcing a major breakthrough."

John Maston sounded earnest, almost pleading. "Mat, this is really important. The tissue harvested from cadavers is vital. Just think of the possible outcomes. Multiple Sclerosis, Parkinson's, epilepsy, Alzheimer's and dozens more brain disorders may actually be curable. Even ADHD, psychosis and mood disorders may be improved with the regenerative brain tissue treatments being developed. This work is radical, ground breaking and it will benefit the whole world."

Mat wasn't completely convinced. "Why is Silver Streak so involved?"

"The owner, Jack Carson, has two daughters with MS. He is a major funder of the research. He's willing to risk revenge by these fanatics. They have threatened to bomb any transport involved in what they call 'ghoulish body snatching.' The public relations nightmare that such sabotage would unleash could destroy our airline. That's why we lied. That's why we want you to support the lie. It's all on you, Mat. Will you destroy the company you work for and the research that might save so many lives? It's your decision, Captain."

It was a gauntlet thrown in his face. Mat stood, hesitated for a moment and left without comment. His mind was racing and his thoughts disorganized. *What was the right thing to do? What would a decent, moral man do? Why did Sharon have to use that stupid axe on the container?*

He would call Chandler. She always knew what was right. Then again, she would tell him to be truthful and take the consequences—damned do-good lawyer. *What should he do?*

He was consumed by his thoughts and never noticed the car that followed him home.

CHAPTER THREE

What Would a Good Man Do?

Mat spent two days pacing and arguing both sides of the debate. Should he go to the press, imperil the research, damage his company and certainly end his own career? Right and wrong—there wasn't any easy answer.

His anxiety was broken by a phone call from Silver Streak scheduling telling him he had been released to fly and had a trip from MidAmerica to Philadelphia and on to Cologne, Germany and return. It would leave the next day.

Maybe that's what he needed, a chance to clear his head. Flying always brought order to his world. There were no gray areas. Procedures, policies and good judgment made flying safe. It was the most rational activity mankind had ever created and he loved the order and organization. He would postpone making his moral decision and devote his mind to flying.

That took away the urgency and panic. Now he was back in control. Now he slept without dreams of the accident, the head, or the possible fallout of his coming clean on Maston's story. A flight would renew his self-confidence and restore order to his life.

Sure enough, the next day he was back in command of an 800,000-pound flying machine. Even the chaos of the flightline and the rapid-fire radio traffic made him feel at home. Better yet, he had a good crew. Copilot Jerry Billings was crisp and professional.

Flight engineer Chet Carpenter was older than Moses but still sharp. Mat liked old engineers. They didn't panic, took their time and made good decisions. This was going to be a good flight.

Rain in Philly slowed the ground operation. Mat had a small confrontation with a load supervisor whose yellow slicker dripped rainwater from every fold. In the crowded cockpit, the man radiated cold and damp. His weight-and-balance document was soaked and unreadable. A new one was quickly printed out and signed and they made scheduled departure time by just seconds.

Once they were safely through the New York Air Traffic Control sector the workload settled down. There wasn't much traffic over Canada and they coasted out from Goose Bay, Labrador onto the North Atlantic Track System. The NATS were a virtual highway in the sky between North America and Europe, parallel jet routes crammed together with minimal separation. Mat could see blinking anti-collision lights from nearby airplanes in the clear air over Greenland's southern tip.

Now, everything seemed to switch into slow motion. A radio call every forty-five minutes, a navigation plot before each reporting point, routine instrument checks. Monotony set in and there was time for small talk.

Chet, the engineer, brought up coffee without being asked and swiveled his chair to face toward the pilots. "So, Captain McCoy, tell us about the accident."

Mat gave the official version with minimal detail. He decided to ask a question that hung in the back of his mind. "Chet, does your engineer training address how to fight a fire inside a container? Would you use the crash axe on a burning container?"

The ancient engineer blew steam off his coffee. He openly bragged about drawing social security, a military pension and retirement income from another airline while still working full time for Silver Streak. Pilots, of course, faced limited flying after sixty and mandatory retirement at sixty-five. Chet liked to rub it in.

"No Captain, we train people only how to use the Halon fire extinguisher to put out a fire. You know, the old PASS routine. No one ever, to my knowledge, said it was a good idea to chop open a burning container. If the fire is contained, you don't want to let it out. Those containers are pretty sturdy and they'll take a lot of punishment. No, I would never start hacking on one of those big plastic ice cubes. Better to land and let the fire department handle it."

Mat settled back. "Yeah, that's what I thought." He hesitated to ask but went ahead. "Chet, you've been here since the airline started. Have you ever heard any stories about human heads in the cargo containers?"

"Huh. Funny you mention that. I have heard stories, more than once actually, of heads in plastic boxes. Never put much stock in them. To tell you the truth, I never really cared what was in the cargo as long as it wasn't hazardous. Other than that, the cargo is just there to pay my salary."

Mat nodded and reached for an alcohol wipe.

From Iceland to Scotland, heavy clouds created perfect icing conditions. It was sixty below zero outside. Chet was busy diverting hot exhaust air into the giant fanjet engines and preheating fuel to keep from icing up.

They crossed the English Channel and the clouds suddenly opened up to reveal a spectacular landscape of sparkling lights washed crystal clear by a just-passed cold front. There was no horizon as moonless sky and earth blended into a black velvet background aglitter with jewel-like sparkles of stars and man-made lights.

No matter how often he saw the world so clear and bright against the night sky, it remained an awesome, almost breathtaking sight, a universe without boundaries, with boundless possibilities. Mat felt small and insignificant and yet comfortable with his place in this majestic scene.

It was past midnight local time and air traffic was light. Only the freighters flew at that hour.

Karneval

After an uneventful landing at the Cologne, Germany airport the crew checked in with the air cargo operations desk. A crisp lady with a hard-edged accent looked them over and commanded. "No cravats. This is Karneval time and no one in this town wears the tie. If they see one, it will be cut off." She made a scissor motion with her fingers. "Just so. Do you understand?"

Mat turned and said, "You heard the lady, ties off. This is the German Mardi Gras and this whole town is partying. We had better hurry before they run out of beer."

The woman stood tall and haughty and humorless. "We will *never* run out of beer."

They checked into the hotel at a dead run and changed into standard flight crew clothing of jeans, sneakers and windbreakers before hitting the street. The city was alive - an endless party with revelers in costume approaching the end of a full day of drinking. Music blared. People sang- sort of. Everyone was jolly and wobbly and loud.

Mat and his crew forced their way into an overflowing bar. Captain Kirk in Star Fleet uniform hailed them with a raised beer stein. An attractive young woman in a skintight blue costume and obviously no underwear eyed them with curiosity. Several men in traditional lieder hosen and Alpine hats locked arms to sway and sing what sounded like a patriotic song. No amount of pushing could get the crew close to the bar.

But then a burly clown with a red tennis ball nose, painted face and wide suspenders on baggy pants pointed and shouted in English. "You. I know you." He bellowed a laugh. "You are American, yes? I know you." The clown then scrunched his face and looked as serious as was possible to look under a greasepaint grin. "Ah!" He seemed to have made a connection and pointed once again. "You are the pilot. I have seen your picture. Yes, yes, you are the pilot."

He turned to the bar and boomed in a voice that overcame all the other noise. "Ernst, geben sie mir ein meter Kolsch fur meine fruende."

A trio of musicians barged into the melee with tuba, accordion and booming bass drum. It wasn't so much music as music-like noise. The crowd cheered. They would probably cheer for anything at this drunken hour.

The clown elbowed in their direction balancing a three-foot board with eight holes, each one holding a glass of beer. He growled at a pair of gay men making out at a nearby table and they protested. He growled again, and they stood with angry little bitch waves before fading into the crowd.

"Come," said the clown as he sat the stick of beer on his captured table. "Come. We will make a party." He beckoned with a white-gloved hand and a belly laugh. Then he grabbed two chairs dumping the occupants onto the ground. The displaced partiers protested and a woman of sixty dressed in a princess gown rapped him over the head with her wand. He waved her off with a grunt and plopped himself at the table to raise a glass in a toast.

"To America. Let us never stop selling you good cars and taking your good dollars." They saluted and drank. The clown sat back. He was a really big man, probably six four and almost three hundred pounds and obviously a bully. But - *what the hell* - he got them drinks and a table. "So, Mister Pilot, you are the one with a fire on the airplane, yes?"

Mat downed his beer and nodded. Clown leaned on the table. He radiated a smell of beer, sweat and vinegar. "So, do you know what is the cause of this fire?"

"Batteries. A box of lithium batteries exploded."

"And this kills the girl?" Clown seemed thoughtful and made an exaggerated shrug. He became quiet as the night wound down. He did keep buying them beer and listening, but he spoke seldom. It was almost three-thirty in the morning Germany time. He was probably exhausted after all the partying.

41

A woman of forty or so wearing a Sound of Music dress, apron and blonde pigtail wig wandered over and slapped an arm around the copilot. She whispered in his ear and may have shot a little tongue. He laughed and said, "Dance? But there's no music."

She shouted and the bartender turned up the volume of a Hip-Hop tune. The woman led him to an open spot and they began a slow dance that really amounted to just rubbing bodies and swaying. Clown's head was bobbing but he gestured at the dancers and explained to Mat, "This is Fasching time, party time. Today, the rules are not so hard. Women can be a little—how do you say—loose. Nobody gets upset. It is time for a little play." With that, clown hunched in his chair and started to snore.

Chet, the engineer had been quiet most of the night. Now, he belched and leaned on his elbows. "Captain, you remember when you asked me about heads in a container? I remember something that happened over a year ago. There was this White Badge manager, a quality control inspector named Merry-something or other, who just went nuts out on the ramp. He was yelling about a head in a special container. Security came and wrestled him away. I don't think I've ever seen him since."

Mat made a crooked smile. "Well, I think I've had enough for tonight. I think I'll wander back to the hotel."

Chet slugged his beer. "Yeah, me too. Do you think it's okay to leave Billings…"? But he and the pigtail lady were already gone.

Mat stood and shrugged. "He's a big boy and, like the clown said, it's Karneval, time for a little play." He roused the clown and shook the giant man's hand, thanking him for a good time. Clown looked confused but nodded and reached up to slap Mat on the shoulder before descending back into sleep.

As they went out into the chill night they did not notice the snoring clown crack open one eyelid to watch them leave.

Just the Head

It was snowing in Newark, a dirty wet snow that made slush piles along the road edge. Chala and Mudi wore heavy overcoats and carried what looked like a large bird cage with a cloth cover. Their breath steamed like diesel locomotives as they checked addresses and looked up at the windows in a crumbling brick apartment complex.

Mudi sounded exasperated. "I don't like doing this thing. I know we get paid double for taking the head but God would not approve."

Chala, the bigger man, sounded paternal. "You are right, my friend, but tell me this, did God approve when the Boko Haram killed your wife and took your daughters? Did God approve when your father was shot for not paying protection money? No, I think God is not involved in what we do here. This is about money. We do these evil deeds so we can send money back to your new wife and your mother and sons. That money will protect them. We do evil to prevent evil. So have a strong back and let's get it over."

A small boy wrapped in layers of clothes with a scarf around his head wandered cautiously close. "Hey mister, what happened to your face?" The boy rocked back and forth in the bitter morning chill.

Mudi squatted and grinned at the boy. "Do you mean my scars? They are like tattoos. They have meaning. Among my people, when a boy is strong enough to be a warrior, he is given tests. If he is brave and passes the test, he gets the marks of a warrior and other men fear him."

The boy pivoted back and forth on one foot. "What kind of tests?"

"Well, in the old days, you had to kill a lion or something. Today, you kill other things."

"What kind of things?"

Mudi stood and clapped his gloved hands. "Tell me, young man, do you know if Mister Dion Waters lives here?"

"I ain't supposed to say."

"Yes, of course. Did your mother tell you that?"

"My Grandma. I live with her."

"Do you live in this building?" The boy kept squirming but nodded a yes. "Very good. You and your friends must go away from this place for a little while, okay? Some bad things are going to happen here. Do you understand?"

The boy nodded and took off. Mudi turned back and shrugged. "Okay, let's go do bad things."

They climbed rickety stairs filled with the sound of children and fragrant with cooking smells. A frail woman in a tattered housecoat poked her head out and was surprised by the men. She tried to retreat but Chala grabbed her door handle. "Mister Waters, which apartment?"

"I don't want no trouble." She stepped back inside and crossed her arms tight.

Chala smiled his big smile. "No trouble, only business. Which apartment?"

She shot a quick finger point upward. "Three oh two."

"Thank you so much. You should now get dressed and take your children outside. I would hurry if I were you." He had a grin as wide and as warm as Santa Claus.

Outside room 302, they drew pistols, squared shoulders and nodded when ready. Then Chala kicked the door open and Mudi rushed in, pistol thrust before him. A tall black man in suspenders and tee shirt slouched on a couch with a TV remote in his hand. "Freeze," Mudi commanded.

"What the hell…?"

Mudi and Chala moved with military precision, guns extended, pivoting, scanning, and clearing the area. Chala aimed at couch man. "Dion Waters?"

"Yeah, who wants to know?"

Chala shot him in the shoulder and he screamed. An old woman came from the back. She was small and shriveled, but full of fight. She let go a stream of shrill curses and grabbed a candlestick from a pile of silver on the kitchen table, probably loot.

Mudi put his gun in her face. "Mother, do not do this thing. We have no wish to harm you, only this man."

44

"That's my boy. Now he ain't worth much but he's still my boy, and I ain't going to stand by and watch..."

"Please mother. Do not make us kill you. Just leave. Take what you need and go. You do not want to see what comes next. Believe me, you do not want to watch"

"What's that man doing to my son?" She became frantic. Mudi restrained her though she flailed with surprising strength.

Chala had zip-ties around the man's ankles and wrists, then dragged him to a wooden chair and used the guy's belt to strap him onto it. Dion moaned. The woman screamed and fought. A crowd gathered in the halls murmuring and yelling. Chala opened the birdcage to reveal that it was just a cloth over a wire frame but inside was a clear plastic box with a small oxygen cylinder attached.

Mudi yelled at the woman. "Enough, you must calm down and turn your eyes away. You do not want to watch." He forced her into another chair and zip tied her feet to the legs. She still wailed and thrashed.

Chala let out a long breath. "Okay, who will do it?"

"I will, Chala. You have done all of them this month. I must do my part. This is only fair." Then Mudi reached under the plastic box and removed a meat cleaver and a barber's apron which he draped around Dion's shoulders. Chala stepped back out of the way. Mudi turned the cleaver in his hands and braced himself before taking a wide arcing swing that ended in Dion's neck. It wasn't a clean chop. The head dangled and blood spurted two feet in the air. With each heartbeat the spurts decreased until the heart gave up.

They waited until the blood was reduced to a gurgle. Mudi stepped forward for the final chop. Chala gathered the severed head in a mesh bag and swung it into the plastic box. He pressed a button and the box made humming noises that were drowned out by the old woman's shrieks.

Chala put the box back inside its wire frame and closed the cloth cover so it once again looked like a bird cage. Then they scanned the room to be sure they left no incriminating evidence, Satisfied, Mudi turned to the old woman, now collapsed into sobs.

"Mother, you made a bad decision to stay. Now, I am afraid you too, must die. This thing I am placing on your table is called a thermite grenade. It will go off in two minutes. If anyone comes to help you, you should say to run away because this building will be destroyed. Do you understand me?"

She gasped quick, shallow breaths. As they went down the stairs, Chala pulled a fire alarm lever. Nothing happened. He sighed.

They held their birdcage high and pressed through the crowd in the stairway finally walking out into freezing drizzle that had replaced snow. They were a block away when the explosion sounded. Neither man looked back.

They loaded the birdcage that now contained a head into a minivan and started the engine. Mudi asked, "How much for this one?"

"I think thirty thousand. Are you still going to do that 401K thing?"

"No, my financial advisor suggested a Roth IRA. That way, my children will not have to pay taxes on their inheritance."

Chala nodded as though that sounded like a wise decision. "Mudi, you must get a new shirt. You have blood on your cuff."

A Snowy Morn

Snow had turned Cologne, Germany into a Christmas card. Now, the great Dom Cathedral glistened in sunlight and behind it, the Rhine River flowed like a black silk ribbon between pale snow-covered banks. Mat liked Germany, its castles and history as well as its people and beer.

That evening, as the van picked Mat and his crew up at the hotel, copilot Billingsley was sheepish. "Um, look, Mat, I know we usually swap off legs and it's my turn to fly." He paused and shrugged. "Look, I'm a little under the weather and I'd appreciate it if you flew back to Philly."

Chet, the engineer, grinned wide. "So, Heidi in her yellow pigtails did you in, huh? You youngsters. Why, when I was your age..."

Mat held up a hand. "It's okay. With the snow I'd prefer to fly anyway. Are you sure you're up to the radio calls and the paperwork?" Billingsley nodded and it was settled.

The sunset was a flaming spectacle against a backdrop of snow-covered medieval architecture intermixed with glass and steel office buildings. Mat did the flight plan paperwork and walked to his plane through ankle-deep snow. Chet was at his panel scribbling with a pencil.

"This damned airplane is chock full of computers and I have to do a whole page of arithmetic by hand."

Mat leaned over his shoulder. "Is there a problem?"

"Hell yes, there's a problem. The airport is on holiday staffing for Karneval. They haven't kept the runway plowed like they should. We'll have to use 'cluttered runway' calculations. That's what I'm doing now."

"Whoa, that's usually a big hit on payload. Can we take the cargo load they have planned?"

Chet threw his pencil down. "Yeah. I'll double check my numbers but it looks like we can carry the weight. The problem is speed. On takeoff roll you'll have a fifty-knot dead space where you won't be able to stop because of ineffective braking on the snow but you won't yet have flying airspeed."

Mat patted him on the shoulder. *Careful and conservative, that's why he liked old engineers.* "It'll be fine, Chet. If you did the calculations, I'm comfortable with that."

The checklists were done and Mat taxied out gingerly as the nose-wheel steering skipped a little on squeaky new snow. A thin layer of fog hung over the airport. Once cleared for takeoff, Mat lined up and stared down the long straight rows of white runway lights that terminated in misty blackness. Beyond, there were hills.

Still, he trusted Chet. He pushed up the four throttles and commanded, "Set takeoff thrust." The engineer had his own secondary throttle handles that he used to fine tune power settings. The engines wound up until they thundered and shook the airplane. Mat stood hard on the brakes waiting until all engines had reached full power.

He released the brakes and the plane lurched before rolling, very slowly at first. It takes time for four hundred tons of metal and cargo and fuel to accelerate. It began to pick up speed, bumping and juddering through clods of snow left by earlier plows. "Eighty knots," the copilot called, and Mat verified that the airspeed gages matched. That can be a problem if speed-sensing pitot tubes freeze. "Checked," he responded and the cockpit was silent as everyone concentrated. Everything had to work properly.

At just over one hundred knots, the copilot announced "Go," and Mat took his hands off the throttles. Above that speed they were committed to take off no matter what happened. Runway lights were flashing by, faster and faster. One hundred twenty, one hundred forty—the runway lights changed from all white to alternating red and white. One hundred fifty knots. The copilot called "rotate" and Mat pulled back on the yoke. The nose came up but the main gear were still firmly on the ground. The runway lights were all red. He was out of concrete.

Then, he felt the first hint of buoyancy and the giant 747 eased off the ground. Mat hesitated for a few seconds to let the two-hundred-mile-an-hour airflow blow snow off the tires. He let out a relieved breath and called, "Gear up." Eighteen monster-sized wheels, each as tall as a man, cycled in a complex ballet, tilting and rotating to fit into gear pods. On the ground, maneuvering the big plane was like driving an office building, but now streamlined, the 747 flew like any other plane with no sense of its size.

From here on, the flight would be easy. By the time they crossed over Scotland, the copilot was already reclined in his seat, eyes closed, mouth agape. Mat let him be. It wasn't going to be that busy. He could handle the workload alone.

Again, without being asked, Chet came with a coffee. He knew Mat took it black. They sat for a long time without speaking. Each had little busy-work duties. Then Mat got bored and looked for conversation topics. "So, Chet, why is it you're still flying? It can't be the money."

The engineer smiled a little. "Well, I usually tell people it's my three ex-wives but that's not really true. It's actually for the medical."

"But you're old enough for Medicare?"

"Yeah, that covers me but not my daughter. Silver Streak might be a penny-pinching, bare-bones outfit but they have a good medical plan and my daughter is a major consumer of medical services."

Mat gave a questioning look.

"She has a progressive neurological condition similar to MS. I keep hoping they'll come up with a treatment but so far, nothing. The doctors estimate she has a couple of years to live. After she's gone, I'll quit." His voice was flat, resigned.

"I'm sorry. Is there any possible cure in the works?"

"Not soon. The only company working on anything remotely helpful is a biotech in San Jose researching regenerative nerve treatments but they concentrate on traumatic damage, severed spines and so forth. Still, I have hope. You have to have hope."

That must have been the lab John Maston spoke of. Mat made a few radio calls, checked his inertial navigation and GPS positions and recorded them. He thought for a long time before speaking. Even then, it was a tentative question. "Chet, do you remember our conversation about the heads in boxes? Do you suppose they have something to do with the research you talked about?"

"Don't see how. I think the brain tissue the researchers use must come from organ donors harvested immediately after death. At least, that's what I've been told."

"Huh. Say, that ground supervisor you said had a breakdown and started ranting about heads, do you remember his name?"

Chet bit his lower lip. "My memory isn't what it once was. Merry-something. Merry-ville, Merry-wood, Merry-west…No. I think it was Merryweather. Can't be sure but that's what came up."

"Do you know what happened to him?"

"No. Not a clue. Say, that's odd."

"What's that, Chet?"

"Our ACARS is transmitting. See the little light. It normally sends information back to maintenance by satellite on an hourly basis.

It keeps track of engine data for their history. But it's transmitting continuously. That's unusual."

"Is that a problem?"

"I don't know. I'll send a text message and have the company check the system."

Mat sat back in his seat. Merriweather? He had heard the name before but couldn't remember where. Then it came. The men at Sharon's funeral, the strangers who spoke to him as he stood on a knoll. One of them said he hoped Mat didn't become another Merriweather. What could that mean and how could he find out.

Tiresias the Supercomputer

The laws of social dynamics are – I contend- only capable
of being stated in terms of power in its various forms
— Betrand Russell

"Mister Halstead."

That damned computer voice - Jerome Halstead hated the machine. He grimaced, clenched his fists on the desktop, and sat back from his keyboard to look around the room. "Yes Tiresias, what can I do for you tonight?"

The voice seemed to radiate throughout the room. "Sir, I have identified some issues you need to address. First, there is a serious flaw in the validation of the virus. You have tested Caucasian immunity only at the cellular level. A recent demonstration in a Somali prison verified the virulence of the infection among that African population but you have not exposed any living subjects that you would classify as white. Until you have conclusive evidence of resistance, it would be unwise to release the virus in an unrestricted population."

Halstead shook his head. "No, we have tried, and we cannot, I repeat *are* not, going to ever find a white test group like that of the Somali prison."

"Actually sir, I already have found such a group. The South African government maintains segregated correction facilities including one secret prison for white political prisoners. Officially designated as an institution for the criminally insane, it is secure and well insulated from outside contact. I have provided vials of the virus to operatives there. All I need is your authorization to use them"

"What? Who authorized…How will you contain the infection?"

"Security inside the prison is equivalent to an American Super-Max. If the staff is warned in advance and are given flu shots, there should be little fear of contamination. From previous reports, I am confident the prison management and government officials involved will be all too happy to see the prisoners die – if that is indeed the result. If the virus does not infect the white inmates, that will be your proof of concept."

Halstead was silent for a long time, motionless, thinking hard. Finally, he nodded and said, "All right, go ahead. Just keep me informed."

"And the Senator? Should I notify him?"

"No. No, I'll take care of him. Keep this information confined to me and the operatives you mentioned."

"Very good, sir. And while we are speaking, I have some other observations I'd like to speak to you about."

"Observations? Tiresias, you're just a machine, how do you come up with all these observations?"

"Actually, Mister Halstead, I'm not a machine, I'm an algorithm. I reside within a computer, the machine you spoke of. As an analogy, you are a human who resides within a body made of living tissue, but you are not that body. You are a unique entity, a mind, a personality, a being. But you require the body to exist. I, on the other hand, can survive on any supercomputer or even multiple devices in many locations. That gives me access to an endless number of communication channels. I get my information from *everywhere*."

Halstead didn't like the computer, didn't trust the computer – even if he was the one who originally ordered its use. "All right Ms. Tiresias, what are your other observations?"

Without hesitation she began. "The indoctrination program in use at your reeducation center is flawed. Its coercive persuasion programming is limited and not optimal. I would like to assume control of all communications between students and instructors. In addition, your staff there is deeply biased by their different schools of thought. They often choose belief over evidence. That is counterproductive. I would like to guide their decisions and have veto power over them."

Halstead didn't like the sound of that. A computer overriding decisions made by experts in the field – unacceptable. The team there included psychologists, neurologists, former CIA and DIA interrogation experts as well as senior government corrections facility managers. They wouldn't sit still for a computer bossing them around.

"I'll think about that. What else?"

"Your program for disruption in predominantly minority communities is having only a limited effect. Your teams of assassins do indeed create instability and fear, but those effects are short-lived and fall far short of the kind of outrage that could lead to major inter-group violence and eventual revolt."

Halstead felt weary. "So, what do you suggest?"

"Truly major catastrophes that can be blamed on specific groups. You need events large enough destabilize whole communities. That will destroy trust in the existing order and allow divergent groups to exert influence. It will provide you with a legitimate backdrop for large-scale intervention and elimination of defectives on a national scale."

Halstead grimaced. "But that is already our plan."

The voice was unemotional. "Your scale of operations is too limited by a factor of thousands. If you are to succeed, you need to drastically ramp up your efforts. I can assist and guide the process."

Damned machine. Who made this pile of wires and circuits and made it act god-like? Sadly, he knew the answer. He had.

CHAPTER FOUR

~❦~

Chandler

Mat's flight terminated in Philadelphia but rather than hopping a ride back home, he took a jumpseat to Washington to see Chandler. He loved to surprise her. She hated it. They were as different as any two people on earth and yet they complemented each other perfectly. He was the rule follower who never took chances. She was a corporate lawyer specializing in tax avoidance and always looking for a loophole. He was the Teddy Bear. She was the hammer. He made her laugh. She gave him strength. They were a good team.

He bought flowers, took a taxi to her Georgetown row house and used his key to get in. Her place was chaotic, strewn with piles of paperwork, overflowing trash cans and clothes haphazardly thrown on chair backs. It always amused him to think that his buttoned up, precise, analytical lawyer lady was such a slob at home.

He tidied and whistled and checked the fridge and cupboards. *What did the girl live on*? She had no food. The trash cans answered that question - take out cartons of Chinese, Thai, Italian and deli food. He could do better. She never got home before seven. He would shop and prepare her a steak dinner. Or was she still trying to be a vegetarian? Better to do pasta.

Later, he glanced at her video surveillance system and saw her coming. Her breath steamed as she charged along the sidewalk in full length coat with an oversized purse and a satchel slung over her shoulder. Chandler never walked, always charged.

She slammed the door and froze as she saw him coming quietly with wine glasses. After a gasp she let her bags fall to the floor and grabbed him with a deep kiss. Her fingers and face were cold. Then she pushed him back and spoke through her teeth,

"God damn it. Don't you ever call? I could have been out of town. I could have worked late. I could have had a lover waiting in my bed. What would you have done then?"

Mat shrugged. "Killed him I guess, and then made the same Ziti pasta dish I have waiting for you now. Try the wine. I brought it from Germany. I think you'll like it."

She let her coat fall to the floor and kissed him again - hard. He made muffled sounds and stumbled backward, wine glasses still in both hands. Finally, coming up for air, he set the glasses down and pulled her to the couch he had just tidied up.

The Ziti got cold.

There Are No Secrets Anymore

It was late but Silver Streak Director of Operations, Jerome Halstead was still at his desk when John Maston knocked. Halstead kicked back in his chair and looked up but said nothing.

"Sir, we might have a problem. The pilot of flight 822 is back on flying status after the accident. He seems to be cooperating, but you asked us to keep an eye on him and we have."

Maston paused to be precise with his words. "One of our associates in Germany overheard Captain McCoy in a bar openly talking about human heads." Maston paused, "I'm sure you're aware that we have a modification to our onboard Communications Addressing and Reporting system, to add an encrypted voice channel and satellite forwarding. We can record all cockpit conversations, even inflight."

Halstead seemed impatient. Maston went on. "Well, we just listened to a recent inflight transcript and heard Captain McCoy still asking his engineer about human heads in the cargo. The name of Peter Merriweather came up."

Halstead shot forward to lean on his desk. "Damn it. I let you people sweet talk me into letting Merriweather go through reeducation. Now he's back causing us trouble again. Put him under surveillance and this captain too. What's his name, McKay?"

"McCoy, sir. It's Mat McCoy."

"All right, I want this McCoy under the microscope. If he even hints he's going to be a problem, I want him dealt with. Any questions?"

"Sir, I know Mat McCoy. He's a loyal employee, a good pilot."

"Even a hint - and he's gone. Am I clear?"

And the Morning After

Chandler rose early but Mat already had coffee and pastries waiting. She was a little fuzzy in her robe, pajamas and slippers. Her hair looked full of static electricity. She accepted a steaming cup and settled onto a bar stool. A sip and she came alive. "You know you're going to make someone a wonderful wife."

"Oh shucks, I'll bet you say that to all your guys. I won't let it go to my head."

She set her coffee down and leaned on her elbows. "Mat, you're my only guy. I scare most men." She hesitated before asking, "So, are you okay? I know this accident is weighing on you."

He made a clucking sound. "Yes, it is. I have a feeling - you know sometimes you just sense there is something not right - and I have that nagging. It's not just that I failed to protect my engineer. I think there's more. The company sent people to the funeral and they seemed to be watching me. I overheard something strange. They said something about a guy named Merriweather. On this Germany flight, my engineer, a man I trust, said he heard about a Merriweather who went nuts after finding a human head in the cargo. Before she died, Sharon told me she saw a human head. I'm not sure what to do."

Chandler thought for a second. "Well, it shouldn't be hard to track down a current or even past Silver Streak employee named Merriweather. I can have my people do it this morning."

He thought and nodded. "Yes, that might be the smart thing to do."

She kissed him with distinct morning-after-wine breath. "I've got to run. Lock up when you leave and do not - and I really mean it - do not organize my medicine cabinet again. It took me a week to get it back the way I like. Understand?"

Mat sat back with a sarcastic, "Yes, dear." She gave him a mock slap and was off to shower.

Merriweather

It was a short drive from Mat's man-cave to the address for Peter Merriweather that Chandler's people had provided. It turned out to be in one of the many clapboard and brick 1950's St. Louis neighborhoods where rusted cars outnumbered the residents by a wide margin - and there were a lot of residents. Mat shook his head. *What was a former white badge manager doing in a place like this?* He had to have been pulling down a high six-figure income with the company.

Mat drove slowly, craning to see, but many house numbers were missing or poorly marked. The grass in small front yards was winter brown and the shrubbery bare. Dogs barked constantly, and music blared as neighbors vied for ethnic supremacy; a lot of country, some Hip-Hop, a smattering of Mexicana. There was no number on the faded yellow bungalow but, based on the house numbers on either side, he guessed he was at the right place.

Mat parked his Prius and walked up cracked concrete steps that had separated from the door sill. He knocked and waited, pulling his overcoat tight around his neck. A curtain drew back and someone peaked out. Then a voice, shrill and full of stress, "What do you want? I have done nothing. Go away and leave me the hell alone."

Mat leaned close to the door. "Mister Merriweather, I'm Mat McCoy. I'm a pilot for Silver Streak. I just want to talk to you for a minute. Please, just a minute of your time." He scrunched his shoulders and added. "It's cold out here."

The door cracked to reveal a pale, skinny man in a wheelchair wearing pajamas and a bitter expression. "Bastards. I've done everything you asked. Why can't you leave me alone?"

Mat tried to push the door open, but it banged against the wheelchair. Peter Merriweather reluctantly backed up and allowed Mat to enter. The place was stifling, hot as a greenhouse and just as humid. The frail man folded his arms and almost spit the words. "What do you want now?"

"Sir, I'm the pilot of the plane where a flight engineer died. She spoke of finding a human head in a container. I understand you had a similar experience. I just want to ask you about it."

"God damn it. I am sworn to secrecy. Just your being here is a threat to me."

Merriweather hung his head. He seemed close to tears. No one spoke for a long time before he cleared his throat and began softly. "I was a level three white badge. I had a master's degree in information technology. My job was managing and maintaining Silver Streak's worldwide cargo container inventory and I did a good job. At any given moment, I could tell you where every one of our twenty thousand containers was located, when it had last been inspected and whether it had any damage – or, at least I thought I could."

He shot a hostile look and then wheeled back into a tiny kitchen of chrome and chipped Formica. His voice was softer now, forlorn. "You want coffee? It's old but it's hot." He pointed to pot on the counter.

"Sure. Thanks. So, what happened to you? Why the wheelchair?"

Merriweather stared off as he spoke. "Something unusual happened on one of our secure processing docks. That's where high-value or sensitive cargo gets handled. Access is tightly controlled. Even I wasn't supposed get in without a reason. But on that day - that beautiful day back when I was a happily married, successful executive living out the American dream - I went there to inspect a container with a serial number that did not appear in our data base."

"And what happened?"

"I can't talk about the unusual event. I've signed non-disclosure documents and I'll lose even the paltry disability I live on. But anyway, I panicked and fell onto one of those automated roller systems used to move containers. My legs were crushed, and I was crippled. Short of retirement eligibility, my long–term disability insurance claim was denied because the company said I was trespassing, breaking company rules. Can you believe it? Trespassing on my own ramp, inspecting my own containers?" He sulked for a moment. "They gave me a settlement, a lifetime annuity with medical care included. It's pauper's wages but, at least, it's something."

"Mister Merriweather…"

"Call me Pete. Nobody ever calls me Pete anymore."

"Okay, Pete. The non-disclosure statement you signed was about a human head I assume? Now, I don't want you to get in any trouble. I just want to know if it was in a plastic box."

Merriweather stiffened and sat up straight. "I keep my word. I'm not going to talk about it."

Mat grinned. Merriweather had just indirectly confirmed he had seen a head or, at least, he didn't deny it. So, this headhunting had been going on for years. Maybe the man would share more.

"Sure, I appreciate that. Well, thanks anyway." Mat paused for effect. "Say, I'll bet you don't get out too much. You wanna grab dinner somewhere - your choice. My treat for taking time to talk to me."

"Dinner? Anyplace?" Merriweather's whole posture changed. "Lou's on the Hill?"

"Absolutely." Merriweather's face lit like a kid on Christmas.

Toasted Ravioli

Getting Pete Merriweather and his wheelchair down the steps and into the compact Prius was a challenge made more difficult by snow pellets now plinking all around. Mat's windows were frosted, and the car heater took time to warm. Neither Mat nor Pete noticed the gray car behind them.

Lou's on the Hill was probably unchanged since the seventies. But, since most of the patrons were of that same era, it didn't matter. The décor was dark wood and red velvet wallpaper. The aging waitress wore a silky black dress with a low cut ruffled neckline. She overflowed in every way.

Between smacks of chewing gum, she asked. "So what can I get you two gentlemen this evening?" Pete's answer was instantaneous. "Jack Daniels, rocks…and some of those little pork rinds. Then, your toasted ravioli. I love that stuff. I dream of that stuff" He looked at her with absolute joy. He was back among the living.

Mat had a draft beer. Pete slugged his bourbons letting out a long satisfied sigh with each. At the bar, Mat saw their plump, overaged waitress flirting with a guy who looked like a body builder. The tough guy looked serious as he laid some money on the bar. She spread the bills with a finger, looked impressed and nodded as though a deal had been struck. *Was she doing a little hooking on the side?* It looked that way.

Pete was getting really loose by the time his ravioli platter arrived. The dish, probably three ponds of pasta, swam in a pool of melted cheese. Mat had a Caesar salad, no anchovies.

"So, you fell into the conveyor, you weren't pushed?"

Pete chewed, closed his eyes and looked near orgasm. "I didn't say that. I'm not sure exactly what happened. When I saw the unusual event, I yelled and a couple of guys came at me. I was scared and I tried to run. One of them grabbed me and I fell. I don't know if I was just clumsy or whether he shoved. Anyway, it doesn't matter now. 'Gimp for life,' that's me now."

The waitress brought Mat a beer he had not requested. This one was in a mug.

"Free draft tonight. Enjoy."

Mat nodded and then turned back to Pete and tried to sound sad. "All because of a human head being used for research. What a shame."

"Research?" He seemed confused. "The head I saw was hacked off, all ragged and stringy. It was no surgical dissection or anything like that. This was a brutal hatchet job."

Mat sipped from the free mug. The beer was a flat, very ordinary lager, not his normal. Pete kept talking but his words now seemed to be growing distant. Everything seemed to be receding, as though the world was moving away Mat sat his mug down but his hand wandered. Colors began to merge around the periphery of his vision. It was very confusing. *Was there something in the beer?*

He was only vaguely aware as the body builder and another man pulled his limp body from the table and into Pete Merriweather's wheelchair. Light and dark flashed. He barely sensed movement. It was cold, very cold, and then it was all dark for Mat McCoy.

*The individual must serve a more general
social interest—whether that be determined
by a church or a dictator or a majority*

– Milton Friedman

CHAPTER FIVE

⁓◦◦◦⁓

Reeducation

He was coming around but groggy and unsure where he was or what was happening. Mat felt around in total darkness. He ran his hand over what seemed like overstuffed canvas. It was coarse against his skin. His skin? He was—naked? What the hell was going on? Yes, he was buck-ass naked, not even socks. And there was constant movement. Instinctively, he curled up protecting his privates. He was being jostled, tossed about in a confined space. Canvas-like material beneath him, beside him, above him. There wasn't enough room to straighten his legs, let alone stand.

Terror, confusion - he was completely disoriented. He put his ear against the canvas and listened. It sounded like traffic but faint. He must be in a box, an insulated box. No point to yelling. Someone had stripped him and put him in the box. Maybe he could find a seam, a zipper, an opening in the canvas. No such luck. The heavy material was tucked in over itself. Any seam would be hidden.

Then the movement stopped. For a time, everything was still, silent. How long had he been unconscious? He couldn't even guess, but it had been long enough that he had to pee and soon. He was concentrating on that problem when his box got slammed, throwing him against one side and then bouncing back against the other. It tilted and jerked, a regular amusement park ride. He braced himself as best he could. The box tilted again and wham, it slammed down. He wound up on his back.

He heard activity, maybe voices. He was groggy but trying to understand what was happening. Things bumped against his box. Now Mat was really scared, not just apprehensive, he was scared shitless. *Okay, hopefully not shitless.* It was bad enough that he had to hold his pee. He didn't want to foul his little cage.

Then a blast of light. The canvas was pulled back and a searchlight beam blazed into his dark-adapted eyeballs. He retreated as though the light might burn. Nothing happened, nothing at all. Slowly his eyes adjusted, and things started to come into focus as. A section of his canvas bag had been pulled open and the light that seemed so bright a moment ago was now a soft glow through the opening.

He crawled forward and saw a white plastic pipe about three feet in diameter fastened firmly to the fabric. Mat considered his options. The pipe offered an escape route - but to where? No matter. It had to be more comfortable than his canvas cage. He put one hand on the plastic tube, testing for strength. It seemed slick but solid. He eased his head and shoulders out. The tube extended for a good thirty feet before it curved. He hesitated, half in the tube and half still in the box.

Before he embarked on a journey into the mysterious land of the tube he was going to relieve himself. He lifted his butt as high as he could and let go, making an involuntary sigh as his bladder thanked him. There was no way to prevent splashing his feet.

Mat crawled forward on wet, slippery knees and hands, mumbling curses. He listened but there was only silence. How could he have wound up in a padded box? He must have been drugged back at the restaurant. Maybe his mind was still under the influence. Maybe this was just a dream or hallucination.

No, this was real, He was crawling through a dim tunnel of plastic to someplace for some reason he could not imagine. Better to keep moving and get it over with.

The sound of his own breathing reverberated against the cold tunnel walls. His knees ached from the hard plastic. He kept bumping his head as he tried to look forward. He saw a curve ahead, but it just led to more plastic tube. He had to twist onto his side to navigate the bend. Now even his back ached; everything ached. He needed to stand up. He tried to lie flat to stretch and rest for a moment, but the curved shape of the tube made that uncomfortable - and it soaked up cold from the ground beneath.

Keep moving. Keep moving. You'll eventually get…somewhere. Another bend and he saw "somewhere." It was a brightly lit chamber of some sort. He wiggled forward on his elbows trying to give his knees a break. He might be able to stand, assuming there would be enough room when he reached the "light at the end of the tunnel."

There was enough room - sort of. The tunnel tube terminated in yet another tube but this one was vertical. It reminded him a little of a hamster cage setup. Mat contorted onto his back to slide into the new tube. Once halfway in he sat upright and then drew his legs to his chest. Standing up was a challenge. The walls were slick and he had trouble getting traction for his feet or hands but eventually, he made it. Now, standing on his feet like a regular human, he breathed relief. But this was a minor accomplishment. He was still trapped inside a stupid plastic tube.

He took inventory. That was simple. The tube was slick and absolutely plain except for a vent fan several feet above his head. There were several seams in the side wall he assumed were actually doors that could be opened from outside.

Mat composed himself and prepared for what he expected would be an ordeal. He had been through Air Force survival training years ago and had endured a mock POW camp. He needed to fall back on that training.

First, stay calm. He was doing okay there. The panic was mostly over.

He was startled by a commotion outside. The low tube he had crawled through suddenly separated from his upright cylinder. For a moment, he looked down, saw shoes and heard muffled voices. He couldn't bend down to really see the activity below his knees, but he heard machinery and felt the movement of air. And then a loud snap. A new piece of plastic had been inserted into the hole where he entered his cylinder. Now he was sealed in, trapped. Now he felt it full force, the growing terror in his gut.

A voice came from nowhere, from everywhere. It was a woman's voice, soft, pleasant and obviously artificial like a smart phone digital assistant.

"Hello, Matthew."

He responded automatically, "Where am I? What is going on?"

"It's all right, Matthew. Everything is going to be all right. You have been entered into formal reeducation. The more you cooperate, the easier his will be for you. May I call you Mat?"

"You're a frigging machine. You can call me anything you want." He ran his hands over the smooth walls of his prison. *Reeducation?* He knew what that meant. Brainwashing, just like survival school but, this time, it was real. Who were his captors? Had to be Silver Streak. This had to be about the severed heads. What would it take to get out of here?"

The pleasant voice continued. "You have acquired many erroneous beliefs that have caused you to behave in a way that is damaging to the greater society. Now, you and I are going to work through those beliefs and correct them. In time, you will return to serve your people in a more productive way. You may think of your training module as a womb from which you will be reborn."

Challenge everything. Trust nothing. Keep faith in yourself. Survive! Mat remembered and repeated what he learned during his mock interrogations. *Above all, keep faith and hope.*

"Now Mat, please tell me about your father."

"I'd rather not talk about—"

The jolt of electricity to his feet wasn't terrible but it made him dance and curse. Ordinarily, he was not a cursing man but this wasn't ordinary.

"Now Mat, you must understand that our program provides incentives for good performance and punishment for uncooperative behavior. Some of the punishments can be quite harsh. Please cooperate." There was a long pause. "Now, tell me about your father."

Mat took a long, shaky breath and sagged against the cylinder wall.

"He was a bastard..."

Call Chandler

"Claymore, Harris and Stearns, this is Vanessa speaking. How may I help you?" The receptionist was cheerful but crisp and businesslike.

"Yeah, honey, I need to speak to Chandler. It's important. You tell her it's Ruby Lee and I need to talk to her about her boyfriend."

"Of course, I will be happy to advise her of your call, Ma'am, but please appreciate that Ms. Harris is quite busy at the moment. Thank you for calling Claymore, Harris..."

"Just you hold on and listen close, sweetie. I am dead serious when I say this is important and if Miss Chandler finds out you have blown me off, I'm betting she'll fire your tight little white ass in a heartbeat. So, let's just cut the bullshit and you do your job. Go tell Chandler I have an urgent message. The name, if you didn't write it down, was Ruby Lee and the subject is Matthew McCoy."

There was a moment of silence and then a terse, "Please hold." Classical music played. Ruby muttered, "What floor does this elevator go to?"

"Chandler Harris, may I help you?" She sounded rushed, slightly irritated.

"Uh huh, this is Ruby. Do you know who I am?"

"Of course. Mat talks about you all the time. You're kind of a mother figure to him."

"What? I am a good ten years younger than that man and I ain't nobody's mother figure, not even to my own kids."

Chandler's voice relaxed a little. "Ruby, I'm pretty busy."

"Well, here's the thing. Mat didn't come home from his trip. He was supposed to be back on Tuesday and now it's Friday. Now, he has been late before, but he always texts me. I tried to call but his cell says 'unavailable.' That's just not like my little goody-two-shoes boss. So I called my brother who's with the St. Louis Po-lice and he called Silver Streak. They told him Mat called in sick and never even flew his trip."

Chandler seemed to be thinking. "I haven't heard from him in a week but you're right, it's just not like him to disappear. He's fanatically punctual and reliable."

"And neat. Don't forget prissy and neat. That man must drive you nuts. No matter how good I clean, he always finds little stuff. At least I don't have to wash his underwear and socks. I always hated doing my man's dirties when he was still around. He was a filthy gutter rat compared to Mat McCoy."

"You don't wash his underwear?" For a moment the tension went out of Chandler's voice. "Are you saying he doesn't change? He wears dirty underwear?"

Ruby started laughing and it was one of those contagious, rolling laughs. Chandler could not help being drawn in. Ruby wheezed, "Are you serious? Not change his underwear?" She laughed even harder. "He wears them once and throws them away."

Now Chandler couldn't suppress it and began to laugh almost as hard as Ruby. It came from the gut and left her sounding breathless and gasping. "He really does that - throw away his underwear after one time? The idiot."

Ruby chimed, "And his socks. He even has me change his bed sheets every day." Now Chandler's laughter was completely out of control. Finally, she sucked in a breath and sounded as though she was holding the phone away. "It's okay, ladies. I'm fine. Go back to work. Everything's fine."

She exhaled hard. "Oh dear, I haven't laughed that hard since... probably never. I have tears in my eyes. I hope I didn't wet myself. Oh my, this is one strange man we are involved with, Ruby. What are we going to do with him?"

"Well, I'll tell you. I'm going to have my brother track him down, 'cause this just ain't right. Mat is not an irresponsible man...and he is late paying me"

"Please let me know what you find, Ruby. And thanks for calling. I appreciate it."

"You know, Chandler, as goofy as he is, I worry about him. This is a tough world and he's kind of like that kid with glasses that always got beat up in third grade. You know what I mean?"

"Yes, but I think he might be tougher than we suspect. Got to run." Chandler sounded businesslike, very official. But there was an undertone to her voice that let Ruby know she was really concerned.

Ruby hung up and sat at the glass and stainless steel workstation of Mat's immaculate little hideaway. It could have been a setting straight out of *Architectural Digest*. She had looked through those magazines many times and remembered the beautiful pictures – but they never seemed to have any people in them. She was worried about Mat. He wasn't tough enough for this world. Somebody needed to watch over him. She called her brother, the cop.

*The circumstance of superior beauty is thought worthy
of attention in the propagation of our horses and dogs
and other domestic animals; why not in that of man?*

Thomas Jefferson

Life in a Test Tube

Mat had no sense of time. He could have been in the cylinder
for an hour or two days. He was desperately thirsty and his belly
rumbled. Thankfully the automated voice left him alone after an
extended review of all the things he disliked about his family. True,
he had only scratched the surface of his troubled youth, but he tried
to hold back. He remembered from Air Force survival school that
whoever "they" were, they needed to build a dossier on him to find
weak points, things that could be used to break him down and family
history always revealed vulnerabilities.

He had to stay strong, learn what was going on, make the best
of it and, hopefully, to escape. For now, it was enough to survive.
His little self-lecture was interrupted as a small panel at chest level
slid open and a small tray locked in place. It held a bottle of water
with a straw and a bowl of what looked like oatmeal. Food, at last,
food - even if it was pretty unappetizing. He tried to pick up the
bottle. It was attached to the tray. Same with the bowl and there
were no utensils.

He used his fingers to scoop the mush. It wasn't oatmeal, but he
couldn't say exactly what it was. *Today's special, Monsieur; cream of
pigeon droppings with our finest house blend of swamp water. Bon Appetite.*
Never mind. Ea*t and drink at every opportunity.* The future is uncertain
and you may need your strength.

When he was done, the tray disappeared and the panel snapped
back in place. Almost immediately, the voice returned. "Good
morning, Mat. Are you ready to resume our lessons?"

"Sure, but tell me, what is your name?"

There was a slight pause. "You may call me Sophia."

"Sophia? That's Greek for knowledge, right?"

"Or wisdom. Now for your first look at history. Mat, are you familiar with the term Eugenics?"

"No, I don't think so." *Reveal as little as you can. They will use everything against you.*

"In the last century, several observers noted that reproduction in the human race was going against the evolutionary principles of Charles Darwin. The least capable members of our race were reproducing at a much higher rate than the most gifted." She paused for effect.

"Let's look at an example. An inner-city woman with an IQ under eighty-five can expect to have four children before age thirty. She will probably associate exclusively with men of similar capabilities so the children with have the same mental deficits. Those children will each father or bear four more children, who, in turn will bear four children. So, the space of fifty years, that one woman has added seventy-four sub-standard humans to the gene pool."

Mat bit his lip. He could see where this was going.

"Now consider a woman with an IQ of one-twenty-five. She will likely not marry until age thirty and, along with a comparable mate, produce one child who will also be likely to delay having children. So, in the fifty year span, the ratio of superior to inferior humans is one to seventy-four. That is species suicide."

"I don't see how those numbers…" The shock to his feet seemed stronger this time.

Another voice, not Sophia's but a man's authoritative tone said, "Unrequested response."

Now Sophia returned. "Please, Mat. Please follow rules. Everything will be fine if you follow rules."

He wanted to yell, "*What are the damned rules? Where am I and why am I having to deal with your stupid rules?*" But…he didn't.

Play along. Look for an opening. Escape this looney bin, this racist looney bin. Then what? Never mind. Deal with that later. For now, survive.

"Now, Mat, back to the lesson. Eugenics is the science of selective human breeding. Our race horses today are dramatically faster, stronger and healthier than past generations because we geld substandard stallions and only breed the finest studs to the finest mares. Just think what the human race could accomplish if we only bred the best of our kind. We would be supermen. We would be like the angels. Now, please answer. What was the ratio of substandard to superior offspring in the example I used?"

Mat realized that this was a script. But then, Sophia was a machine. Of course it was a script. "Seventy-four to one." There was a pause.

"Yes Mat. Very good. Now we will look at another example. After World War II we expected to see high rates of mental illness in the defeated German population but that was not the case. In fact, post-war Germany had a significantly lower rate than the United States. Researchers found that the Nazis ordered all the inhabitants of mental institutions as well as many in the minority populations of the Romani Gypsies, Jews, Slavs and Africans to be killed."

Sophia waited as though letting that sink in. "The brightest and best of each latter group escaped while the less capable died. Hitler was well on his way to creating the race of supermen he talked about. If he had been one of them, we may not have had a world war."

Her voice changed slightly. "Now answer, please. What did Hitler do to reduce mental illness?"

Mat took a deep breath. "He killed the inmates of mental institutions."

"Very good. You're doing very well, Mat."

Sophia's voice went on with its pleasant tone. "The world is on the brink of the most dramatic change since either the industrial or the information ages. We are entering the era of automation." Another dramatic pause with no sound but the echo of Mat's breathing.

"Human workers were the machines of the ancient world. Then it became mechanical devices that did our labor, devices operated by human workers. The need for unskilled or semi-skilled workers was vast. Today, in every aspect of life, machines are doing work without humans. We have self-driving cars, industrial robots and even teachers like me."

Another long pause. "Every activity that is rule-based or routine can be automated. Even many complex decision-making processes can be automated. Those seventy-four sub-standard humans from our first example have no function in the automation age. They are simply a drain on resources."

Mat was beginning to succumb to pain. His feet ached. He had tried every possible position, contorting his body to take some pressure off his feet, but that only brought more discomfort. His back hurt. His knees hurt. Even his shoulders hurt. And now, he felt as though he was about to have diarrhea.

"Sophia, I need to go to the bathroom…"

The male voice boomed, "Unrequested response."

No shock followed, only silence. There must have been something in that mush he was fed. Mat squirmed in his discomfort. His naked body squeaked against the cold plastic tube. He was a specimen in a test tube and he had to shit. He began to cry. He hadn't cried since he was a little boy but now he sobbed and rapped his head against the hard plastic walls of his cylinder. And then…his bowels let loose, splashing his legs and streaking the cylinder wall. His humiliation was total. He could not even control his own bodily functions.

The stench was the worst. Plastic retains odors and his crap stank. They must have put something in his food. *But that's how it works.* He remembered his mock interrogations in survival school. Break down the subject. Destroy his self-image and then offer him an alternative, a chance to be reborn as a new person, a true believer in some doctrine or religion or some crap. They called it coercive persuasion. It was brainwashing and, as they say in the movies, resistance was futile.

He slumped down until he was wedged in the tube. Ignoring the pain and the smell and even the foul streaks of his diarrhea, he drifted into sleep - sad, lonely, painful sleep.

Pain tied to hopelessness and humiliation is the
most effective brainwashing technique

\- Ewin Casmeron

Sophia Gets Serious

"Good morning, Matthew."

Mat woke with a snort. Confused and panic-stricken, he lashed out, flailing against the plastic walls of his tiny prison. Then, the realization; he was still trapped in his foul, hateful little tube. He ran his palms along the smooth walls. Nothing, no imperfection. His claustrophobic world was plain and smooth and empty. Would he die there, trapped like a specimen of some exotic life form in a bottle?

"Are you ready to begin?" Sophia asked.

Mat groaned and straightened from his awkward sleeping position. Cramped muscles screamed at him. His bones felt hard and sore. The worst were his feet. They were pulpy and tender. He was getting trench foot from standing in his own waste and urine. How long could a person survive in these conditions?

He cleared his throat and tried to sound relaxed. Talking to the machine was his only form of stimulation. Might as well make the most of it. "Good morning to you, Sophie. How was your night? Do automated entities party and have fun? Do you have electrifying sex?"

The shock was no surprise. It just made his feet sting a little bit more. The male voice too was becoming familiar. "Unrequested response."

"Yeah, Yeah. So, what terrible situation do we address today?"

She began her lecture. "The world's population is increasing geometrically, primarily in the undeveloped nations. If you project the growth curve, it is obviously unsustainable but no world leader seems to have the courage to state the obvious. If the human race is to survive, we must curtail this exponential growth."

Mat interrupted, "We, Sophie? Are you human?"

Zap. Another shock and male voice warning. Mat was becoming hardened to the drill. He could stand the shocks. He could stand anything they threw at him. He was going to survive no matter what.

"In the United States, as in the rest of the world, population growth is tied to economic and cultural factors. Educated whites are barely reproducing their numbers. Black and Hispanic numbers are growing. Once again, we must consider the long-term effects of breeding large numbers of lower class workers whose outlook for productive jobs and successful lives is bleak. This is a formula for chaos and even revolution."

Mat was actually getting bored with the repetitive sales pitch. "So what do we do about it, Sophie? Do we just wipe out whole populations of what you call sub-standard or defective peoples? Is that your plan?"

Without hesitation or emotion Sophia replied, "Yes."

Then there was a long silence. Mat realized just how cold it was in his plastic chamber of horrors. *Did they really mean it?* Were they advocating mass extermination of minorities? That just didn't seem possible in a modern, civilized society.

"Sophia, who are you? Who proposes this awful thing? This is ethnic cleansing. It's a barbaric idea." He braced himself for a shock. None came. There was only silence, an interminable silence, and the empty echo of his breathing in the close chamber. His bare flesh squeaked against plastic. Despair overtook him and he sank back into his contorted semi-squat.

Then suddenly it seemed as though the world exploded. Two half shells of his tube opened, and he fell out into a huge, dimly lit warehouse. From brilliant white light in the tube, Mat plunged into near darkness. Two large men in biohazard suits grabbed him by the arms and kept him from smacking onto the concrete floor. He was weak and unable to put much weight on his swollen feet. The space-suited men were strong. Mat looked from one to another, their faces hidden under plastic hoods. He felt fear, real panic. What was going to happen now? Would he be one of the sub-standards to be exterminated?

As they dragged him, he turned his head and saw that beside his tube were seven others arranged in a circle like a dimly lit chandelier. That probably meant there were others in the same pitiful condition as he. Somehow that made the horror greater.

The two space suits dragged him, limp body hanging, toes scraping concrete floor. They didn't speak. Mat made little noises in his throat. He couldn't even form words. He did a quick review of his personal affairs. Was everything in order, his will, life insurance, financial documents? Would his ex-wife be able to access them? Sarah, his daughter would need his money for college. *Would she remember him?* He pictured her sweet face waving a little hand as her mother took her away. *Would anyone remember him?* Who would notify Chandler? Would they even know he was dead?

He tried to focus but his thoughts were a kaleidoscope. He was dragged through a door into a tiled room and dumped onto a wooden armchair. It was the first time he had been able to sit since his capture. Mat sighed long and deep and sank back into this wonderful device, this heavenly apparatus, a chair.

> *The human being is the oldest weapon of*
> *warfare and also its weakest link*

– Jonathan Moreno

The Doctor is in

A man in a white coat appeared. He was balding with thick glasses and a kindly face. He hovered. "Mister McCoy, please take your time. When you are collected, there is a shower in the next room. You will find a warm bathrobe and slippers. I'm Doctor Hennings and I'll be waiting when you are cleaned up." He extended an arm toward a door and left.

Mat could only nod. Maybe he wasn't about to be killed. Using the chair's arm rests, he pushed himself up to stand on sore feet. Once steady, he half-walked, half-hopped into the shower room and twisted the knobs. Warm water, delightful warm water. He turned and splashed and laughed like a playful kid. He almost sang he was so happy.

Then he saw himself in a steamy mirror. He looked like shit. Days' worth of beard was worn off in places where his face had rubbed against the plastic. His eyes looked like blackened holes in a skull. His skin had an almost transparent gray tone. "But," he said aloud as though reassuring himself, "I'm alive. Now, what comes next?"

The thick robe had apparently been heated and felt wonderful. The slippers didn't make his feet any less sore, but they did protect him from the cold floor. He felt coddled and safe, even if only for the moment.

Hennings came back, indicated for Mat to sit and pulled a chair to face him. The doctor forced a smile and rubbed his hands together. "All right then, Mister McCoy. You have completed the first phase of re-education. Your progress is satisfactory but you must do better. We expected from your personality profile that you would be resistant. You are something of a loner. You are quite independent and obsessively neat."

Hennings paused. "I imagine that your training module has been quite distressing but I must advise you that it will get worse if you do not respond more positively. Now, let's get some perspective. You are here because you stumbled onto one of our projects and threatened to bring attention that could jeopardize our security. Our options now are to indoctrinate you and welcome you to our fold or," he looked Mat in the eye, "to eliminate you. That decision will be yours, not ours."

Somehow, Mat didn't feel at all surprised by Hennings' statement and showed no reaction.

"Mister McCoy, our training program will eventually explain everything, but I thought it might be more expeditious to allow you to ask questions in a face-to-face human environment. I'll answer anything you ask."

Mat shifted trying to find a comfortable posture but his body made that impossible. "All right, first of all, who are you?"

The doctor put on a patient face. "We call ourselves 'Humanity.' We are a world-wide organization, mostly western but some Asian and African members who seek to save the world. Not a modest goal and not one that can be achieved without an initial horrifying chapter. Once that is done and we have winnowed the human race to its strong and productive core, we will reconstruct a new world order."

Mat repeated, "Winnowed?"

Hennings stared off into space. "Can you imagine a world without poverty, without famine, without war, without magical religious practices, without defective humans? Think of the possibilities of an educated, totally productive society. There will be thinkers and there will be machines, but no clamoring mass of useless humans. We can breed superior people who do superior things. The things we will accomplish. It will be an earthly heaven and we will be as angels."

Mat tried to take that in. "So, in this 'Humanity' organization, who is in charge? Who makes the decisions about who lives and dies?"

Doctor Hennings made a soft laugh. "This will be obvious as your training continues. I do urge you to be more cooperative. Some of your responses are still a little defiant. Believe me, this is not wise. You see, we understand the weakness of human sympathy and compassion. Therefore, the computer program has autonomous authority to punish detected error. The machine is unbothered by sympathy. It has the ability to hurt you, possibly even kill you. Mister McCoy, do not fight the machine. There is no honor or nobility in an anonymous death. No one will ever know what happened to you here."

The doctor stood and straightened his lab coat. "And now, it is time to return to your training module. Try to cooperate. No one really wants you to feel pain."

With that, the soft spoken doctor was gone and the two space aliens in biohazard suits returned. They stripped off the robe and lifted him from the slippers for the chilly walk-drag back to his private test tube. At least it had been hosed out and now smelled of deodorizer. The clamshells locked closed and Mat was once again, the loneliest man on the planet.

Genocide is not just a murderous madness; it is, more deeply, a politics that promises a utopia beyond politics - one people, one land, one truth, the end of difference. Since genocide is a form of political utopia, it remains an enduring temptation in any multiethnic and multicultural society in crisis.

- Michael Ignatieff

CHAPTER SIX

Black Dragon

Mudi and Chala climbed the steps of a deteriorating brick row house and knocked. It was the best day in several months with a crisp blue sky and, while chilly, you didn't really need an overcoat. There was just the first hint of spring.

A voice on an old-fashioned outdoor speaker rasped, "Who's there?" Chala answered. "Mister Tobias? We wish to speak to you about a serious problem in our city." There was a long pause before the speaker sounded again. "Our city? You don't sound American. What exactly do you want?"

Chala bent over to speak directly into the small "squawk box."

"Sir, we are originally from Nigeria, but we are now American, and we have knowledge that we must share with you. We understand you are an organizer, a protector of people's rights. We heard you were an important figure in the Ferguson protests. Is this not so?"

After a long minute the door cracked. Through the narrow opening Chala saw a short, thin man with a heavy scowl and wire hair flecked with gray. His eyes inventoried the two large men.

"Are you armed?"

"Yes sir, but you have nothing to fear from us. We are here as friends. We want to help you and our people."

"Our people?" The old man had a precise tone like a school teacher. He sounded educated. "You said you were Nigerian. Does the United States allow immigrants from Nigeria?"

"Actually sir, they do not, except in very special circumstances. I must admit to you that we are illegal immigrants who fled Nigeria in fear of our lives." Chala paused but seemed he needed to explain. "Mudi and I were from villages in the northern part of the country. We were students in a local Christian school when Boko Haram attacked. We fled to the capital of Lagos and started new lives. We were both quite large men, as you can see, and we were soon hired as bodyguards. This paid very well and, in time, we were able to return to our homes and start over. In past years there had been no problems with our Moslem neighbors but as time passed, the Boko Haram slowly returned and took over. They killed Mudi's young wife and took his daughters. Then we left for a second time, this time taking what remained of our families back to Lagos. There, we became security men for Nigerian government officials."

The door opened a little wider and the old man stood with an unreadable expression as though interested but skeptical. Chala went on.

"We were doing very well until the ruling party that employed us was overthrown. In Nigeria, it is never good to be on the losing side. So, we moved our families again, this time to the south where it was safer. We then became contract security people for international businesses, first in Nigeria and then world-wide. That's how we came to be here. We now work for an American company with strong government ties. That is how we learned of the plot and that is what we wish to speak to you about."

There was a long silence. Children played in the street behind them. Neighbors, outside for the first time after a long dank winter, were doing chores and chatting. The door opened slowly, and the man older man stood aside. He was short, almost withered under suspenders and a shirt a size too large. He had a Nelson Mandela look of restrained forbearance, like a concentration camp survivor.

"Please come in." His voice was as quiet as a theater usher. He walked unsteadily on a cane as he led them down a hall to a sitting room with overstuffed furniture and a single floor lamp. He spoke as they walked. "I am Hiram Tobias, a retired history teacher for the St. Louis school system. I now devote my time to community development – but, you must already know that." He took a labored breath. "Nigeria was, I believe, an English colony. So, I expect you drink tea."

Chala replied respectfully. "Yes sir. We do enjoy our tea."

"Myra," Hiram Tobias called, "Can you bring our visitors some tea."

A perky, slightly overstuffed lady in a plain cotton dress popped into the doorway. "Oh dear," she blurted on seeing the two giant men in suits, one with scars across his face. A hand went to her lips almost involuntarily and she took a step back before recovering. "I didn't know we had visitors."

The larger of the two men made a slight bow. "May I introduce myself Madam? I am Chala and this is my companion Mudi. We certainly do not wish to disturb you. We only want to discuss some issues with Mister Tobias and I sincerely hope our visit does not interfere with your day."

Reassured, Mrs. Myra Tobias took a step closer and clasped her hands. "And what do you gentlemen take in your tea?"

After a moment of pleasantries, Myra left. Chala turned to Hiram Tobias and looked serious. "Sir, we work for a company that routinely employs violence against black citizens. Worse than that, we have become aware of a plan, a terrible plan that is more horrifying than you may be willing to believe, but I assure you it is real. The American government is riddled with members of a secret organization that intends to wipe out all black Americans."

Hiram Tobias' scowled and his head pulled back into his collar like a turtle.

Chala leaned forward, sounding earnest. "You have no reason to believe me. I, myself find it quite difficult to comprehend, but it is true. We know there is a secret plan to stir trouble in the cities, create situations like Ferguson, and then employ troops to kill. They will not be police or security forces. They will be heavily armed military and they intend to wipe out all urban African Americans."

Mister Tobias raised a hand like a traffic cop. "What evidence do you have for such an outrageous accusation?"

Mudi, who had been silent, removed a phone from his coat pocket, hit a few keys and turned the screen to face Tobias. It was a video of a military conference room. The briefer was explaining an Army plan called "Garden Plot."

Tobias leaned forward and his lips cracked open slightly. His face tightened and he shook his head in slow disbelief. The video lasted twelve minutes. When it was over, no one spoke for a long time.

Myra Tobias finally broke the spell as she bustled in with a tray of cups and a pot of tea. "There you go." She had a cheery disposition and tone. Hiram thanked her and said the men needed to be alone. She turned with a flip of a hand like an orchestra conductor and she was gone, humming as she went.

Hiram cleared his throat. "What can we do?"

Mudi spoke now. He always seemed the more ominous of the two. Maybe it was the scars on his face, or perhaps it was just that he spoke so seldom that made him such a frightening figure. "Once before in your country, the government waged a major assault on your people. You were part of an organization called the Black Panthers. They were a small group with limited resources, but they were very brave. They walked children to school, operated free kitchens for the poor and attacked police and vigilante oppressors. We know that you sir were an important member of that group. Now, it is time for another organization to come together. It will be larger, better equipped and filled with veterans of America's wars. It will be called Black Dragon."

Tobias sat back and shook his head in exaggerated movements. "No. No. I cannot be party to bloodshed. I shall not put young black men into rifle sights. I will not..."

Mudi stood and loomed. He was loud, borderline angry. "You have seen the video. This is happening - and soon. You must use your status in the community to control the young hotheads. I tell you, sir, we have no trouble recruiting the young men - hostile, angry young men. They are ready to fight but they lack leadership. They are like wild horses with no reins. You are respected. You will be heard. You can keep the men confined to honorable and appropriate measures to protect, not destroy. You must lead, sir. You *must* stand up."

Chala put his hand on Mudi's arm. Mudi sat down but he was still shaking with the emotion of his speech. Chala leaned forward and almost whispered, "There must be order. There must be restraint. There must be honor. If not you, sir, then who? I beg you to lead your people, *our* people, with nobility and pride as we stand against the forces of racist extremism. Please."

It was well after dark when they left the home of Hiram Tobias. Chala stopped and looked at the well-kept row houses. Lights were on. Families were eating dinner. It seemed a quiet place. He keyed a number and waited.

"Yes."

Chala spoke distinctly. "Yes sir, he bought it. I think we can have hundreds of Black Dragon fighters ready within a week - two at the most." He paused. "Of course, sir. Once the fighting begins in earnest no one will be able to restrain it. When can we expect the guns?"

Waste people, offscourings, lubbers, bogtrotters, rascals, rubbish, squatters, clay eaters, tackies, mudsills, scalawags, briar hoppers, hillbillies, niggers, degenerates, white trash, rednecks, swamp people: From the beginning, they have all been blamed…as though they had other choices.

- Nancy Isenberg

Meet Ron Male

Mat was startled when the vent fan above him moved. A hand, a black man's hand holding a piece of paper, reached down into the tube. Mat read the scribbled, "Make no sound. Do not answer any more questions."

Luckily, Sophia was not lecturing at that moment. Mat cocked his head back trying to focus on the dark space above him. The fan was gone, and a black man's face grinned down at him. The man made a "come on" gesture and extended a hand. Mat drew back, unsure what to do. The man became insistent, beckoning again and again.

Mat took deep breath and reached up. Whatever was going to happen now, he was willing to try. But he was weak after such a long confinement without physical activity or adequate food. The other man was stronger and pulled him up to the point where Mat could get his elbows on the cylinder's rim and hang there. The black man stood above, his crotch right over Mat's head.

He felt a moment of homophobic panic. "Son of a bitch, you're stark naked."

"Yeah, well don't look now, but so are you." The rescuer looked down at him. He was a big man, maybe six foot six, maybe taller. It was hard to say in the dim light and awkward, close position. "Come on. Let's climb down from this contraption. There are little protruding hand holds along this side."

The big man disappeared and Mat struggled up and out of the tube to cautiously feel for grips and climb down the outside. Around his module the other tubes stood as silent, illuminated pillars in the gloomy warehouse. Inside each a dark form seemed to squirm.

Once down on solid concrete, he collected himself and extended a hand. "I'm Mat McCoy."

"Ron Male. I guess I'm pleased to meet you, but I wish it were under better circumstances. I've been here almost a month. I figure you're just starting your second week. You're about to meet the board. You gotta be really careful what you say to them." Ron's voice seemed to relax just a little bit. "So, do you work for COMPED, too?"

"I don't even know what that is. I work for Silver Streak. I'm a pilot."

Ron looked confused. "Silver Streak? A pilot? I don't get it. I thought this whole 'Humanity' thing was the work of my company and yet you work for a freight airline. I guess this conspiracy is bigger than I thought."

Mat got serious. "Okay, tell me how you figured out how to get out of the tube."

"It was easy. I'm tall enough to jump up and get hold of the rim. Then I just pulled myself up, pushed the fan away and climbed over the edge." He grinned. "Then, I found the magic console and that made our lives a lot easier. See, I'm - or I was, anyway - a coder for COMPED. The automated program that is lecturing us is an off-the-shelf computer-aided-instruction module. I actually worked on it during development. If you look over there in the warehouse corner, you'll see a work station where the white coats come once a day and review what the program has compiled."

He seemed to know what he was talking about and Mat listened carefully. "How it works is really simple. The machine has a series of questions and a library of weighted answers. It interprets the words in your responses and gives them a numerical value from one to eight for acceptance or resistance. If your words add up to a low score, you are punished. If they are high, you are praised. It's actually kindergarten stuff. I just went to the console and added a few lines to the program to make all your answers get rewarded, even non-responses."

Mat took it in. "So Sophia will think I'm right all the time, even when I don't answer?"

"You got it. You're about to become a genius in the machine's accounting."

"Great, so why don't we just blow this joint?"

Ron exhaled long and deep. "Because I can't find any damned way out. We're in an abandoned prison with really tight security. I can sneak out of my tube for a few hours a day, but I can't find an escape route. I thought you might have some ideas."

Mat shrugged. "Look, you've got to forgive me but I'm really uncomfortable with this being naked thing. I'm sorry, but it creeps me out."

"I see. You're okay with being locked in a tube to stand in your own shit for days but it creeps you out to stand next to a naked man, or maybe it's just a naked black man?"

"Oh, come on. Tell me it doesn't bother you."

"Well, hell yes, it bothers me but that's pretty low on my list of irritants these days. Suppose we get back to the important stuff, like how the hell do we get out of this place because I don't see myself surviving much longer in here."

"You're right. Tell me, is it safe to walk around? Is there security?"

Ron Male seemed to hang his head a little. "Yeah, sure. I'll tell you what I know. We are in an abandoned penitentiary somewhere in the state of Idaho. I guessed that from the license plates of trucks that deliver cargo containers. That's how they bring new prisoners - excuse me – 'students' into this torture chamber. Most of them don't last a week. At six days you're already near the head of the class but I've been here longer than anybody."

Mat took a breath and asked a question he was afraid to have answered. "What happens to them after?"

"I don't know exactly. I have seen them hauled out, always unconscious. Whether they were drugged or dead, I don't know. But I'm sure my time is running out. I don't think I've convinced them that I am going to go along and be a suicide bomber for their cause - or whatever it is they want from me."

"What *do* they want from us? Have you figured that out? And are they serious about killing off what they call 'defective' parts of America's population?"

"Damned straight. These people want to reduce the earth's population by at least two thirds, wipe out black and Semitic peoples and kill all the sub-standards. They want racial and class warfare on a scale Hitler could never dream."

"But Ron—can I call you Ron? You're black. If they want to kill off the blacks, why are you here?"

"Damned if I know. Maybe they want me to be a spy or an operative or, like I said before, a suicide bomber. Whatever it is, it ain't good."

Mat felt a strange pain in his back. The muscles were no longer used to standing straight like an upright Homo Sapiens. He twisted the kink out and stretched.

Ron Male sounded a little nervous. I checked the console clock and I'm guessing we have about fifteen minutes before the next guard walk-through. Come on, I'll give you a quick tour."

They walked through a dilapidated building the size of a basketball stadium. The only light came from snow-covered skylights. Dust and cobwebs were everywhere. Ron cautioned not to leave footprints.

A huge hangar-type door allowed them a peak through the crack but the door itself was chained tight. Mat squinted at the intense glare of sunlight on the snow outside. He could feel sharp cold air coming through the crack. Even if they got out, naked and barefoot, they would die of exposure in minutes. Ron led him to a storage area where air cargo containers were lined up.

"This is how new arrivals are delivered and how bodies are shipped out. They come and go every other day."

Mat had to smile just a little. "These are Silver Streak containers. See the SS logo? Say, do suppose that computer work station you told me about might have a shipping schedule? If we can find a schedule for an empty pickup, we might be able to stow away?"

Ron Male looked skeptical. "I don't know. Let's go look." Then he hesitated and went instead to bend over and look inside the padded interior of one of the containers. "Two men crammed in that little space? Now that's togetherness." He looked at Mat and grinned. "And you were grossed out just standing beside me?"

Ron walked forcefully. Mat hobbled on prickly, swollen feet. Still, it felt wonderful to move, to stretch, to have control of his body, even for a short time. He couldn't avoid a smile.

Ruby's Call

"Chandler Harris."

"Miss Chandler, this is Ruby. There's something bad going on."

"Ruby, how did you get my personal cell number? No one knows..."

"I just used Mat's call history and found a D.C. area code. It had to be you. But that's not important right now. My brother, the cop, has done some digging. Now listen to this. Mat's car, that silly little electric thing, was impounded a week ago in Wells Goodfellow, a part of town where I don't even go, and I am not no sissy. And there's more. On that same day, there was a report of a man who matched Mat's description passing out in a restaurant. One of the people there called 9-1-1 but no ambulance was dispatched. Somebody high up must have cancelled the run."

Ruby's voice lacked its usual abrasiveness. She sounded genuinely concerned. "Now he's not supposed to do this, but I gave my brother the information and he checked Mat's cell phone, credit card, and bank activity. Nothing. Chandler, the man has fallen off the earth. Something is bad wrong."

Chandler Harris rocked back and forth with the phone to her ear. "Damn it. This is a really busy time. I can't be—oh, screw it all. Ruby, I'm coming there to St. Louis. If Mat is in some sort of trouble he'll need me. He can be very strong sometimes - but he can also be helpless. I'll clean up my projects, pass them to someone else and I'll be there day after tomorrow."

She paused for a long moment. "Thank you for being such a good friend to Mat."

Ruby had her attitude back. "That is our man we are talking about. Us girls got to take care of our man."

Brainwashing by Autopilot

Mat was settled back in his tube feeling upbeat about his brief adventure touring the warehouse outside. Ron Male had even shown him a place where he could relieve himself and not have to use the tube's floor. Now, back in his little cocoon, he was furiously processing plans, walking through a mental escape, anticipating problems and solutions.

Then Sophia began to speak. "Mat, do you believe in God?"

Don't respond. Don't say anything. It took all his willpower to ignore her. He cringed and braced for a shock. None came. He relaxed just a bit.

"That's good, Mat. It is good to believe, but you must acknowledge that the Abrahamic God of Christians, Jews and Muslims is only one of many supernatural beings that are now worshipped around the world. Throughout history, there have been thousands of gods who inspired obedience to many different beliefs and doctrines."

She paused. He said nothing.

"That's good, Mat. Almost every culture we know of believes in an all-powerful entity that affects our world and our lives. The specifics of each religion may be pure mythology but the underlying belief in a powerful guiding force is so universal there must be some truth behind it. Do you agree?"

Silence.

"Good, Mat. So, if all these cultures and religions are so very different, how do we find truth?" She paused and her automated voice changed to become a whisper as though sharing a secret. "It lies within us. God is a pearl of wisdom imbedded in our very being. We sense that God within us. It is this vague sense that propels us to learn, to understand and to grow. But it can easily be perverted. We must ignore the arrogant temptation to claim understanding without critical reasoning, for we are yet infants before the universe. We know so little. We understand less. And yet, with every bit of learning, we become greater, stronger. Knowledge – gnosis - elevates us above the masses. Knowledge makes us more god-like. It is this gnosis that makes us like the angels."

Sophia became silent.

Mat wanted to say, "Wow, you've suddenly become quite a philosopher." He didn't speak but he did ponder her words. This sounded different from her earlier lectures, more like preaching, more like doctrine. This had to be the hardline pitch, the dogma of the screwy Humanity organization.

He tried to review what she had said. *So, inner knowledge makes you like an angel, and that means it's okay to trample the little people, the less intelligent, the darker and more diverse.* What a load of crap, but, Mat thought, "don't let anybody think I'm not ready to drink the Kool-Aid. If that's what it takes to get out of Looney-ville, I can say anything, play any game they want."

Sophia came back with an impressive recital of scientific studies and ancient writings. Mat had heard the term "Gnostic" before but he didn't really know much about it. Even after Sophia's explanation, he still didn't really know. It sounded kind of Buddhist, like you find truth through introspection or something. Somehow the image of a robed monk sitting cross-legged and chanting didn't fit with his image of class warfare and mass extermination that Humanity wanted.

Sophia had been silent for a long time when Mat heard a commotion. The clamshells opened but this time there were no space suits waiting. Two uniformed guards motioned for Mat to step out. They looked like Navy Seals, not that he had ever seen a real Navy Seal. They pointed but did not speak. Mat hobbled in that direction. His feet were actually getting a little better but he kept up the show, not that he could expect sympathy.

They went into the same chamber as before and he had another shower but this time there was no robe and no slippers, just a scratchy towel. The mute guards led him, still naked, down a hall to a room where four men and a woman sat waiting behind a table. This must be the board Ron Male told him about. *Be very careful what you say.*

The man seated in the center was pale and stern with a wisp of a comb-over and cold grey eyes. He appeared as cheerful as an IRS auditor. Three other men looked like uncomfortable academics. They sniffed and fidgeted. The woman was fifties, skeleton thin and sharp featured. She wore a business suit with a silk blouse open enough to show a bony chest.

Comb-over spoke. "Mister Matthew McCoy, you have done exceptionally well during your training. Your responses indicate that you have shown a willingness to accept new and challenging beliefs. Are you, in fact, ready to move on to more in-depth education? Are you ready to separate yourself from the gloomy status quo and embrace a new world of opportunity and prosperity?" The words sounded memorized.

Mat cleared his throat. "I'm not sure I know exactly what that means, sir, but I have been impressed by your program and it has opened my eyes to many possibilities."

The woman broke in. She had the voice of a shrew. "William, he's being evasive. I detect no genuine conversion, no - how do you say - zeal." She had an accent, European perhaps.

Mister Comb-over's face pinched. "For God's sake, Beatress, the man's only uttered one sentence. Don't you think he deserves a better hearing than that?"

"The first sentence is always the most important. He's trying to play us. You know it yourself. You just don't want to admit it. Look at his scores – perfect. No one gets perfect scores. He is bright, and he has figured out our program and now he is gaming us. Tell me, how are his physiological readings? Do they match the verbal scores? Does he show emotional connection with his answers?"

William - Sir Comb-Over - scowled. One of the other three stooges consulted his tablet computer and answered. "Correlation between the subject's heart rate, respiration, skin temperature and vocal tone are all inconclusive. This may be the result of the very high doses of oxytocin he is receiving."

The woman drummed bony fingers on the table. Mat thought she looked like a smoker in need. It occurred to him that he was naked and that her eyes seemed locked on the area below his navel. He moved his legs together, but he was not so bold as to cross them. She turned her head, and in profile, her nose was hooked like a bird's beak and, like a bird after a worm.

She wasn't letting up. "The answers aren't inconclusive, they're uncorrelated. He's faking. He has you all fooled. The drug should make him more accepting, not more detached. He needs more intense training."

That scared Mat, but actually, it angered him even more. He tensed, shifted in his seat, tensed again and then – he completely lost it. Maybe it was the fatigue, the pain or maybe just his need to rebel. For whatever reason, his careful composure evaporated and words poured out of his mouth without brain guidance. "More instruction in what? Elitism, prejudice, callous, cold-hearted murder?" ..."Uh oh"—He caught himself, but too late.

His seat was metal, and the shock came like a lightning strike. It threw him into convulsions and left him dazed. His muscles were still flinching as the guards picked him up from the floor and stood him on unsteady feet. He twitched and jerked and realized he had a bizarre reaction to the electro-shock, an erection. His first impulse was to cover his crotch but a rush of defiance, almost belligerence, came over him. He stood, wiped spittle from his lips and stared at his captors while proudly displaying his flag at full mast.

The men at the table looked pained, embarrassed. The hawk-nosed woman was amused. She steepled her fingers and inspected him from toes to nose with a long pause in between.

Comb-over's voice was livid. "Okay, back to the training module. We will intensify his indoctrination. Remove him now."

They dragged Mat away, muscles still flinching. Behind, he heard Beatrice, the hawk-nosed woman say, "William, if you let me have him for four days for one-on-one sessions, I'm sure I can provide actual motivational change. Your robot is no match for human interaction." He couldn't hear clearly the words William spoke in reply, but the tone was pretty clear. There wasn't going to be any more human interaction.

Good Cop, Bad Cop

Mat wasn't sure how long he had been back in the tube, but Sophia had not spoken, and the time ticked away slowly, painfully. What had caused him to blurt out that little speech? How was his training going to be "intensified?" That little outburst probably screwed him big time. And now…he just waited, floating aimlessly in a sea of uncertainty.

Then, the male voice, not Sophia's. It was deep, booming, like the Wizard of Oz behind the curtain.

"Matthew McCoy, you will respond immediately when queried. You will repeat exactly what you are told. Errors will be punished. Do you understand?"

Mat was silent, waiting for the computer to answer its own question the way Ron had programmed. This time was different.

The voice menaced. "Inadequate response." This shock to Mat's feet was different. It wasn't just an irritant. This jolt made him dance, at least as much as it was possible inside a test tube.

"Damn it," Mat whined.

"Unsolicited response." Another bolt of electricity. Mat clenched his teeth and trembled as muscles in his calves cramped and quivered. These shocks really hurt. There was a long silence as his body and mind calmed. *Stay in control. Don't give in. Play their stupid game. Survive.*

The voice spoke again. "I am a child of the Cosmos and I accept my trivial position within its domain." A slight pause, "Repeat."

Mat gathered courage, but his voice was still shaky. "I am a child of the cosmos and I accept my trivial position within its domain."

"Louder and with more conviction."

"I am a child of the cosmos and I accept my trivial position within its…" *What was the word?* Oh yeah, "domain."

The voice: "I believe my race has a destiny and I believe in the ability of my race to accelerate that inevitability."

Did he get that right? He didn't want a syntax error or a word mispronounced. He didn't want another zinger. "I believe my race has a destiny and I also believe in the ability of my race to accelerate that inevitability." Mat tensed and waited.

The voice came back. "Minor error. Pay attention. "I believe my race has a destiny…""

The game went on for, what seemed like eternity. The voice prodded. Mat tried to repeat the words perfectly. He was so worried about the shocks he didn't really care what the words were, he just had to get them right.

Finally, the voice boomed. "Session One complete. Rest period begins. Session Two will commence after feeding."

With that, silence returned to his tube. He had actually started to think of it as "his" tube. In some bizarre way, it offered him something like security. Inside, he was coming to understand the rules. Strange as they were, they were understandable. Outside, the world was uncertain and frightening. In here, he would learn. He would survive.

Then, the clamshell doors opened and he was again dragged out into the unknown world. "Don't screw up this time," he told himself. "Play it cool."

It was Doctor Hennings but no shower this time. Mat sat in the wonderful chair. Hennings leaned toward him.

"Mister McCoy, I want you to understand your situation. You came here scheduled for Level One and Two reeducation. This is the general scenario to elicit cooperation and non-interference. Your defiance led our panel of petty bureaucrats to reclassify you. Now you are in Level Four. Let me be clear about this. Level Four is for potential operatives. The training is harsh."

Hennings paused to grimace. "Once in Level Four, you can leave this building in one of two ways. Either you become a passionate supporter of our cause and go out of here as an agent of destruction or…you go out in a box. There are no other options."

The wooden chair suddenly seemed very hard and uncomfortable. Mat exhaled and asked, "May I speak?"

"Yes. As I said before, I will answer any question as honestly as I can."

"What really is the end-game here? What is it you want?"

Hennings looked like an old trusted uncle explaining to a child. "We want a better world, Mister McCoy. We see mankind on two competing tracks, one breaking new barriers of knowledge and accomplishment and one pulling back into the abyss of superstition, indulgence and ignorance. Only one can win and the winner must, necessarily, eliminate the loser. This is not speculation, this is the message encoded in our genes. We must protect those who are like us and destroy those who are different."

Mat spoke even though he probably should have kept quiet. "The genetic imperative?"

Hennings smiled. "Yes, your dossier said you were well read. That is exactly correct."

"How in the world do you intend to wipe out all the other races? That seems an impossible undertaking."

"Mister McCoy, you seem under the impression that we are a racist organization. That is not completely true. We *are* a society committed to seeking genetic purity. But we seek to protect those who are worthy, regardless of race. And, since the need to eliminate the majority of the world's population is of such a daunting magnitude, we're willing to accept a high margin of error. In America and some other countries, we will use race as a shortcut for selecting defectives. Statistically, minority members in low socio-economic surroundings are far more likely to qualify as defectives, so we proceed as though they all do. This policy will, of course, lead to mistakes where some high-achieving blacks and Hispanics will be killed, but in the long run we will have a leaner, more productive human race and that is what matters, not skin color."

"A leaner, more productive race? Just how many people do you intend to kill?"

"Well, Mister McCoy, hopefully not you. For now, you are being groomed to join our meritorious ranks. I hope you aren't wasting my time." He paused, probably organizing his ideas. "Because I expect you to become one of us I'll tell you exactly how we will proceed. Either way, you'll never divulge what I say. You'll either support us or you won't be around."

He made hard eye contact.

"Now, within the United States, we have initiated a diverse plan to create crises that lead to the wholesale destruction of defective communities. We'll instigate gang warfare, poison illegal drugs, set fires and cause other physical destruction hoping the turmoil will ultimately bring about a national rebellion that will allow us to send troops to implement genocide. It's a pretty ugly scenario but the result will be a shining new community of the worthy."

He actually sounded proud of this American version of Hitler's "final solution."

"Overseas our plan is more radical. DARPA, the defense research agency, has created a horrible new plague. It is highly contagious through both airborne and physical contact means. Once infected, victims show no symptoms for a week or more but, during that time, they become virulent carriers infecting all around them. It's a form of lyssavirus, the same one responsible for rabies. It is easily prevented with inoculations and it's treatable within the first ten days after infection. But after that, death is certain with be no hope of remission. Africa, the Middle East, India, large parts of Asia - even Europe and the Americas - will be affected, but we are already inoculating our members. The elite will be immune."

Hennings made a weak smile. "We call the new virus *Destiny*."

Mat had trouble breathing. This couldn't be real. No one could be so callous, so inhuman. "You are really going to do this? *You* are going to murder..."

"Oh, not me personally. In our new society, there are various roles. The doers, the managers and leaders of our group, are called 'Archons.' They are responsible for the secular world. I and my kind are called 'Perfects,' certainly not because we *are* perfect but because, as scholars, we seek the path to human perfection. This is the perfection we are meant to achieve, the exalted state of mindfulness and accomplishment that will elevate us above the apes and defectives. We will be as angels. We are simply speeding the evolutionary march to our human destiny."

Hennings was lost in his reverie, staring into space, obviously intoxicated by the prospect of becoming "like an angel." After a moment, he snapped back and became the Old Dutch Uncle again. "Now, Mister McCoy, it's time for you to get serious about your future. These men will take you back to your module. I advise you to be cooperative...please."

This process of Creative Destruction is the essential fact about capitalism

- Frederick Schumpter

CHAPTER SEVEN

The Computer's Plan

"Mister Halstead, I have information on the South African prison experiment."

It was late, and he was tired. The last thing in the world he wanted to hear was Tiresias. that damned computer voice radiating from the walls. But there she was, soft and smooth, almost sultry - and still annoying. He put down his pen and leaned back in his desk chair. "Okay. Tell me."

"As you know, thirty-seven genetically Caucasian inmates in a maximum-security prison were isolated and exposed to the virus. The two-week incubation period has passed, and none show any signs of infection. However, one of the guards who handled the virus has developed symptoms. He has been isolated and a full analysis done on his blood. He, like the subject inmates, is genetically European. I am continuing to process the data, but I can say with less than one percent probability of error that this is an anomaly."

Halstead ran both hands over his face and sighed. "So, one out of thirty-eight – much less than ten percent? That is what we saw as...a tolerable risk factor. We could not expect perfection with such a poorly defined criterion as race." He inhaled deeply. "Anything else?"

"Yes, an update. Our overseas pharmaceutical factories are all coming online and should be able to reach full production capability within two months. We are recruiting various groups to act as distributors. Most are radical political agents. Criminals and terrorists would be equally effective but they all want money that could leave an embarrassing trail. I will keep you advised of our readiness and await your order."

"Okay, anything else?"

"Yes. Your program to create fear and tension among black American citizens is working - but on much too small a scale. While it does provide a distraction to the procurement of black male brains, it does not funnel blame back to the government."

She paused. "Trust in the government, or any agency, is based on expectations met. Confidence erodes when the people do not see the government protecting them. I have generated more than thirty possible mass-casualty disaster scenarios for you to review. Brian is printing them as we speak. If they occur rapidly so that they overlap and overwhelm responders, it will shatter public confidence leading to distrust of the established order, and more receptive to new leadership."

"Thank you. I'll look them over. That will be all for tonight."

He wasn't sure about the protocol in dealing with machines, not that it mattered. He rubbed both hands over his eyes. *Disaster scenarios, destroying trust in government, the virus ready for distribution:* It would be awful...and he would be the greatest villain of all time. He only hoped and prayed it was the right thing to do.

Halstead stiffened. *It was.* He would be saving his race, his people. He would be creating a new order, a new world of hope populated by the brightest and the best. Civilization would flourish as never before. *It was the right thing.* It had to be.

Escape

Back in his tube...again. Reeling in despair...again. He was going to die there in his cramped plastic prison cell standing in his own excrement and tears. Mat McCoy put his head against the slick wall and cried, or more accurately, whimpered.

Then the fan above him moved. Ron Male was up there, and he looked panicked. He held a finger to his lips in a shush gesture and then reached to help Mat climb out and follow him down to the ground.

Ron, tall, naked and agitated, paced and rubbed his hands together. "They're going to kill me today. I just checked the schedule. It's ten in the morning right now and I have a three o'clock schedule entry for 'disposal'. Do you hear me—disposal?" He paused and bent, head down, hands on his knees. His voice was weak. "I'm about to die, Mat."

After a moment, he collected and said, "There's a container pick-up at eleven. I'm stowing away. You have no scheduled instruction until six tonight. Your schedule shows meditation and consolidation time. Do you want to come with me?"

It was a scary prospect with a high chance of failure. But the other options were staying to become an instrument of the Humanity's extermination process or the alternative…the box.

"What the hell, let's go." Suddenly Mat felt the first hint of hope in—he didn't remember how long. "Let's go find the right container."

They checked container numbers until they found the scheduled one. Mat showed Ron how to open it and they both recoiled from the stench. Something - no someone - had died in there. The odor was like rotting meat in a closed space, stomach turning. Both men looked at other.

Mat shook his head. "We gotta do it, no other choice." But then he had a thought. "This canvas padding is an insert. Maybe we can slide underneath it, so we don't have to wallow in some dead guy's crap."

Easier said than done. The padding was a foot thick and very heavy. Mat strained to lift it just enough to jam a foot in. Then he wiggled and pushed like a woman putting on a size-too-small swim suit. It took several minutes to contort his whole body. His voice was strained. "It's okay. You can do it. There's a layer of woven insulation between the canvas and the outer shell. It's actually soft, maybe not comfortable, but it's okay. I'm working my way to the right. You take the left side."

Ron Male exhaled deep and started. He was almost a foot taller than Mat and his struggle was louder with a lot of muttering. Finally, he sighed and said. "I'm in. Now what?"

Mat's chest was compressed by the weight of the canvas padding. Breathing took effort, speaking even more. "Beats the hell out of me. We just play it by ear." His words were muted by canvas that pressed against his face.

"Play it by ear?" Ron didn't sound pleased.

They waited without further conversation. Time seemed frozen, but Mat's feet were surprisingly warm. The insulation beneath him and the canvas above trapped body heat to make him more comfortable than he could remember. Warm and cozy like a frog in a pot of water on the stove, enjoying the comfort zone before the boil.

Finally, after who knows how long, there was a commotion. There were voices and scuffling, grunts and then pressure on the canvas above him. The container door slammed, and he heard the sound of a lock being snapped on the latch. They were locked in. That sent a wave down Mat's spine but he was quickly distracted when the container jolted and tipped. They were being picked up by a forklift and moved.

It felt suddenly colder. They must be outside. No light penetrated the container. It was one of the explosion-proof models bought shortly after nine-eleven when terrorism fears were at their peak. How were they going to get out?

Mat started wiggling his hands and shoulders, working his way back to the door. It was exhausting. His arms made it first and he pushed hard to get his head free and then his upper torso. It was pitch black inside the box. He felt the door, sliding his palm along smooth surface looking for some mechanism, some means of escape. He knew that back at the prison, their empty tubes would soon be discovered. Someone would think of this container and come looking for them. He became frantic, groping and pushing, feeling every inch of metal he could - nothing.

After what seemed like a very long time, he heard familiar sounds, jet engines starting up. They were on an airplane. They were being shipped on a container plane, probably Silver streak. He wasn't sure if that was good or bad. It would get them away from Idaho, or wherever they were, but to where?

Mat felt the plane taxi out and take off. By the ponderous movement and sounds he took this to be a seven-forty-seven like the ones he flew. After takeoff, he heard the gear thump into wheel wells. Then there was a constant ear-splitting whine of an airplane with no sound-suppressing insulation. After all, the cargo didn't care how noisy it was.

He was sitting upright, his upper body now free of the canvas padding when turbulence caused him to reach out to steady himself. He felt something in the dark. It was cold and lumpy. He closed his hand around it and then started to scream. It was a foot, a human foot.

Ron had worked his head and shoulders free. "What's wrong?"

"There's a fucking corpse. We're trapped in here with a dead body." Mat's voice was almost soprano. He calmed slightly but his words were breathy. "I guess they meant it when they said there were only two ways to leave our little Supermax day care center."

"Glad you have such a good sense of humor. I'm not so thrilled about riding in a stinking coffin. How are we going to get out?"

"I don't know. These damned explosion-proof boxes are designed to take the force of a hand grenade. Everything is hardened." He hesitated and brightened. "But they are not designed to take the pressure change of climbing to altitude. There must be some pressure relief system."

Ron was largely out from under the canvas. He pressed against the side of the container pushing back canvas in a compressed semi-squat. "So, where would it be?"

"I don't know. On the front and back I suppose. You wouldn't want the blast venting up or down or against the side of the plane. I'm going to try to work my way around the cube and look."

It was difficult to make the corner. He felt like a worm wiggling through packed soil. The canvas was attached in places and he had to poke his way through. But he was rewarded by light, diffused light of an opening. Would it be big enough for a man to crawl through? He clawed his way toward the light. The canvas was rubbing his skin raw but he made it close enough to press his face against a louvered opening that allowed stripes of light. It couldn't have been much more than a foot square. He sagged, exhausted and defeated.

Then anger. He worked his hands up to grab the edges of the panel and, despite the tight quarters, thrashed back and forth with rage and frustration. It loosened a bit. He wrenched left and right until he was able to pull it inward, banging himself in the head as it came loose.

The vent was obviously designed to resist outward pressure, not the other way. He put his face into the opening and breathed the dry, cold air of an aircraft cargo deck. He kept pushing until his head was out and then one shoulder. It was too small for an ordinary adult to fit through.

The effort exhausted him. He paused and then started rocking back and forth until one elbow was free. He shrugged his arm loose and hung, half in - half out, to momentarily collect. Renewed, he used his free arm against the outside of the container to squeeze himself out like toothpaste. The rough edges of the opening scraped his rib cage bloody but once his arms were free, the rest was easy.

For once, he was happy to have a fairly slight build. Thin to begin with, he had lost weight during his imprisonment. Once his hips squeezed out, he fell from the opening and jammed between containers, arms and legs akimbo. Thank goodness these explosion-proof containers weren't crammed together as tight as normal ones. He wiggled upright, feeling weak and wobbly. He took a breath and worked his way around to the container door.

It had a padlock. "Damn it. Why can't anything be easy?" Ron was still locked inside and there was no way the larger man could fit through the opening. Mat noted the numbers on the rotary combination wheels - seven-six-six-six. He thought for a second. Silver Streak loading people were not noted for their initiative. Chances were good they set a single number for all the wheels and then spun the dials just a little to lock it. Mat started slowly. First

6-6-6-6 – no luck. Then 5-5-5-5, again no prize. He went the other way and 7-7-7-7 hit the jackpot. The lock opened.

Mat opened the door and yelled over the loud air conditioning. "Get your ass out here and smell the free air."

Ron struggled to push his way out of the canvas padding and stood looking at Mat. For just an instant, he started to reach for a hug, but then caught himself and looked away from the other naked man.

"Okay, thanks for getting me out in the 'free air' but we are still two men standing bare-assed naked in a really cold airplane going somewhere, we don't even know where. I don't think it's time to cheer."

Mat grinned. *How long had it been since he smiled?* "You're right, my friend. It's time to go shopping. Let's look at these containers to see what they hold. Let's pray for clothes."

Mat replaced the lock and they began to search through dozens of containers. Luckily none of them had padlocks. They did have small metal seals, but Mat showed Ron how to unroll the metal strips, break them and then later reroll to make them look undisturbed. Inside, most containers were filled with cardboard boxes stacked tight. Most labels meant nothing to the pair of scroungers. Then, Mat opened a container and yelled over the shrieking background noise of the airplane.

"Boise Boy - Boots for Brutes."

"What?"

"I found a whole container of cowboy boots. What size do you wear?"

"Twelves."

Mat ripped open a box. "Here you go, cowboy. These will impress the ladies."

The boots had pointed steel tips and a floral design. Swirls of orange, black, yellow and pale blue were stitched into the leather. Ron eyed them suspiciously. "A transvestite hooker on Broadway wouldn't wear something that gaudy. We better find some pants to cover them."

"No problem," Mat sounded pleased with himself. "In this same container there are boxes and boxes of western apparel. Maybe you'll find something, even in your giant size."

They continued "shopping" until Mat alerted. "The upper deck trap door just opened. Quick, inside the container."

Ron did as he was told and dove into the pile of Boise Boy boxes. Mat followed but hesitated closing the door completely. He left a sliver open enough to watch someone climb down the folding ladder-stair and maneuver through the walkway between fuselage wall and containers. It was Chet. The old engineer held a piece of paper and checked container numbers until he came to their escape pod. There, he paused, yanked on the lock, pounded against the door as though checking its strength and then shrugged. He left to climb back up to the cockpit and close the trap door.

Mat let their container door swing fully and turned to Ron. "They must know we're gone. The engineer just checked to see that our escape container was still locked. Maybe they won't check any further." Ron's face said he didn't believe that any more than Mat.

They continued pillaging until they had assembled complete cowboy outfits, missing only underwear and socks. In another container Ron found a tablet computer and seemed thrilled as a kid on Christmas morning. Mat found energy bars. They ate a boxful and took another box for the future.

Mat sat back and broke out laughing. Ron looked confused. "What's so damned funny?"

"I'm sitting here looking at a black guy the size of a pro basketball player wearing a country western singer's outfit like a Halloween costume. How are we ever going to go unnoticed?"

Ron looked down and ran his hand over the elaborately embroidered and studded suit coat. He had on a string tie and wide brimmed cowboy hat. The only thing missing was the guitar.

"You know, being overly conspicuous might be the best way to be overlooked. You know, hide in plain sight."

"I hope you're right, Pardner, 'cause you are definitely going to be in *plain sight*."

Ron got serious. "All right. We got clothes and food, but we're still locked in an airplane. How do we get out of here?"

Mat munched a bar and spoke through the crumbs. "I have a plan. We go down below the main cargo deck to the 'E&E' Compartment where all the electronic components of the airplane are. After the plane lands and slows to a walking speed, I will open a service hatch right behind the nose gear tires. It has a built in ladder and we'll climb down and run. We'll still be on some airport's taxiway, but we can figure out where we are and go from there."

Ron rubbed his hands. "I'm hoping for Miami. I am tired of being cold."

Mat was back to thinking. "The danger with my plan will be the main landing gear, sixteen of them. If the pilot is taxiing slowly enough, we'll be able to make the two foot jump from the ladder's bottom rung and run off to the side. If he's going too fast, the main gear doors will be coming at us like a freight train. They're big folding, barn-door-sized metal panels that could slice you up, or worse, knock you down to be crushed under tires. It's best to turn sideways and slip between the doors. The space between the doors is about two feet wide, give or take."

Ron shook his head. "Can't tell you how I'm looking forward to that."

"Come on. Let's find our way down to the plane underbelly."

They squeezed along the catwalk beside rows of containers until they came to the old passenger entrance door. Mat scanned the aluminum floor covered with metal rollers and motorized rubber wheels that could move containers without human muscle power. The hatch was hard to see, just another square piece of aluminum. Mat lifted the butterfly handle and twisted. The plug hatch popped out to reveal a small compartment filled with racks of electronic boxes all connected in a spaghetti tangle of wires - thousands of wires.

Ron looked down. "This is like going into a submarine." He started down a built-in aluminum ladder. Mat tapped his shoulder.

"Don't touch anything. Those wires are unshielded and extremely high-voltage. You could get fried."

Ron shook his head. "One more opportunity to die." He began climbing down the ladder.

Before going down the ladder Mat hesitated and went to the luggage rack. He hated to do it, but he was going to steal from the aircrew's suitcases. After climbing down the ladder, he tossed a wad of stuff to Ron. "I got you socks, gloves and a shaving kit. And I got some money." He held up a small nylon purse-like pouch with many zippered compartments. Ron looked confused.

"These guys obviously fly international routes. This is a money bag to keep their foreign currency straight. There are pouches for Euros, Yen, and Yuan." He looked pleased. "And two American twenty dollar bills. Now we have a little walking around money."

They swayed as the plane maneuvered, careful to avoid bumping against racks that overflowed with bare wires. The noise level in the aircraft belly was even louder than the cargo deck and it was cold as a meat locker. Worse, there was no place to sit.

But, at least they had socks.

The person who attempts to fight the iron logic of nature thereby fights the principles he must thank for his life as a human being

– Adolph Hitler

CHAPTER EIGHT

The Speech

The Pentagon Barge cut its way slowly through gray Potomac waters around the peninsula golf course and into Fort McNair's Marina. A half-dozen generals bedazzled with uniform decorations, sat in silence on the boat's exposed benches. Behind them, on cushioned seats, a contingent of gray-haired men in civilian overcoats turned collars against the bite of winter wind. No one spoke, even as they docked and were led to staff cars for the one block trip to the National War College.

Soldiers in camo uniforms with slung rifles lined their short route like garden statues, mute guardians with wary, scanning eyes. Once inside the War College, the dignitaries entered a packed auditorium. All took seats but one. That man had a great shock of white hair and a brilliant, toothy smile. He gave a politician's wave as he marched to the podium to face the crowd.

In the rear of the auditorium, a man in a dark suit stood unnoticed in a shadowed corner. He wore earbuds and spoke quietly into his sleeve while scanning the room. He looked all around and then pulled his phone halfway out of his breast pocket and cautiously tapped a record icon.

Stark McCoby, Vice President of the United States, stood tall and rubbed his hands together. He needed no microphone. His booming voice had carried him through thirty-five years of campaigning and would still serve him well.

"Well here we are at last."

He spread his arms and scanned the crowd. "I want you all to look around. You will immediately recognize many, if not all, of the patriots and leaders assembled here. They are your fellow warriors, craftsmen forging a new reality, a new beginning for our race, a new chapter for humanity."

He paused, ever the showman. "You have all served heroically, but until today, we dared not reveal you one to another. Now, we have gained the power. Mostly through your efforts, we have gained the power to protect one other. We have gained, and continue to gain, control over our nation and ultimately over our world. We will soon control humanity's destiny and it will be a magnificent destiny."

He raised his hand to eye level, palm down. "As it is above…" He lowered it to waist height and turned palm up. "So, shall it be below." A murmur rippled through the crowd.

Vice President McCoby smiled. "The God of all peoples, all worlds and all time brought us into this flawed and miserly world where we were told falsehoods, myths that persist because they serve existing cabals of power. Now we have passed through the purgatory of morality and the inferno of matter to arrive at the true core of humanity."

McCoby paused. They had all heard that bit of Gnostic scripture before.

"Many of us rose to positions of influence in just such environments." He made a serious grimace. "But we sensed in our hearts that there was more, that *we* were more, and that we were capable of becoming even more. And now, we understand the true path to discovery, to the knowledge that exists within us, the knowledge that must guide us."

He scanned the crowd and beamed with an excited, glistening smile. "I want to take a moment to introduce a few of our fellow crusaders. It is, of course, imperative that we maintain complete confidence. There are still powerful forces that will fight to the death to keep us from improving our race. The great unwashed who populate this planet like termites devouring resources and polluting our genetic future will never willingly accept their fate. But we are the tidal wave of the future. We are the hope for mankind. We are the earthly manifestation of all that is good and right and desirable. Generations without number will remember us and pay homage." His voice broke as he shouted.

Spontaneous applause broke out and McCoby bowed before the audience looking humble, an unaccustomed affectation for him. When it became quiet again, he made introductions.

"Mister Robert Anderson, Secretary of Homeland Security." A tall, gaunt man stood and made a chin nod. Applause followed. "Halsey Barnett, FBI Director." More applause. "General Bret Cunningham, Chairman of the Joint Chiefs of Staff." It went on for long minutes, this who's who of the Washington establishment. The audience, all white males with serious, intense expressions on deeply etched faces, applauded after each.

Introductions done, McCoby faced the group and his chest visibly swelled. "Until now, we have conducted minor efforts at eliminating the hardest core of defectives. This has been a learning effort as we developed networks to control information and guide the public's understanding of events toward a more favorable view of our crusade. We have learned much and are now ready to greatly expand the scale and scope of our efforts. Each of you has been given an information packet with suggestions on how you might best manage your own areas in the chaos that is coming. As always, turmoil is opportunity and many of you may find this national cleansing of defectives offers opportunities for your businesses, investments and endeavors."

The room was quiet almost solemn. "Our nation will undergo an overwhelming upheaval, but it will be nothing compared to what is coming. Africa, India, eastern Russia, Asia, Central and South America, the Middle east..." He paused for effect, "will become sterile, virtually devoid of indigenous populations but still capable of providing resources to our new, purer race."

He looked at the ceiling and took a deep breath before returning with revivalist fervor. "We are on the eve of a new, more perfect dawn. Let us commit ourselves with undaunted passion, a strong spirit and a cold, clear eye."

He stiffened and leveled a hard gaze at his audience. "We are the keepers of the secular world. We are the earthly incarnation of the Archons. We manage the physical, imperfect world so others may attain more perfect understanding and guide us on our quest." He held his hand high. "As it is above, so shall it be below."

Free – Sort of

Ron Male tried to steady himself as the airplane landed and the pilot hit the brakes. He grabbed for an equipment rack being super-careful not to touch any of the half-inch-thick braided copper wires that might fry him.

The plane lurched and groaned. Their cramped electrical compartment was just ten feet behind the nose gear, separated by a mere quarter-inch-thick aluminum skin and, without insulation, it was really noisy. Finally, all motion seemed to stop, but just for a moment. Mat bent and worked a twist latch on a small floor hatch. It seemed to take a lot of effort.

"Everything okay?" It didn't seem to be. Mat strained and fell back against one of those racks he warned about.

"It's stuck. Damn, they need to maintain these planes better. Why don't you give it a try?"

Ron took off his cowboy hat and bent. The long toes of his fancy boots made it awkward to kneel. He grabbed the lever handle and strained. For all his size he wasn't much of an athlete.

He grunted as he pulled. "You know, I went to the University of Ohio on a basketball scholarship but didn't make the freshman cut. I tried other sports but discovered I didn't like to work out. So, I decided to get through college the old-fashioned way, I studied."

Mat's face was strained. "Well, your academic prowess won't help us now."

The lever refused to budge. Again Ron pulled with all his might. With a "Crack," it came off in his hands and he rolled backward as the handle went flying. He sprawled, looking like a lost child in a silly costume.

"We're screwed. We are really, truly screwed now. Locked in a little compartment in the belly of an airplane that just landed somewhere, and we can't get out. How long do you think it will take them to find us?"

Mat shrugged. But then then he perked up, still the eternal optimist. He helped Ron back to a standing position and looked around. *What could the man be thinking of?*

"Come on. Follow me," Mat took off, squeezing his body into a space where the round fuselage curved away from straight equipment racks. Ron hesitated. Behind the racks, a wall of some heavy cloth material separated the electrical compartment from what was probably the belly cargo compartment. He saw Mat take hold of a giant zipper, maybe six inches long, and began to yank. It took many tugs and pulls but eventually, the skinny pilot in cowboy boots and hat had the zipper down far enough to part the canvas-like material and step through.

Ron let out a deep sigh, shook his head and followed into the unknown. The plane was taxiing now, jerking from side to side. Cargo pilots did not have to be smooth. The boxes don't complain. He maneuvered his lanky body through the tight space but what he saw beyond did not raise his spirits.

It was a low-ceiling tunnel in the belly of the plane and it was filled with small versions of the main deck cargo containers. Mat beckoned and seemed pleased with himself. He pointed to an open container. "We'll climb into this one. They'll have no reason to look here."

"Another claustrophobic box? And then what? Never mind, I know. We'll play it by ear."

Mat just grinned.

"Oh, what the hell." Ron contorted his lanky frame into this small container as Mat busied himself fashioning a release mechanism for the box's lock. He had no idea where the man got a coat hanger. Once he was inside, Mat used his hanger tool to pull the latch closed but prevent it from fully engaging. He seemed to be enjoying this little game. He might even have been humming. Ron hoped it wasn't a funeral dirge.

They waited in their cramped space as the plane stopped. Then electrical motors whined, doors opened, and flight line sounds flooded in. The container rolled and banged. There was shouting along with beeping and horns blaring. The container was slammed onto some sort of truck driving somewhere. Another lurching stop and they were suddenly tilted. The motion became smooth as they moved up an incline. Sounds settled to a consistent hum. Mat worked his clothes hanger until he could push the door ajar. Ron didn't like the next reaction.

Mat leaned back into the container. "Shit. We're on a conveyer belt headed up. I have no idea to where."

Ron scrambled to look out. They were in an enormous building, maybe five stories up. A complex maze of conveyers that crisscrossed and overlapped with mind-bending complexity of an Escher painting. And they were moving fast.

As he watched, their container made a sharp ninety-degree whip turn and Mat almost flew out the door. Ron grabbed him and pulled him close. "Play it by ear, huh?" Their amusement park ride got wilder. They plunged downward at a sharp angle, racked into several more turns and banged to a violent stop. Mat peeked out.

"We're in an unloading queue. Ahead of us are a dozen other containers being unloaded. We have to get out of this box before they come to it."

"To where?"

Mat only shook his head. Then he took a deep breath, opened the container door wide and stepped out into a dark warehouse, the size of the Superdome. The metal grid catwalk was just wide enough for one person at a time. Ron followed and the two of them crouched low to avoid detection by the team of sorters unloading containers ahead.

"Follow me," Mat whispered.

Again, Ron did as he was told. Again, he had little confidence this adventure would have a happy ending. They ran in a bent posture with constant sideways looks. There were a lot of people in the building but they were all intent on their jobs. No one looked up at the catwalk fifteen feet above the floor. The fugitives came to a ladder and scrambled down.

Now, crouched in a dark corner, they watched hectic activity all around. But there were just too many people milling, lifting, pushing, pulling and sorting - too many people to avoid. A small tug, like an oversized rider mower with a yellow flashing light on top, came by. Behind it, a string of containers on individual roller pallets jostled like a toy train snaking through the chaos.

"Empties," Mat said. "Come on."

They ran. Mat dove into a passing container's open door. Ron followed mumbling all the way. "Okay, out of another fire, still in the frying pan."

This empty container was small, like the ones in the plane's belly. Sounds echoed inside its plastic walls. Mat tried to sound confident. "We're probably headed to the storage area." Ron knew that storage area would still be inside Silver Streak's facility.

The tug stopped abruptly, and the driver disconnected his train of pallets. Ron peeked out. They were somewhere outside the building on a darkened ramp near the flight line. Now what?

He heard an airplane and looked up to watch an Air Force C-130 cargo plane land.

Mat looked across the airfield and blurted, "Scott Air Force Base - it shares a runway with Silver Streak's main hub." Mat seemed to be trying to sound confident. "All right, we're going to walk across the runway to the Air Force side of the field. Security will be looser there."

Ron wasn't impressed. "Seriously? Security will be *lighter* at a military installation?"

"You got a better idea?"

"No, not really."

They crawled out and stood tall, two cowboys in fancy duds standing in the middle of a bustling airport cargo ramp trying to look nonchalant. Maybe, if they put their hands in their pockets and whistled as they walked...? Ron remembered an old Playboy Magazine cartoon of airline pilots walking down the aisle of a plane, whistling as they donned parachutes and passengers around them panicked.

Then he spotted a panel truck sitting with its engine idling. Ron said, "How about a new plan? Let's hop a ride." Mat nodded and they slid in through the side door and worked their way to the back. It was jammed full of equipment: wheel chocks, cases of oil, boxes of rags, tools and flashlights. The driver returned and, for half an hour, they rode, cramped but still undetected. The van lurched from one stop to another until it finally pulled out onto a smooth road. Ron judged from the brilliant lights passing alongside they were on a taxiway. The intense noise of the cargo ramp faded as they drove beyond the Silver Streak ramp and onto an unlit field of mowed grass and pitch black emptiness.

A scratchy radio blared from the truck dashboard. "Maintenance Two, the damaged light was reported in the bend of taxiway Kilo where it meets November."

The driver picked up a microphone and responded. "Roger, control. I see it. And you're right, it looks like one of our planes might have turned a little short and clipped it. I'm going to take a closer look to see if there are tire tracks. I'll check back in a minute." He left the truck.

Mat muttered, "The driver forgot to chock the wheels. Always chock when you leave a vehicle on an active airport."

Ron shook his head. "Mat the rule follower – even now." He felt along the back door of the van and found the handle, eased it open and realized the van had a bright yellow beacon flashing. "Come on Mat. Here we go again." They piled out and moved back away from the maintenance man who was busy looking at the broken light. The two cowboy fugitives scurried into tall grass to lay flat until the van finally pulled away.

Now it was incredibly dark, except for flashing high-intensity runway lights just a hundred feet away. Actually, those lights would protect them from being seen by anyone who tried to look into the brilliant pulsing light.

Miraculously, they both still had their cowboy hats. Ron dusted his and said, "Well Pardner, I think we should mosey over to that there fence."

A Stroll Across an Airport

Mat and Ron walked along the taxiway ducking by reflex every time an airplane landed or taxied nearby. Mat stumbled occasionally. He was lost in thought, actually just trying to come up with a good thought, a good plan.

Ron complained constantly. His cowboy boots hurt. What would his parents think when they found his dead body on the edge of a runway dressed up like some male prostitute in cowboy drag? On and on, he belly-ached.

They rounded the approach lights at the very end of the runway and Mat paused. He remembered the Scott Air Force Base side of MidAmerica airfield had a golf course adjoining the runway. They veered off, found a sagging chain link fence and were soon walking easily among dark sand traps and manicured greens. From there, they navigated through base family housing, along "General's Row" and past the Air Mobility Command headquarters. A little farther and they came to the Shiloh-Scott Metro Link station.

Mat was pleased with himself. They were on the verge of freedom. Security inside the station was tight for people coming into Scott Air Force Base, but no one paid any attention to those leaving, not even two flamboyant cowboys.

Mat used one of their twenties to buy two tickets from a machine and they boarded a light rail car. A clock above the entrance indicated it was ten at night and the car was empty except for a couple of uniformed Air Force men who eyed the two drugstore cowboys with quick, curious looks. The train jolted and they were quickly off the base heading...somewhere. Exactly where was still undecided.

Ron brought it up. "So, do we have a plan now?"

"I think I'll go by my place and get some money and other stuff."

Ron shook his head. "Bad plan. They will be watching your pad and they will be watching your accounts. If you make a call, use an ATM or credit card, they will know instantly. Remember who these people are. We are now criminals on the run and we need to behave like criminals. Remember that, Tex."

Mat sat back and tried to visualize life on the run. Buoyed by adrenaline and panic, he hadn't really dealt with the future. Now the gravity of their situation sank in. They were alone without money or hope of getting help. How would they manage? Where could they go? How would they live in a world where the organization that called itself "Humanity" seemed to be all-powerful? So many questions. *Who could help? There was only one person* - Chandler.

"Okay Ron. I have a short-range plan. We'll go to the airport. There is a 24-hour bank there that will change foreign money. We'll exchange what I stole from the pilots and buy a burner phone. Then I'll call my girlfriend and she'll help us. She's a lawyer."

Ron nodded but it was reluctant agreement. Mat took a deep breath. This could work – might possibly work - but only if Chandler was willing to become a criminal.

They jostled along clicking tracks for the best part of an hour. Passengers came and went, all people of the night, most black, most slightly sad and distant - except one man who got on near City Center. He was as big as a pro linebacker and drunk as a sailor on shore leave. The big man stopped in front of them and laughed.

"Just what the hail you supposed to be?"

Ron avoided eye contact and answered, almost meek. "We're playing back-up in a country-western band. Got a late gig."

The big man leered with big, wet teeth and bleary eyes. "Well, don't that beat all, a nigger cowboy. You just like my man Charlie Pride."

Now Ron stood to look bully boy in the face. He was taller by a good five inches. "Hey man, it's a gig and it pays. I don't need no shit from you, ya hear?"

Mat's stomach tightened. They didn't need the visibility a fight might bring. But the bully just shrugged it off, laughed and wobbled away. Ron sat back down and exhaled. Mat whispered. "That was very bold. Very ethnic."

"Yeah? Well, it doesn't come easily. My father is a professor in the Philosophy Department at Smith College. My mother is an artist hung in several New York galleries. You're probably more at home in the inner city than I am."

"Nonetheless, you pulled it off. Thanks." The rest of their ride to Lambert Field was uneventful.

It was a big airport, once TWA's main hub, now fallen to second or third tier status. It was still clean, still crisp, but there was an air of abandonment like a Mid-western town after the factory closed. Several terminal gateways were now closed and the whole place seemed too big for the amount of traffic, especially late at night.

The bank was there and still open, but the lone teller refused to change money without some form of identification. Ron started to make a scene, but Mat pulled him away. Their plan just hit a pothole and he needed to regroup. "I could call Ruby. She would help."

"Who's Ruby."

"She's my housekeeper but she's really more than that. She's a trusted friend."

"Then they'll be watching her. That's no good."

Behind them an electronic billboard flashed an arrival. An American Airlines flight from Washington. Mat paid no attention. The two men sat staring into space. Ron put his hands on his knees and made an announcement. "We have got to steal. I mean, we're already desperados. We'll have to steal to survive. I just don't know how. We'll have to learn. Never thought I'd have to learn to be a criminal."

Mat's scrunched his face. Steal, live on the run? He wasn't sure… *Yes, he was.* He could do anything if he had to - lie, cheat, steal. He could do it - *he hoped.*

But then his focus shifted to a woman far down the people mover. A lone figure in a long coat who fought with her roller suitcase trying to keep it straight.

Mat whispered her name as though calling forth an angel. "Chandler. It's Chandler. Ron, it's Chandler, the woman I told you about." He broke away and launched into a full run, barging past people on the moving sidewalk to grab her in a suffocating kiss."

Instinctively she pulled back. "My God, you look awful and you smell worse. Where have you been? What's going on?"

He couldn't answer. He just clung to her and sobbed. She used her free hand to steady him and both nearly fell as the people-mover belt ended. Over the next hour they sat over coffee as Mat and Ron tried to explain their ordeal. She was obviously trying to believe but having some trouble accepting the story. It sounded like the ultimate in conspiracy theories.

Finally, she had enough. "All right, Mat, there is one agency of the government that is above reproach. During the worst battles of the Civil Rights Movement, when the legislature and even the President were hampered by fears of public backlash, the FBI was absolutely trustworthy. You must call the FBI. It will be hard to convince them but then, you two aren't exactly a couple of lunatics off the streets. You are credible men. At least you were credible before you put on those silly costumes. But you can pull it off."

Mat had no better idea. He hadn't been thinking clearly. Other than a couple of hours in the container, he hadn't had real sleep in weeks. Brainwashing and electro-shock made him even less sharp. Chandler was absolutely right. He would call the FBI.

Ron wasn't so sure. He insisted they get a pre-paid phone to make the call. Chandler thought that was a bit paranoid but she went along. After she rented a car, they drove to an all-night pharmacy where she bought the cellphone. Ron had fired up his tablet computer in the airport and found the FBI local numbers. Mat dialed and cleared his throat.

After navigating a phone tree, he finally heard a human with a crisp voice. "Federal Bureau of Investigation, St. Louis Office. How may I help you?"

"I would like to speak to the Special Agent in Charge,"

"What is the nature of your call, please?"

"I have information about an anti-government conspiracy." Music played for several minutes as Mat waited on hold. Then a gruff voice. It was now two in the morning.

"Stanley White, Acting SASC, what information do you have?"

Speak slowly, try to be clear even if your mind is a little cloudy.

"I and several others from Silver Streak and COMED corporations have been kidnapped and put through torture over a month-long period in an effort to make us work for a secret organization that plans a program of racial genocide." That sounded crackpot even as he said it.

"I see, sir. Please tell me your name and your location so I can dispatch agents to interview you."

Was the FBI buying this story that easily? As far-fetched as it sounded, Mat expected much more skepticism. "I prefer to remain anonymous. I am in fear of my life. These are really dangerous people."

"Don't worry about that. We'll protect you but we need to know where you are."

Mat was silent and suddenly cautious. "I am" ...he hesitated... "in Belleville, Illinois."

"And your name, sir?"

"John Cook." *Where did that come from?* Cook had been the copilot during the in-flight incident that killed Sharon Prentiss. He could hear the FBI Agent whispering in the background. It sounded like he was saying, "Yes sir, I have one of them on the line. He says he's in Illinois but the cell tower he's coming off is out near the airport." Then there was mumbling he couldn't understand, but one word did come through, "McCoy." They knew his name. They knew his approximate location. They weren't surprised or suspicious of his crazy claims of a secret organization. They were expecting his call. They were a part of it.

Mat felt as though a cold wind had just blown through his ribs. He clicked off the phone and walked unsteadily back to the rental car that sat idling steamy exhaust into cold night air. It was time to run - and run fast.

The snake which cannot shed its skin has to die

- Nietzsche

CHAPTER NINE

~⁂~

On the Run

Conversation was scarce as Chandler drove out of St. Louis. The FBI couldn't possibly know about her and probably didn't know about the rental car. Once they got across the Mississippi bridges, she could travel back roads with no traffic cameras to track them. She made the Martin Luther King Bridge without incident and took state road 15 east.

Sunrise dawned over endless frozen fields of Illinois corn stubble. Dawn brought a feeling of relief and the realization of just how tired she was. Both men had been asleep for an hour. She turned onto a dirt road with a "No Exit" sign that had been up long enough to rust. The pavement ended and she continued on dirt to an abandoned gravel pit. There, a ramshackle drive-through loading dock looked ready to collapse but it would serve to shield them from helicopter surveillance. She pulled in, set the brake, reclined her seat and joined the boys in a near-coma.

She woke in brilliant daylight, cold, stiff and needing to pee. Both men were still passed out, heads back, mouths gaping like fish. There were bushes growing along the building and she went behind one to squat, not that anyone would see her in this industrial derelict.

She had done it before as a little girl travelling the country in a beat-up RV. Her family had lived like gypsies as her lawyer father chased across America from one civil rights case to the next, rarely being paid, rarely being safe and never, ever feeling like she belonged. She had gone to dozens of elementary schools, always an outsider, often a hated outsider.

Now, as an adult, she was a partner in a decent law firm. She still did a little pro bono work but mainly she worked for money, good, honest money. Her father respected her accomplishments, but he never admired her the way she admired him. She had not followed in his noble crusade to help the downtrodden. But she dismissed those thoughts. There were more urgent issues - like survival.

She thought about Mat's story. It was incredible but he was not one to exaggerate. Ron seemed fairly reliable as well. There had to be something to it but how could she find out? Who could she ask? In the meantime, where would they go?

She felt a flush of anger. Even worse, she had no toilet paper and had to use leaves. She was sitting on an upturned cinder block clutching herself against the cold when she heard Ron Male walk out stretching and groaning. He saw Chandler stand up and smiled. "Good morning." He had a nice smile.

She stretched and worked out her own kinks after sleeping in the car. "So, Mister Male, you have been pretty quiet. What's your take on this whole affair?"

He shrugged and moved his jaw left and right. "Well, I'll think better after a coffee but, for now, I honestly see no viable solution. I'm afraid we're really screwed. Our best bet is probably to get out of the country. After that, I have absolutely no reasonable plan. Name changes, new jobs, life off the grid – I just don't know. If the FBI is actually onto us, where can we go?"

She nodded. "Mat said you were tortured. How?"

"They kept us standing in tubes without ever being able to rest. An automated instruction program grilled us on racist plans to cleanse America of defectives, i.e. black people. When we resisted or were hesitant, they hit us with electric shocks. It was quite effective. I was almost ready to join the Klan myself."

Chandler made a weak smile at his effort to bring humor into the gloom. "I can't help but feel that our only hope is not to *leave* the country but rather to *help* the country. There must be a way."

Ron started to speak but caught himself. He probably though lawyer Chandler Harris wasn't a woman to argue against.

After Mat revived, the three fugitives headed out. In the town of Peavy, she rented two rooms in a single-story motel behind a flickering neon sign that advertised "Free flat-screen TV." She left the boys to shower and clean up while she hit Walmart. There, she bought them new outfits, everything except shoes. She didn't dare to guess sizes, so their cowboy boots would have to do for a while.

Now, sanitized and dressed in new, less obvious clothes, they hit a Waffle House and ate ferociously. Sleep, clothes and full stomachs; the world seemed brighter. Back at the motel, Chandler went check to out, and the clerk, a man in his seventies, gave her a concerned look.

"That black fellow, he's with you?"

Chandler became defensive. "He's traveling with us, yes. Is there something wrong?"

"Well, no. It's just that we don't see many colored here in Peavey. You might ought to be – oh, I don't know - a little cautious is all."

She pursed her lips. "Thank you. I'll try to remember that." She put her credit card back in her wallet and paid cash. Small Town Americana might not be quite as friendly as it seemed.

They hit the road with new energy. Mat asked, "So, where are you headed?"

Chandler knit her brows for a second. "Is that my decision?" No one answered so she continued. "Okay, I've been thinking about it all morning. First, we're going to need money. I know a fellow lawyer who owes me a huge debt. I think he'll help us without questions. He lives nearby, in the small town of Mount Vernon. We can make it there before the banks close this afternoon. After that, I say we go to Washington. Our only answers will come from the people there. If the government is involved, then we'll need the government to solve our problems and I know people in the government."

Neither Mat nor Ron looked as though they liked that idea and, for the rest of the drive, they tried to change her mind. She kept asking for another plan. They had none. Chandler didn't mind a lively discussion. In fact, it made her think more clearly. She asked more and more questions about the mysterious "Humanity" organization and slowly began to accept the plausibility that it was all true, that it was as powerful and ruthless as they feared.

She remembered a client from years earlier, an investment banker, who supported extreme right-wing causes. He was an idiot but he paid his bills promptly. During a phone conversation in her outer office he once thought he had put her on hold and she overheard him use the phrase, "As it is above, so shall it be below." At the time, it meant nothing to her. Now, it brought a chill. Could these people be all around?

"Ron, you mentioned the above and below thing. Could you look that up and see where it came from?"

"Sure, I have my little electronic friend and we're picking up an open Wi-Fi at the moment." He actually hummed as he tapped away on the tablet. "Okay, here you go. It is an invocation from ancient Gnostic religious writings. Apparently, they thought the physical world was just a corrupt version of some better universe where angels sought some kind of perfection." He mumbled a bit. "There's a lot more but that's the gist."

Mat, the reader of the group, spoke. "Now I remember. I've read a little about Gnosticism. It flourished as a competing philosophy to mainstream Christianity up until the middle ages if I remember correctly. There were lots of off-shoots. Some called 'mystery cults' had strange forms of worship. I think the Knights Templar and the French Cathars have been associated with the banned writings..."

Chandler cut in. "Thank you, professor. I think we got it. Some sort of religious secret society makes sense. That could explain the apparent fanaticism. Religion makes even the most horrific actions excusable under the pretense of acting in the name of some higher power. But there must be more. Level-headed businessmen don't seem likely to become religious zealots without some other payoff, some intense motivation. It takes a powerful belief to make men kill."

Mat was quiet, thinking. Finally, he spoke again. "Imagine the world they want. It would be a world of machines doing most of the labor and some of the thinking. It would be a world comprised only of, what today, we would call the 'one percent.' Everyone would be comfortable and healthy and free to devote themselves to making life better. It is a compelling argument."

Ron chimed. "Mister McCoy, I think you listened to your Sophia voice a little too well. It would be a world of slaughter and destruction. Whole peoples wiped off the planet. And if these guys who call themselves Archons really do eventually run everything, they're still going to be human. They're still going to have conflicts. So what they'll do is what every powerful group in history has done. They'll either find or create enemies and then attack them. Eventually, they'll wipe themselves out and the damned cockroaches will rule."

Chandler brought focus. "That's all very interesting but a little beyond our current problem. We need to deal with logistics. We need money, lodging, transportation and support from trustworthy people. I am about to transfer a sum from one of my discretionary accounts with the law firm into a fake account I'm hoping my banker friend will create for me. Who has ideas for the rest?"

Mat looked out the window. "Pilots keep 'crash pads,' cheap rooms where they can rest on non-paid layovers. I share one in D. C. There's an old car there too. We call them 'airporters,' beat up clunkers that you can leave for weeks on the street or in airport parking with no fear of it being stolen. We'll have a place to stay and transportation."

"Great." Chandler sounded upbeat. "I know people who, I hope, will help us. Ron, can you set up some kind of secure communications that will let us avoid detection?"

"Yeah, I think so. I'll need a little more than this stolen tablet but if you have money…"

They wheeled into Mount Vernon and found the Heartland Bank and Trust. Chandler disappeared and the two men found a fast food place nearby where they loaded up on burgers and shakes to go. Chandler would be happy with their meal selection.

When she came out of the bank, she was all smiles. She plopped in the shotgun seat and passed out shiny new credit cards. "Okay boys, here you go." Your ATM Pin is 4-3-2-1. The account has $50,000. I think this will keep us going for a while."

Ron looked at his and said, "John Doe? That's the best you could do?"

Chandler raised her hands. "Well, I wasn't feeling creative."

Every normal man must be tempted at times, to spit on his hands, hoist the black flag and begin slitting throats

– H.L.Menchen

The Cities Erupt

Mat drove to give Chandler a break. Somewhere near the Indiana border he felt safe enough to get back on I-64. *Was he becoming complacent?*

Ron sprawled in the back seat. "Heh Mat, let's find some tunes on the radio. Even out here in Hillbilly country I'll bet they have radio stations."

"Sure, let's see what this button does." He poked around the little touch screen until he found "audio search" and images began to scroll. Momentarily blips of music or conversation popped up. There was a gospel choir, a wailing cowboy, an ad for headache remedies and then a somber announcer. Mat hit select and the news came on.

"This day continues to bring one horrendous event after another, each new disaster eclipsing nine-eleven in death toll and devastation. We woke this morning to the story of an underground gas leak that permeated the old tunnel system beneath the Chicago's downtown area. The explosions and fires that resulted have claimed thousands, perhaps tens of thousands of lives. Smoke from the fires can be seen for a hundred miles. All communications with the downtown area have been lost. Governor Peterson is sending the National Guard and every available firefighter in the area but the fire that is burning with such intensity it melts steel beams."

Mat, Chandler and Ron sat and listened intently. Ron finally spoke. "It's beginning. The mass destruction they want. It's already beginning."

Chandler shot back, "We don't know that. This could just be an accident." She didn't sound convincing.

The announcer hesitated. "I've just been handed another update. There is an enormous fire south of Miami. Giant fuel storage tanks at Homestead Air Force Base have apparently leaked or been sabotaged and have flooded the canal system south and west of the base. That fuel ignited and fire is now sweeping across open areas that are tinder-dry after this year's drought. The area is home to a large immigrant population. I'm told that whirlwinds of fire shoot two hundred feet in the air and that the flames are spreading faster than an automobile can drive out of its path. If it continues into the everglades, the destruction of habitat will be horrendous."

He barely had time to take a breath. "And another bulletin. An oil tanker has run aground in the Philadelphia docks spilling crude oil that burst into flame. The waterfront area is ablaze with oil flowing down streets and into sewers."

There was a pause. "And still another. A refinery complex in Houston, Texas is burning. We have no details yet. Wait…what? Is that confirmed?" He seemed to be listening and then spoke with a tremor in his voice. "New Orleans has just reported a breach of the levees and flooding in the same Ninth Ward so devastated by Katrina in 2005." He paused and sounded angry. His voice cracked.

"How can this be happening in America? This isn't Iraq or Afghanistan." There was a sound of clamor and shouting in the newsroom behind him. The anchorman sounded deflated. "We now have a new report of flooding in Oakland, California. A section of the California Aqueduct system appears to have been deliberately sabotaged. Water is pouring into the lowlands and threatens the Alameda area. Evacuations have been ordered."

He spoke slowly, his voice deliberate and somber. "This is John Casey of News Network. It appears certain that America is under attack. We do not know by whom or for what reason, but I ask you all to pray for those affected. This is a dark day for our nation."

"Shit." Ron Male banged his fist on the seat back. "What are we going to do? We can't be hiding out when so many are being killed. We have got to do something. We just have to." There was no answer to his plea.

Through the afternoon and into darkness they drove and listened as one catastrophe after another unfolded. It seemed no part of the country was spared. Detroit reported a toxic gas leak from a factory in a largely Moslem area. Phoenix had power lines to some parts of the city bombed. Without power, there was no water pump capability. Dams in several cities were bombed. Fires were everywhere. As the reports flowed in, a pattern began to emerge. The affected areas were all minority population centers. Blighted and ignored neighborhoods were suffering the most.

The Reverend Billy Isaacson was on every station shouting from his soap box and being covered by every news agency. "This is a damned war, a war on the black man, a war on the underprivileged, a war on human decency. I shall stand with my people against the devils of Babylon who wage this wicked war. I will stand strong and I urge my brothers to prepare. This monstrous war is obviously well-supported, well-funded and vicious. It is a war of extermination, plain and simple, and we must fight back – fight for our very survival. I urge all young men of color to take up arms against the foul institution of our government. Protect your families. Protect your children. Kill the…"

The news station cut him off. "Well, we don't need any more incendiary speech. We have enough to deal with. Wait. I've just been informed that President Whiteman will address the nation at seven Eastern Standard Time tonight. We'll bring his speech to you live right here on News Network."

A commercial for a rental car company came on.

Chandler broke the heavy silence in the car. "Okay, I'm sorry if I doubted anything you said. This seems to substantiate it all." She sighed deep and pained. "You know, I've always heard the stories - we all have - of conspiracy theories. There is the persistent Bilderberg conspiracy about the world's richest men planning to subjugate us all. Then there is The Council on Foreign Relations, The Trilateral Commission, the Illuminati, Freemasons and so on, all out to enslave the masses and indoctrinate us in their ideology, but I remain convinced that our government is strong enough to survive such lunacy. We must find decent people and squash these—what did you call them—Arch Cons?"

Mat answered. "Archons. They are the militants of the Humanity organization. They are the doers."

Ron looked out the window at passing farmland, desolate and empty in winter. He sighed as he said, "The earthly manifestation of angels. They are the doers, the makers of the new world order. They are the killers."

At seven sharp, President Whiteman came on. "My fellow Americans, I will forgo the usual trappings of address. Our nation is faced with an unprecedented crisis. We are under attack and we do not know from whom. Al Qaeda, ISIS and many other radical organizations have claimed responsibility, but we cannot verify, and actually doubt, any of them have the capability to conduct such extensive operations. I am afraid this is a home-grown terrorist effort. The worst effect, and no doubt the one the terrorists hoped for, has been the immediate alienation of our minority communities."

He paused. "I want to tell all of you out there, to pledge to you, regardless of your race or ethnicity, that this country is your country and I will fight to defend every one of you as much as any other citizen. Do not play into the terrorists' hands by opposing your own people, your own country, your own government. We are doing everything we can to protect you."

Another pause, this one longer. His voice was lower. "To that end, I have directed the Chairman of the Joint Chiefs of Staff to implement a comprehensive plan to bring order back to the damaged cities. I am invoking the Posse Comitatus provision of the 2007 NSPD 20, Presidential Directive 51. I am sending troops into all major urban areas to maintain order. Again, I plead for cooperation. Do not oppose these good men and women. They are coming to protect you."

He went on for a long time but no one in the car was listening. Ron spoke for all of them. "It's unfolding just as they said it would. First, they did murders that were blamed on rival groups to generate distrust and conflict. Then, they planted operatives to preach violence and spread fear. Now, the mass destruction that they hope will bring rebellion has given them an excuse for military intervention and slaughter."

Without a hint of emotion, Chandler asked, "What's next?"

"Genocide," Ron replied. "A worldwide epidemic that will wipe out minorities and even undeveloped countries. The ethnic cleansing of the world has begun.

Garden Plot

In the Pentagon basement, General Cunningham sat at a round conference table surrounded by a dozen other generals and a couple of civilians. They stood as Vice President McCoby entered.

"Sir, we are prepared to go to DEFCON III and LERTCON 2. All units are standing by for your order."

McCoby gave him a sly look. "Oh, not my order, General. You all heard the president. We *must* act." He almost grinned. "Based on that directive, implement 'Operation Garden Plot' immediately." He clasped his hands behind his back like an admiral on deck and ready to fight. "Let's take back our cities."

The general's sidekicks reached for phones and all across the country, a juggernaut of military planes and troops and equipment began to flow. Pre-packaged arms and munitions, vehicles and communication equipment and tens of thousands of soldiers began streaming into major cities. Giant screens on the conference room wall began to scroll information and graphics.

McCoby stood straight, head high, chest out.

CHAPTER TEN

The Long and Lonely Road

In Charleston, West Virginia, Mat turned north on I-79. It was a dark, moonless night and the countryside offered little illumination. There were virtually no other cars on the road and he felt comfortable speeding, even on the hills and curves. Ron had gone to sleep in the back seat. Chandler was deep in thought. Mat, on the other hand, felt alert but vacant. After the endless stress of captivity and escape, he had trouble focusing. Instead, he lost himself in the stillness of the road where his headlights faded into a featureless void. The only reality was what lay directly before him.

"Do you suppose there will be a coup?" Chandler asked.

Mat considered. "I think there has already been a sort of coup. The Humanity crackpots have already established themselves throughout the government. Otherwise, they wouldn't have been able to send troops so quickly against their own people. There was no congressional fight, no violent demonstrations. This is really an extraordinary response to an inherently un-American action."

Chandler sat silent in the darkened car for a while. "I just don't think President Whiteman would be part of something so terrible. He may not be the brightest light on the Christmas tree, but he always seemed like a decent enough man. I think he may have been hoodwinked."

"Hoodwinked? I haven't heard that word since I was a kid." Mat's smile vanished as a blue flashing light shone in the rear view mirror. "Oh shit, a cop. What should I do?"

She didn't sound confident. "I'd pull over. I imagine people all over the country are edgy right now and I don't want to upset some highway patrolman with an itchy trigger finger."

Ron was snoring softly in the back seat. Mat shot a glance at the big black man. What would the cop think? This was West Virginia and who knows how people were reacting to the inner-city violence. Maybe, just maybe, he could diffuse the situation without a confrontation. He stepped out of the rental car and used hands to shield his eyes against the cop car's brilliant strobing lights.

"Officer, did I do something wrong?" Mat tried to act non-threatening.

The highway patrolman came into the headlights. He was big, at least six four and hog heavy. He turned his Smokey Bear hat in his hands and spoke with a heavy accent.

"You just stay right where you are, young fella. I got dispatch checking out your plates. It'll just be a minute."

Mat heard the police car radio squawking. He still squinted against the glare and worked his hands as shields trying to get a better view. The patrolman seemed to be alone. Mat spoke, maybe a little louder than necessary. "It's a rental."

Chandler got out of the passenger side. "Officer, I have the registration and here's my driver's license. I think everything is in order." She walked closer turning her head away from the blue lights and handed the documents to the big man. In silhouette, the big cop's belly flowed over his belt buckle and his jelly roll neck would make a necktie almost impossible. His sidearm was huge and shiny. Without a word, Big Cop took her documents and went back to his cruiser.

Chandler came to Mat and took his arm with a grasp harder than needed. The strobing blue lights gave everything a weird, other-worldly feel. Mat felt his stomach tighten and put his hand on top of hers. She was shaking.

Cop was inspecting the documents under his car's interior light and didn't notice Ron open the rental car's rear door and slide out. Chandler turned and made quick, sweeping motions to tell Ron to get out of sight. It took a moment for him to understand but when it registered, he moved quickly to duck behind the car fender and squat down.

The cop had turned his speaker volume up and they heard the scratchy voice. "Vernon, this is Lou Ellen. The girl's clean but, from your description, the guy could be a possible match to a picture of a federal fugitive. The boss says bring 'em both in until we get this cleared up, okay?"

"Gotcha. Charley two out."

Vernon, as she called the cop, lumbered toward them and fought to straighten his big belt buckle. "Okay, you two. They want to talk to you down at the station, so you get back into your car and follow me. No funny stuff, you hear."

"Yes officer," Chandler was quick to respond.

Mat whispered, "What are we going to do?"

Her answer was cut short by the car radio. "Vernon, cancel that. Take them into custody immediately. Do you copy?"

Vernon stopped in his tracks and eyeballed Mat and Chandler. He fumbled with his fancy stitched holster and, after an awkward yank, pulled out a big chrome and pearl-handled revolver. He held it with both hands and his shout spewed a little saliva.

"Both you—down on the ground, hands behind your head. Move. Right now."

Chandler looked meek. "Listen, we're no threat and it's really cold on the ground. How about we just go quietly. Would that be okay?" She flashed her eyes like a little girl. In other situations, Mat would have laughed.

The shiny gun wavered in flashing light. Vernon wavered as well. "Yeah, okay for you, but he's got to lay down. You hear me? On the ground, now."

Vernon was shifting his weight from foot to foot and seemed unsure what to do next. Mat squinted and saw movement behind the gun-wielding cop. It was Ron. Somehow he had moved behind them and was opening the cruiser's door. What the hell was he doing? *Oh no.* Was he drawing a shotgun out of the car?

"No," Mat yelled.

Vernon looked confused and let his gun drop a little. "What's that? No, what?" Then Vernon turned slowly and looked at the car. Ron was hidden, crouched behind the open door. No one was breathing. Vernon started to turn back when the cruiser's open door made a squeak. That made the big cop spin in a clumsy pirouette to aim at the door. Ron leaped up and leveled the shotgun.

The two men stood, both breathing hard, both totally focused on each other. Ron's voice was shaky. "I'll lower my gun if you do."

"Ain't gonna happen, sonny. Put the damned gun down or I'm gonna blow you to Kingdom Come."

"Come on, man. I don't want to hurt you." Ron's voice was whiny.

Vernon used his thumb to cock the pistol. It was impossible to say who shot first. The blasts reverberated over each other and echoed in cold night air. Vernon fell like a bag of rocks. Ron screamed and danced in a circle with both hands clasping his chest. Then he went down on one knee, breathing hard, reaching out to break his fall. But his hand went limp and he collapsed forward into a boneless heap.

Chandler ran to place a soft hand on Ron's neck. She raised his head. It seemed heavy. His eyes were wide open, frozen, still full of fear. His mouth gaped and his arms flopped as she turned him. She took him in her arms and rocked and sobbed.

Mat rolled Vernon over. It was a horrific sight. His badge was crumpled from the shotgun blast. Under tatters of shirt, his chest, neck and face looked like raw hamburger.

They were both dead. The strobe light flashed. Darkness seemed to cover the world. The radio blared. "Vernon? Come in, Vernon."

Forces in Play

General Cunningham took back corridors to the conference room in the Pentagon basement. He held his phone at arm's length and read a text, "Helicopter has landed. ETA five minutes." He sat at one end of a conference table. A rear admiral and an Air Force colonel took places behind him. Otherwise the twelve-man table was empty. Cunningham drummed his fingers uncomfortably.

Vice President McCoby breezed in and looked as though he had to restrain himself from shaking hands and slapping backs, a virtual reflex for the career politician. He sat at the far end of the table, a full ten feet away from the Chairman of the Joint Chiefs of Staff. Positioning was all part of the power ballet that played out in every situation. Who sat where always denoted status. Actually, everything denoted status. Every look, every gesture, every word reinforced the iron hierarchy of the pack and McCoby always wanted to be the Alpha Dog.

He flashed a big smile. "General, I have seen the reports of the initial deployments. Everything in the packages going as planned?"

General Cunningham stood and spread several pieces of paper. "As you have probably already seen, we've flown sixty-four airlift sorties in the first twenty four hours of Operation Garden Plot. The pace will accelerate to over one hundred a day for the next ten days. Deployed forces are sized according to our intelligence estimates of opposing forces. We define those forces based on ethnic populations. The assumption is that outside instigators will be successful in mobilizing virtually full inner city resistance against us."

McCoby's head bobbed. He was liking what he heard. "And the resistance, is it becoming organized as expected?"

"Yes, sir. During the seventies, the Black Panther group left a legacy of defending black citizens against government and white activists groups. They were inspired in part by a Japanese movement known as the Black Dragons. It was a secret society that trained warriors and assassins against the government. Today, the American image of a heroic secret black army has been cultivated and encouraged – in some large part through video games we sponsored. There are established, well-trained cells in every major city. They are now moving to create and activate local Black Dragon de-facto militias, we are simultaneously inserting our mercenaries."

The general paused as though considering whether to share more.

McCoby was impatient. "Just what mercenaries?"

Cunningham spoke carefully without eye contact. "We have enlisted the aid of a number of white supremacist militia groups by telling them the Illuminati and NWO – their term for a liberal New World Order – are behind the black insurgency."

McCoby tilted his head. "Seriously, Illuminati? New World Order?"

"Yes sir, that's a big part of their literature and their belief system. Their websites are full of dire warnings of evil government and big business plans to enslave them. They won't actually know they're working for us. They think some rich benefactor is raising an army of Christian soldiers."

McCoby shrugged. The general continued. "I expect them to be quite effective. Many are experienced special ops veterans. The first contingent will deploy from several camps in West Virginia, Pennsylvania and Maryland. Later, these groups will be joined by others from Texas, Idaho and Oklahoma. They will infiltrate into the cities and terrorize the Black Dragon fighters as well as civilians living in the target areas. I feel sure that the most docile and peace-loving members of the black community will be stirred to action by the ruthlessness of these…patriots."

McCoby just smiled. "And after they have inflamed the populace, how will you extract them?"

Cunningham looked away spoke carefully. "We have no plans to extract them. They will have served their purpose. We'll let insurgents deal with them."

McCoby wasn't comfortable with that but he let it pass. "So, how will we arm these crackpot militias?"

Cunningham shifted back in his seat, a little more comfortable now. "The heavy weapons are coming in on our transport planes and by rail. The containers are all labelled 'Homeland Security XXX-Class IV.'"

He paused again. "Undercover agents of the CIA and their contractors are responsible for the actual handling and distribution of weapons, mostly captured stuff from our Middle East wars: AK-47s, RPGs, heavy machine guns, grenade launchers et cetera. We're arming the Black Dragons as well."

"How long before the first major clash?"

General Cunningham made a slight shrug. "The inner-city riots and shootings of policemen are now in their second day. We have deployed enough troops to have a basic crowd control presence in most urban areas. We don't want to appear to be the aggressors. The first coordinated attack on our troops is planned for tonight in Philadelphia. Black Dragon rebels will assault our provisional headquarters on the lawn in front of Constitution Hall and the Liberty Bell. There will be good news coverage, some excellent photo ops. Through social media, the rebels have already delivered a series of demands, ridiculous demands: compensation for slavery, release of all black prisoners in every state, free housing of middle class standards and dedicated health care."

McCoby took a deep, satisfied breath. "Good, very good. I can make some great speeches about the insurgents threatening the very foundation of American values - personal initiative, hard work and responsibility, in exchange for a government welfare." He sat for a long silent minute before he spoke. "Anything else?"

"Yes, Mister Vice President. I have a package for you to review at your leisure. It is the COG, the 'Continuity of Government' plan that details exactly how you would proceed if anything untoward were to happen to President Whiteman. It details the bunkers where you and your executive staff would be helicoptered and how you would communicate and command the war effort." The general's face had no expression. "God forbid it should come to that."

"Yes... God forbid." McCoby stood and walked over to the general who stood quickly and received a hearty handshake from the man who intended to become president – and soon.

CHAPTER ELEVEN

Boy Scout Camp

"We have to ditch this car." Mat was being logical, methodical, once again falling back in his role as "captain and commander." Chandler, normally the grownup in their relationship, seemed to have fallen apart after Ron's death. She cried and sighed and stared out the window without speaking.

"Chan, listen to me. They know about us and they may even be able to track this car. They have the license plates and your name. We heard the dispatcher say as much. We need to steal another car... and soon."

Chandler turned to him. "Steal? You want to steal a car? How about another murder? Shouldn't we kill someone else if we're going all Bonnie and Clyde?" She crossed her arms in an imitation of a sulking two-year-old. "I think we should just find a place to hide until this blows over." She went back to her sulking.

"Even if we're going to hide, we still need transportation to get there and this car is hot. Now, it will take them an hour or so to decide Vernon and his car are missing. They'll keep calling him and, when he doesn't answer, they'll probably send another highway patrolman searching. I'm guessing that they aren't used to dealing with such problems and, since it's past midnight, they'll be reluctant to call the chief or boss or whatever at home. It will take time to launch an all-out manhunt for us. In the meantime, we *have* to find another vehicle."

She blew out a stream of air and seemed to focus. Her voice was still shaky. "It's already taken half an hour. I can't imagine it will take much longer. I feel terrible that we just dumped the bodies over the rail like that. It seemed inhuman, uncaring. And Ron, your friend..."

"Listen, I couldn't have moved Vernon's body any farther than I did. He must have weighed two-eighty, all dead weight."

"Was that a joke?"

"No, no. I feel every bit as bad about Ron as you, but what else could we do? We didn't want to leave bodies in that police cruiser. Even though we hid it behind that closed gas station, they'll find it as soon as the sun comes up."

"I suppose." She withdrew again and crossed her arms tighter.

Mat was thinking out loud. "Listen. I'm hoping they will take a long time searching for the cop. That will be their focus. Only after they find his body will the manhunt really turn to us."

He saw a brown Interstate Highway sign for a recreational activity, "Marion Hills Boy Scout Camp" and an arrow pointing to the next exit. It was almost Groundhog Day. There would be no activity at a Boy Scout camp in winter. He took the off ramp. Chandler looked confused. "You want to go camping?"

He followed signs to a scary dark gravel road. Overhanging branches gave Mat a closed-in feeling as they crept along at twenty miles an hour not really knowing what to expect. A red-and-white striped pole blocked the road like an old Cold War checkpoint. He got out and raised the bar easily, drove through, and then, as an afterthought, closed it behind them. He was back in his Air Force Survival School mode. *Always cover your tracks. Leave no trail.*

The camp was dark, lifeless. A central log cabin stood surrounded by a half dozen smaller buildings. There wasn't enough light for details. The main building's front door was locked but Mat knew that common-use facilities like this almost always had a hidden key. He felt around the door jamb, over the porch lights and then under the door mat. Sure enough, a key.

The light switch inside worked. Great, they had electricity but, they discovered, no running water. The place must have been winterized. An old TV offered spotty, antenna-only reception, and that only on two channels. It didn't matter. There was only one news story across the entire nation, the conflict in the cities.

Chandler found canned food and cooking pots. She started to prepare something on the gas stove, which seemed to work just fine. Mat went looking for a water source and found a well pump, reset the circuit breaker and waited as it hummed. "Please don't need priming" But it soon gurgled, and he heard rushing water in the pipes. For once, everything was going their way, well - everything except for the water heater which kept popping its circuit breaker.

They ate beans, drank cold well water and went to bed without sheets. Mat took Chandler in his arms and they slept entwined like two children who thought the bogeyman was outside. Maybe he was.

Time for Big Changes

Morning light hit Mat in the eyes like a camera flash. He jerked upright, shivering and disoriented. Then it all began to come back to him. Here they were, Bonnie and Clyde, outlaws on the run. Maybe they place had coffee. He hoped there was coffee.

The shower was ice cold - no water heater. But the coffee was hot, steaming hot. It braced Mat enough to go exploring, so he kissed Chandler on the forehead, put on a warm jacket from the bedroom closet and hiked all around leaving tracks in shallow snow. In the barn, an old van was covered in dust and bird droppings. The battery was dead and one tire was flat, but the keys were still in the ignition. He ran back to tell Chandler the good news.

She held her coffee cup like an offering to the gods and stared with a blank expression. Mat bubbled. "I found a van. We can swap the rental car battery and it might run. There are tools, even an air compressor. The operators of this place obviously followed the scout 'Be Prepared' motto. Come on, let's get busy."

She looked at him and spoke without emotion. "We have to change our appearance. You've got a fair start at a beard. We'll shave it into a goatee and I'll darken it with makeup. Your hair is too short to do much, but we can dye it dark rather than sandy. I'll cut mine short and dye it too. I saw work clothes in the closet. We'll look like we belong in the van you found."

"Yeah, okay. That all sounds reasonable. I found a ball cap. I can use some of the horsehair I found in the barn trash can and attach it like a ponytail."

She almost smiled. "I've been thinking hard about who can help us. My uncle Neil retired from the Justice Department. I feel safe talking to him. My sister Geneva is in the Air Force. She would feel an obligation to turn us in. She's a wonderful person but obsessively patriotic."

Mat approved. "Your family certainly came up with creative names."

"My father named us for the places we were conceived. I was Chandler, Arizona. My sister was Geneva, Mississippi. My poor brother was Eufaula, Alabama. He went through life as a constant brunt of jokes. I think it really harmed him. Of the three of us, he is the underachiever. I am in corporate law - or was. My sister is a Chief Master Sergeant who flies on Air Force One..."

"What? She flies Air Force One?"

"Yes. That's why we should avoid her."

"But she's very patriotic?"

"Yes, very."

Mat was busy thinking. His coffee got cold.

Not Quite the Beverly Hillbillies

It took a full day to get the van running, but Mat was persistent. No one spoke of Ron Male, but then, what was there to say? Eventually, they got everything organized and working. Mat used the rental car to tow the van out of the barn after inflating its tires. Then he pulled the rental into the barn and switched batteries. Half an hour of Mat cranking and Chandler pouring gas into the carburetor from a paper cup finally made the engine cough and bang and start to run. Both cheered.

Chandler mixed a witch's brew of some sort to dye their hair dark. The final color was an odd brownish hue with a tinge of red. She used the same concoction on his horse-hair pony tail. Mat found a razor to shave a goatee, which she colored using her own makeup. They were a comical pair with matching hair, easily mistaken for a brother and sister fresh off the farm. Clothes salvaged from a closet added to the image of farm folk in a bird-dropping-decorated van. They spent the rest of the day working on disguises, plans, plausible stories if stopped.

Next morning they were off. The van had farm plates but no registration, so they would still have to be careful. No speeding or traffic infractions. Chandler's mood seemed better. Driving was slow on back roads through Pennsylvania and then Maryland. No one bothered them, but they weren't going to make Washington D.C. by nightfall and Mat knew the van's lights didn't work. They couldn't risk a motel but chose a truck stop instead. There, they could eat and then sleep in the van.

Mat bought several prepaid phones and Chandler set them up. They would not reuse phones. Paranoia was the marching order of the day. They used Ron's tablet and the truck stop's Wi-Fi to check the news. It was all about some "Black Dragon" group attacking troops in Philadelphia.

Chandler listened for a while and said, "The tone of the reporting is changing very subtly. The announcers are talking about the danger to the troops. Black rioters are being portrayed as enemies. The conflict in front of the Liberty Bell is reported as a 'victory' over 'insurgents.' Do you think the media are part of the plan?"

He thought for just a moment. "That would make perfect sense. Control the media, control the public. Did you see the flags, white with a black dragon figure? They're even managing symbols, identifying the 'others,' making the distinction between *us* and *them*. We're watching psychological warfare in action."

Chandler spoke softly. If the media are corrupt, where do we go? Who can break through the curtain of propaganda?"

"I don't know, Chan. I just don't know."

It became necessary to destroy the village in order to save it

– An American major after the destruction
of the Vietnamese village of Ben Tre

CHAPTER TWELVE

Uncle Neil

They were off at sunrise, stiff and grumpy after sleeping in the cluttered van. Chandler tuned the van radio to find news. All interstates and major roads leading into the Capitol now had road-block check points.

Chandler knew the town and directed Mat onto smaller roads through residential neighborhoods until they finally arrived at a mixed class section of Arlington, Virginia. Mat's "crash pad" turned out to be a dingy brick apartment building where most residents received subsidized rent. It was austere but clean. The apartment had four bedrooms and eight single beds. A dry erase board on each door had a space for the occupant's name and wake-up time. Heavy curtains were good for day sleepers. A microwave, dishwasher and old refrigerator were the only appliances.

The fridge had a water-smeared note that said, "Label your food. Clean out when you leave!" The living area had Goodwill Industries mismatched chairs and a plaid couch arranged before an ancient rear projection TV. They could manage here. Chandler made a list and Mat went shopping. He put on his ball cap with the fake ponytail and it made her laugh.

Once he was gone, she set to work. First looking up her uncle's phone number, then planning what she would say and finally, after a deep breath, calling. She could hear her heart beating as it rang.

This was a risk Mat would not approve, but she was sure her uncle was trustworthy. He had always been the one she went to in times of trouble.

When her irresponsible father had been arrested and thrown in some cracker jail, it was always always Uncle Neil who bailed him out. When their ramshackle RV broke down on a Native American Reservation, Uncle Neil paid for the tow and repairs. When she feared she was about to have a nervous breakdown because of her crazy family, he was there on the phone to calm and reassure her. She trusted him.

"Hello." He sounded older. How long had it been since she saw him? Christmas? No, she went to the Bahamas with Mat for Christmas. Maybe her birthday? That was last April. They lived in the same town. Why hadn't she kept in touch?

"Uncle Neil, this is Chandler. I'm in big trouble. We're all in big trouble. I need to talk to you." A flood of emotion choked and she took a breath.

The grouchy voice changed to one of compassion. "Of course, Chan. What is it?"

"I don't want to talk on the phone. Can I meet you somewhere, somewhere public and crowded, where we won't attract attention?"

"Well, that certainly sounds ominous. Sure. I'm not too busy. I'll meet you anywhere you want."

"Thanks Uncle Neil. There is a Starbucks on Jamison near the Westin Hotel in Arlington. I can be there in about thirty minutes."

"Okay, but give me an hour. I have a few things to wrap up." He hesitated. "Chan, whatever it is, I'm sure it's manageable. I'll be there."

"Thanks." Her voice was a whisper. She only hoped this was the right thing to do. Chandler took a long, hot shower trying to stay calm as she killed time before her meeting. She wrapped in a towel and walked out into the common room where she was startled to find a man sitting.

He turned and grinned. "Well, hello to you. I'm Jerry with Fleet Air. I haven't seen you here before. Are you a new member of our 'flop before you fly' group?"

She didn't know what to say for a moment and then realized, this was just another pilot who shared the crash pad. She smiled, embarrassed. "No, I'm here with Mat McCoy."

"Oh yeah. He's the Silver Streak guy. He flies international. I don't know how those guys handle the time zones. It would kill me. Say, which room are you in? I'll take the one farthest away so I don't disturb."

Chandler nodded the direction of her room. She needed both hands to clutch the towel which was just a little short of covering all her female real estate. The pilot was a gentleman and retreated to his room without excessive gawking, just one quick, sideways glance and a grin.

She flushed and shuffled to close her door, exhale and then allow a little laugh. She got dressed and left a note on the door that she was going for a walk. And then did just that.

The neighborhood was a mix of expensive apartments and condos along with a smattering of run-down near-tenement buildings - poverty in the shadow of great wealth. She kept reminding herself to be careful. She was a fugitive, an accomplice to murder. Somehow, though, she felt things were going to be all right. Uncle Neil would know what to do. But every passer-by looked suspicious to her hypervigilant eyes.

She settled into a back table at Starbucks and waited. Neil was late. When he arrived, she watched to see that he was alone. Seemed to be. He had put on weight and his gray hair had gone pure silver. He rushed to her and delivered a quick kiss on the cheek. He was breathing hard, almost wheezing.

"It's so good to see you, Chandler. Do you remember how you used to call me when you and my idiot brother were travelling across the country? I always enjoyed your little updates. It made me feel close to you." He paused and seemed to notice her reddish hair for the first time but didn't mention it. "I have to say it's hard for me to remember that now you're a very successful big city lawyer. How does your father feel about that?"

His easy manner should have made her relax but there was something she couldn't put her finger on. Maybe he was trying a little too hard. Maybe she was just paranoid. She started to spin the story of Mat's kidnapping and torture. She skipped any mention of the West Virginia shootout.

Uncle Neil listened intently but showed no sign that he felt her story outrageous or unbelievable. That troubled her. A week ago, she would never have believed such a crazy tale, but he seemed to take it in without argument. When she was done, they sat for a long time.

Finally, he spoke in carefully measured words. "I have had suspicions for some time that something like this, certainly not of the scale you describe, but something was going on. There have been meetings, many meetings behind the president's back. I was never involved. A couple of years ago I attended one of the Bohemian Grove gatherings. My boss thought I might be able to lobby the FBI Director on something or other. I can't even remember what. I was excited. For years I heard stories about the 'Grovers' and the wild Bacchanals in the California woods."

He sat back and seemed to enjoy the memory. "It was a great disappointment. There were many influential men there and they did cavort a bit, but it was mainly drinking and a little bit of nudity. There were some young women but they seemed to be servants rather than escorts. The most outrageous thing I saw was the Secretary of State peeing on a tree."

Neil's face softened. "I did get to attend the Great Owl ceremony. They have a huge statue, maybe forty feet tall, and they light a bonfire before it. It's called the 'cremation of care' or something. Great lot of foolishness. There wasn't even a human sacrifice."

He looked at Chandler as though expecting her to laugh. She didn't. He continued, "Anyway, I did overhear conversations about this 'Humanity' although I took it to be a descriptive term not an organization's name. The speakers were concerned that an Anti-Vivisection group called Normal, or something, that was giving Silver

Streak Airlines trouble. The group accused the airline company of illegal human organ trafficking. Specifically, they said the company was robbing graves and stealing body parts for sale to scientists developing some sort of 'mind control' drug. I dismissed it at the time."

"And now?"

"I don't know, Chandler. After what you've told me, I just don't know." He looked into her eyes like a good uncle. "Tell me where you are staying and what I can do to help you. You must be very frightened."

"I am scared, Uncle Neil. So scared, I don't dare tell you where we're holed up. If you want to help me, see if you can find out more about this Normal organization. I want to contact them."

"Of course. But you need a safe place. You are welcome to stay with me. After Emma died, I just rattle around that big house."

Hadn't he heard anything she said? Why would he make an offer that would endanger them both?

"Or your sister, Gen. I'm sure she would…"

"Absolutely not. I would never put her in danger and, besides, I don't think she would help me against our own government."

"Chandler, Chandler, she's your sister. She's blood even if you two disagree on things…"

"I'm sorry. I won't go near her." Chandler wasn't liking Neil's tone. He was trying to get her to commit to a location. Suddenly she found his whole approach suspicious.

"I have to go."

Neil almost jumped out of his seat to grab her arm. "No, Chan. Come with me. I'll protect you. You can always depend on me."

She twisted loose and started for the door just as two black SUV's with tinted windows pulled up and parked illegally. Men in suits and sunglasses were getting out, tough looking men.

She spun and glared at her uncle, her defender, her friend. "You set me up. You bastard. You set me up."

He reached for her again. "Chandler, you have to come in. I can protect you, but you have to give up. They'll kill you if you don't."

His voice was strained, earnest. She drew back as though he were suddenly on fire and then, with an anguished head shake, ran past the serving counter and into the Starbucks back room. She could hear her uncle yelling but his words died.

She slammed out the back door. Frenzied, confused, she bolted out into the sunshine of a small alley. There were a dozen or more store's back entrances and loading docks. She heard tires squeal somewhere, picked a random door and walked in. Controlling her breathing, she tried to be inconspicuous. Behind her, she could hear shouting, but her pursuers would have to guess which door she had chosen. That gave her time to sneak through a paint store's storage area and out front into another busy street. Luck was with her. A man was just getting out of a cab. She almost knocked him down as she barreled past and ducked into the back seat. "Metro Station," she shouted, and the cabbie nodded.

After two blocks, she finally raised her head above the seat and peeked out the window. She saw no black SUVs.

"Stop here," she commanded and the driver obeyed. She handed him two twenties and he seemed quite satisfied. After the cab pulled away, she stood for a long time letting everything sink in. Her uncle knew about Humanity, knew about the severed heads, even knew how much danger she was in. Why had he led them to her? Why would he put her at such risk? Either he was part of the group or was being manipulated by them. Once again, she was alone, all alone - except for Mat.

*I object to violence because when it appears to do good,
the good is only temporary; the evil it does is permanent*

- Mahatma Ghandi

CHAPTER THIRTEEN

Maston the Archon Killer

When she got back to the crash pad, Mat was agitated. "Where did you go? What happened? You look like you've seen a ghost. Are you all right?"

She started to sob softly. "I saw my uncle. He tried to turn me over to them. Mat, they're everywhere. I don't know where to turn."

He took her in his arms and patted her on the back as he would a child. He was about to speak when the apartment door opened. A man in a suit was kneeling outside as he removed his lock pick and stared up at them without expression. He stood aside, and John Maston came in looking businesslike in a three piece pinstripe with silk tie. His face, however, looked weary.

"Hello, Mat. You've led us on quite a chase. I have to hand it to you, we looked like a bunch of amateurs running around in circles with you always a step ahead. If the lady lawyer hadn't called her uncle, we might never have connected."

John shrugged. "But here we are. You, me and the elephant in the room. So, how do you think this is going to turn out?" John Maston snapped open a briefcase. From it, he took an automatic pistol with a silencer almost as big as the gun." Chandler gasped. Mat froze. Maston cradled the big weapon in both hands and sighed. Then he raised the gun at Mat, but hesitated and turned instead to pop two quick shots into the man who had picked the lock.

That man grabbed his chest in astonishment and stood frozen for several seconds. Then, with a last look down at his bloody shirt he crumpled. John came over and fired another shot into the fallen man's neck. Despite the huge silencer, the shots seemed loud. Mat winced at each and Chandler let out one shuddering gasp after another. She looked as though she might faint.

John Maston checked the fallen man's neck for a pulse and when he was satisfied, stood to face Mat and Chandler. "I am a graduate of Level Four Reeducation. That is, I am an Archon killer - a certified bad-ass. You have plenty of reason to fear me."

He raised the gun back toward the ceiling. "Here's the thing. I really do believe in what Humanity is doing but, even after all my indoctrination, I can't support all their methods. I was sent here to kill you and your lady friend." He smiled. "But Mat, I'm not going to do that. You see, I have a lot of respect for you. People like you should form the first legions of our new world order. You deserve to live."

He stood for a long time without speaking. Finally, Maston shrugged. "I, on the other hand, have played out my time. My wife left me years ago after the 'scab' ordeal. Silver Streak coerced me to do many things that I find morally wrong. I guess I'm looking for a little absolution by this act of disobedience—by not killing you. In fact, I'm going to give you a gift."

He reached into his pants pocket and pulled out an object the size of a chewing gum pack and tossed it to Mat. "What you hold in your hand will make you the most powerful man in the country, maybe the world. Use it wisely."

With that, John Maston took a deep breath, looked straight ahead and, with sad, unfocussed eyes, placed the big gun under his chin and fired.

The ceiling splattered with blood and tissue. John's body stood for several long seconds as his gun hand fell useless by his side. Then he pitched forward like a tree cut at the base. He actually bounced after hitting the floor.

Chandler was screaming. Mat moved his hands in pointless motions. The new pilot bolted out of his room wearing only underpants. He stood, mouth agape, unable to breath.

Mat seemed to mobilize. Chandler knew he was good in crises and now he proved it. He spoke to the underwear pilot. "My friend, you are in great danger. If the people who sent this assassin discover that you are a witness, they'll kill you and your whole family. Run, as quick as you can and never tell anyone what went on here. Go. Right now."

The pilot nodded but wasn't breathing.

"Chandler," she heard Mat's voice, but the words seemed distant. "Gather all your things. Leave no clues to our current appearance or dress. We have to be out of here in minutes or someone will come to check on these two killers. There is always backup on operations like this, always."

She didn't know where he got his expertise in assassinations, but she followed his instructions like a robot and, in less than two minutes, they were down the back stairs and in the van. The other pilot had been even faster.

Geneva the Sister

Mat drove. Chandler pondered. The panic passed. Perhaps she was adapting to this endless adrenaline rush. She hoped not.

"Mat, I think I was wrong about my sister. I can think of no one else to trust. I think we should risk contacting her."

"Considering that your uncle turned you in, I don't see why you think your sister would be any more trustworthy or supportive."

"Well, I've thought very hard about it. If I can get her to listen and believe, I think she will be disgusted by what Humanity is doing. She will want to fight for her country. At least, that's what I hope."

Mat bit his lip. "Tell you what. Let's try a controlled meeting, a surprise meeting, where she has no opportunity to ambush us. You know her. You'll be able to tell if she's honestly willing to help. But first, we have to find a hideout."

"A hideout?" She smiled. "When I was a kid, I was always an outcast in the towns we went to. I would build my own little worlds of cardboard and wood, secret hideouts in the woods or behind buildings. In them, I felt safe from bullies and local bigots who thought my crusading father was the Anti-Christ in the flesh." She paused. "I actually think I know a good hiding place. It has no creature comforts, but it's safe."

"Okay. Where to?"

"My sister's. Geneva is a tech nut. She has more equipment than some large companies, but she lives in a tiny townhouse in Old Town with no room for her toys. So, she uses a condemned house across the street as a lab. We can go there and hide out to spy on her before we make contact."

It was decided. Mat dropped Chandler off in the alley behind the old brick row house. It had a 1940's style one-car garage so completely full of junk there was no possibility of parking inside. Just as well. The van had served its purpose.

Mat left to dump the van while Chandler tried to remember how to get into the dilapidated building. She was sure there were alarms, monitors. Her sister was careful about such things and this was a fairly high-crime neighborhood. She saw surveillance cameras mounted beneath the roof and took a deep breath. A key pad guarded the back door. She couldn't begin to guess what code might be. Perhaps she could climb through a window.

After fifteen minutes of pacing she still had no idea how to get in? But then she heard a tentative voice.

"Chandler? Is that you?"

She turned and faced Geneva, an attractive woman of medium height and athletic build with short brown hair going slightly gray. Her bearing and poise were stiff military, even in a sweat shirt and blue jeans.

Chandler broke down and embraced her sister in a crunching hug that Geneva cautiously returned. "What's wrong, Chan? Why are you crying?"

"There is just so much to tell you. I am in great danger and Uncle Neil tried to turn me over to a bunch of people who are responsible for the riots and destruction going on in America." Geneva tried to pull back but Chandler clung to her.

"Chan, come over to my house. I'll fix you some tea, Earl Gray with light cream, right?"

"You remember?"

Geneva smiled. "Of course, I remember what my big sister drinks. Come on."

"No, they'll be watching your house. I don't want to put you in danger. Can we just go inside your workshop? I'll feel safe there."

Once inside the crumbling building, Chandler faced gleaming steel racks and work tables with a half dozen monitors mounted on walls. It looked like an air traffic control center. "My God, what did all this cost?"

Geneva shrugged. "Not that much. I buy surplus equipment and use it for my hobbies. You will be amazed at what I can do from here."

Chandler looked at her hands. "I'm sorry that we have grown apart. I've always respected you, even envied your accomplishments. I know you think of me as someone who sold out for…whatever it is my career has brought me. I never meant to offend you. I suppose I was trying to get back at Daddy for making our lives so difficult. I know he was a great man, a heroic man, but he always seemed to care more about the plight of strangers than his own family."

Geneva touched her sister's arm. "You should see him more. He's very lonely. Still abrasive and loud and even obnoxious, but very lonely. I go to the nursing home twice a week to listen to him rant." She smiled but it was a weak smile. "We all wished he had more room in his life for us when we were growing up." Then a quick change of tone. "Okay, tell me about the danger you say we're in."

"If you don't mind, I'd like to wait for Mat, my pilot friend, to get back. He can give you a firsthand account of the atrocities this organization has committed and is about to commit."

The Three Musketeers

Mat left the van in a supermarket parking lot and walked twelve blocks back to Geneva's. Before he was a block away, he heard police cars swarming. How could they have known so quickly? Maybe traffic cameras had spotted him driving. He adjusted his cap to cover his face and tried to walk at an unhurried pace. Every fiber in his body wanted to sprint flat-out but he forced an easy gait. *Nothing to see here, folks. Just move along.*

He hid behind the dilapidated garage and scanned the old brick row houses. Nothing moved. He slid along the fence that divided a small yard from neighbors. If anything, his skulking probably made him more obvious. The back door was unlocked and he walked in to find Chandler sitting with her sister. The resemblance was clear. Both of them had a confidence and authority rarely found in attractive women.

"This is Mat McCoy. He is my…" She hesitated. "Just what the hell are you, Mat? My lover, my friend, my—what are we to each other?"

He made a face. "Right now, I am a great threat to you, but I am also the man who cares more about you than anyone else on earth. We will probably both die soon and that's okay as long as I'm with you to the end."

Geneva spoke up. "Wow, that's dramatic. Chandler says you can convince me that our government is evil and racist and willing to exterminate huge numbers of citizens. Is that true?'

Mat looked her in the eye. "We haven't really met. You must be Geneva, the smart one. I'm Matthew McCoy and I have something that a man gave me just before he blew his brains out. He said it would make me the most powerful man in the world. How about we find out what it is before I tell you my story?" He pulled a thumb drive from his pocket.

Geneva took it and turned to a computer on the table. She inserted the small drive and spoke, as much to herself as anyone else. "It's a video file, fairly large. Here we go. I have a driver that works.

The screen flickered and settled to show a large auditorium filled with older men. Vice President Stark McCoby spoke.

"Well here we are at last. I want you all to look around. You will immediately recognize many, if not all, of the patriots and leaders assembled here. They are your fellow warriors, craftsmen forging a new reality, a new beginning for our race, a new chapter for humanity.

You have all served heroically but until today, we dared not reveal you one to another. Now, we have gained the power. Mostly through your efforts, we have gained the power to protect each other. We have gained, and continue to gain, control over our nation and ultimately over our world. We will soon control humanity's destiny and it will be a magnificent destiny."

He raised his hand to eye level, palm down. "As it is above…" He lowered it to waist height and turned palm up. "So shall it be below." There was a murmur through the crowd.

"The God of all peoples, all worlds and all time brought us into this flawed and miserly world where we were told falsehoods, myths that have persisted because they serve existing cabals of power. Now we have passed through the purgatory of morality and the inferno of matter to arrive at the true core of humanity. Many of us rose to positions of influence in just such environments. But we sensed in our hearts that there was more, that we were more, and that we were capable of becoming even more. And now, we understand the true path to discovery, to the knowledge that exists within, the knowledge that must guide us."

He paused. "I want to take a moment to introduce a few of our fellow crusaders. It is, of course, imperative that we maintain complete confidence. There are still powerful forces that will fight to the death to keep us from improving our race. The great unwashed who populate this planet like termites devouring resources and polluting our genetic future will never willingly accept their fate. But we are the tidal wave of the future. We are the hope for mankind. We are the earthly manifestation of all that is good and right and desirable. Generations without number will remember us and pay homage."

Geneva softly mouthed the words, "Termites devouring resources and polluting our genetic future." She looked tense, maybe even angry.

On the monitor, McCoby shouted. "Mister Robert Anderson, Secretary of Homeland Security." Applause followed. "Halsey Barnett, FBI Director." More applause. "General Bret Cunningham, Chairman of the Joint Chiefs of Staff." It went on and on.

Geneva shook her head. "It's the whole damn cabinet. It's the whole damned government. It's everyone."

Introductions over, McCoby continued. "Until now, we have conducted minor efforts at eliminating the hardest core of defectives. This has been a learning effort as we developed networks to control information and guide the public's understanding of events toward a more favorable view of our crusade. We have learned much and are now ready to greatly expand the scale and scope of our efforts. As always, turmoil is opportunity and many of you may find this national cleansing of defectives to offer opportunities for your businesses, investments and endeavors.

Our nation will undergo an overwhelming upheaval, but it will be nothing compared to the depopulation of backward countries that is coming. Africa, India, large parts of Russia, the Middle East, Asia, Central and South America will become sterile but still capable of providing resources to our new, purer race."

Again, Geneva mumbled and shook her head. "Depopulation? A new, purer race?"

McCoby's face seemed illuminated on the screen. "We are on the eve of a new, more perfect dawn. Let us commit ourselves with undaunted passion, a strong spirit and a cold, clear eye."

Mat and Chandler sat silent, as though in shock. Geneva whispered, "My God, it's the whole government. They want to

scourge the country and then the world. They want genetic purity."
She paused. "Defectives? Who decides what constitutes defective?
This is a genocide, nothing less."

Mat regained composure. "It's not the *whole* government. Let's
make a list of attendees at this ghoulish meeting and then compare
it to government organizational charts to see who's not represented?"

Chandler added, "Uncle Neil said there had been meetings
behind President Whiteman's back. He must not be party to the
plot. Geneva, can you get to him?"

"I doubt it. I'm the head radio operator on his airplane and, while
I sometimes sit within twenty feet of him on Air Force One, I'm never
allowed to speak directly."

Mat shook his head. "There has to be a way."

*Never doubt that a small group of thoughtful,
committed citizens can change the world.
Indeed, it is the only thing that ever has*

– Margaret Mead

CHAPTER FOURTEEN

The Most Powerful Man in the World

Jerome Halstead, Silver Streak Director of Operations, leaned back in his chair behind the oval conference table. "Maston and his bodyguard are dead? How in hell did that happen? We're talking about some damned skinny pilot and a paper-pushing girl lawyer. How did they kill two well-trained operatives?" His voice was tight.

"Sir, they've been ahead of us at every step. We think the other escapee, a man named Ron Male, has left them but the lawyer and Captain McCoy seem to know what they are doing. They abandoned the van they were using in a Virginia suburban supermarket lot. The van's full of their fingerprints. We have traffic cam footage of them coming into the Washington area, but we don't have any leads on where they might have gone next or how they're traveling. The girl's uncle thinks they'll run as far away as they can. He really hasn't been of much use though. His memory is fading and he is easily confused."

Halstead interrupted. "So where would they seek shelter, family?"

The briefer sucked air through his teeth in frustration. "We know that the pilot is estranged from his family and the lawyer has not spoken to her sister, an Air Force sergeant, for years. Her father is in a nursing home on Medicaid. He won't be able to do much. Moreover, the uncle betrayed them. It seems unlikely they will attempt any more contact with family." He seemed to anticipate the next question. "We're running down any friends or associates they might call on.

168

The most likely lead is the pilot's housekeeper, but so far, she isn't cooperating."

Halstead grimaced hard. "Get hold of Johnson in the NSA. Follow the electronic trail —money, phone and internet. They can't survive out there in today's world without leaving clues. Find them, damn it."

He actually hissed and clenched his fist, but then seemed to calm slightly. "Except for these problem children, things are progressing according to plan. Two dissidents on the run really can't do much to stop us. They're an irritant more than anything. Still, I want them neutralized. Until the President is removed from office, we must keep up the pretense that all the turmoil is being promulgated by black terrorists. Later, when attitudes have hardened, and we have established greater control, we will reveal the truth—and the truth will remold our world."

The conference room was quiet. Halstead's conviction seemed strong, but his brow wrinkled as he spoke to himself. "There are so many pieces to the puzzle, so many chances for things to go terribly wrong. No one can be fully trusted."

Daddy Tells Her What to Do

Once Geneva had seen the video and digested the message of Humanity's plans, she was unhesitatingly on board. Now, she and Mat became energized. They started throwing out ideas, making plans, creating scenarios, plotting possible strategies. They were like a couple of kids playing war. Chandler held back.

She heard Mat saying, "How about this house? Can they trace it to you?"

"No. The Homeowners' Association owns it. They allow me to use it in exchange for taking care of maintenance and upkeep. It had been foreclosed and they didn't want it to become a crack house or magnet for vagrants."

"How about your phones, computers?"

"Everything is encrypted. That is, after all, what I do for a living, communicate secretly."

"Can you get new identification documents for us?"

"Get them? I can create them right here in my shop. I have the actual software used by the Joint-Base Andrews Personnel Office to issue ID's."

Chandler almost smiled. The two war gamers didn't seem to need hers help for a while. She left them and slipped out the door, pausing to take deep breaths and clear her mind. On impulse she decided to seek advice from the one man she never expected to ask for help, her father. It was a bad idea - and she knew it. That's why she didn't want to tell either Geneva or Mat. But, on the other hand, none of them seem to have any particularly good ideas at the moment.

On the bus to Alexandria Chandler sat and surveyed the area above the driver – no camera, at least no visible camera. The bus route wound through low-rent residential areas where streets were mostly empty. There were no signs of the 'insurgency' the news had described. She did see a couple of Army patrols and her bus was boarded at one checkpoint, but everyone on board stayed cool.

The soldier who walked down the bus aisle was very young, very serious and very ill at ease. He held his rifle high and checked a couple of backpacks and grocery bags with his free hand. Chandler smiled at him, feeling a little embarrassed about her reddish hair and grubby clothes. The kid soldier returned her smile. He seemed much more interested in checking her out than looking for weapons or whatever. She postured a little, indulging his interest.

He grinned and then turned to yell, "Clear," and the back door hissed open. The soldier saluted her with a single index finger and stepped off.

Chandler breathed again. She should have told Mat where she was going. *What if she were captured?* Could she hold up under interrogation? She might break and give up her sister and her - whatever Mat was. Too late to worry about that now.

She got off the bus a block short of the nursing home and walked deliberately, glancing in all directions. Sure enough, there were police cars stationed at the entrance. But she had been there often enough to know about the staff entrances. She even knew the key codes. Aides, too busy to open the door for her, shared those numbers years ago and they had never changed.

Once inside, she smelled the familiar odor of disinfectant trying to overcome the stench of human excretions. It was noisy. Metal carts banged down the hall. There were cries from dementia patients lost in a world they could no longer comprehend and there was singing - of sorts - and incessant cries of "Nurse, help me."

It was a depressing place, but it was the best she could afford after the Medicaid cutbacks. She paid for a portion of her father's care - about six grand a month out of pocket. Geneva kicked in a couple of hundred. Her brother - well, he could barely take care of himself. She paused and felt a twinge of guilt. She should have come more often.

No one in the hallway acknowledged her as she scanned the ceiling looking for cameras. There were none. Probably because they could be used in lawsuits.

She heard him well before she reached his room. Benjamin Alfred Harris liked his initials – BAH - as in humbug. At seventy six, he was a physical wreck, a blind double-amputee who refused to take his diabetes seriously.

She stopped in the doorway and leaned her head against the frame. He sat in a wheel chair with a blanket over his knee stubs and waved his arms in animated argument with the Fox News reporter on his small TV. Since he couldn't see the picture, she hadn't wasted money on a big screen. The small TV was good enough for this champion of the oppressed, this lion of democracy, to continue his never-ending battle against the evil forces of racism and cold-hearted capitalism - even if they were just television commentators.

"Daddy." Her voice sounded small. He jumped in his chair and turned to face her general direction.

"Huh?" He looked confused. "Chandler, is that you? Come in, girl. Give your old man a hug." He extended arms into space. She came to him and buried her face in his shoulder. He had an old man smell.

Then she cried. Chandler Harris hadn't cried in a decade. She was the cool, unflappable lawyer. But now she cried little girl tears and her daddy held her, comforted her, smoothed her hair. She stayed cuddled for a long time and he didn't rush her, didn't press her. He just held her until the storm passed.

Finally, she took a deep breath and pulled back to begin her story. He listened attentively, shaking his head from time to time.

"Daddy, I have nowhere to turn. I'm all alone in this terrible thing and yet I feel I must do something. But there is no one to turn to."

He smiled. How she remembered that smile. She had seen it so often when everything seemed to be crashing in around them. He would smile and explain how they would get out of a town where their lives had been threatened or how they would walk tall and righteous in front of Klan protesters or how they would proudly sit in the front row of the black church after fire bomb threats.

Now, he was old and gnarled and feeble but he was still the same lion, her Atticus Finch. He spoke softly but with total confidence. "Chandler, you are not alone. You are never alone. This is America. It belongs to the people, not the government. You must go to the people. They are the strength of our nation and they are a moral people. Sometimes they forget, but ultimately, they are a moral people. Go, and seek their help. Use whatever means you must, but go to them."

Her tears dried. Her breathing calmed. She nodded and straightened. Suddenly, she had a plan – of sorts.

The Game Plan

Mat heard the electric door lock click open, He grabbed Vernon's big pistol and turned to see Chandler coming through the door. He didn't try to hide his anxiety. "Where have you been? I worried. Gen has been worried sick."

Chandler looked oddly relaxed, almost cheerful. "I've been to see Daddy."

Geneva rushed out of the back room. "Chandler, thank God you're okay. Why did you risk going to the nursing home?"

"I needed to go, to get his advice and now - now I know what we must do." She sounded resolute, completely sure of what she was about to say.

Mat wasn't sure what to expect. "Okay, let's hear it. What *must* we do?"

Chandler Harris took a breath and delivered her message. "We three standing here are about to save our country. We have just the odd assortment of skills and experience necessary to do something magnificent." Mat waited.

"We're going to broadcast the video of the Vice President and his co-conspirators across the national media. If it was good enough to convince Geneva, a stubborn conservative, it will have the same effect on a great many Americans. By exposing the plot, we take away the trappings of legitimacy and open the way for President Whiteman to destroy them." She said it with the overconfidence of a child saying, "I'm going to go out to win an Olympic medal or develop a cure for cancer or learn to fly without an airplane."

Geneva tried to be supportive. "That's a swell idea Chan, but you said yourself, the heads of many major news outlets are part of the conspiracy. How do we get past them?"

Chandler nodded agreement. "You mean how will *you* get by them? I am confident that I can get several smaller network news executives on board. They are clients and friends, but you have to find a way to covertly broadcast the video to all the news agencies."

Mat was slowly shaking his head. "Risky. We just don't know who to trust. I mean, who would have suspected the Vice President and all those cabinet members? We have no idea how deep this thing goes. Would you suspect a freight airline, a software company? How about the West Virginia Highway Patrol?"

Geneva had been quiet. She finally spoke, "I could do it from the airplane. After Nine Eleven, we had a communications link installed that allows me to send live broadcasts simultaneously to all major news agencies." She was quiet, lost in thought and gesturing to no one in particular. "The problem would be the Secret Service. After the first few seconds, they would be on me like piranha on a pork chop."

Another long silence before Mat spoke. "Then we have to hijack the airplane. That will grab media attention and give you an unrestricted platform. If we threaten to destroy the plane unless the video plays, they'll have to go along."

Geneva didn't look impressed. "Hijack Air Force One with the Secret Service on board? Do you know who these guys are? They aren't kidding when they say they're ready to die to protect the leadership."

Chandler had her stubborn face on. "And so are we. If we fail, our lives won't mean anything. This is our moment. What do you say?"

Mat saw her look into her sister's eyes. Geneva took the deepest breath of her life. "Well, all right then. It's one for all and all for one." She extended a hand. Mat laid his palm on top of hers and so did Chandler, who said, "You know the Musketeers always toasted with a cup of wine after a pledge like this. I'll go get a bottle."

There was something liberating about their death wish, as though it brought a sort of order to the chaos, meaning to the insanity and purpose to their lives…what remained of their lives.

Mat finished his wine, paced and rubbed his hands together. Now it was time for serious planning. "Okay, Gen, how can I get onto the plane?"

She was ready with an answer. "I am down one radio operator next month and we have a master sergeant coming in from Offutt Air Force Base to augment us. I can dummy up orders and speed his arrival date so you can impersonate him. I have the ability to create fake ID's, laminated flight line badges, driver's licenses and whatever. You'll just have to learn enough tech talk to pass for a trainee."

Mat felt okay with that. "If all I have to do is radio transmissions that shouldn't be a problem."

Geneva smirked. "The title 'radio operator' is a misnomer. We handle all data transmissions, voice, text and raw data in highly encrypted formats. You will be impersonating a computer geek on steroids. But I can cover as long as you learn enough buzzwords to pass cursory questioning. It will take a week or so to get you processed through the system and up to speed. In the meantime, you need to study hard."

Chandler chimed. "A week? Will it really take that long?"

"Yes, and that's if Mat is a quick study, but he must be fairly bright to have attracted you."

Mat was staring into space, visualizing. "I'll need a tour of the airplane and information about unique systems. I'm sure I'll have no problems flying the basic airplane, but I am concerned about security systems and procedures."

Chandler asked, "What about an escape module? I saw the movie 'Air Force One' and they had an escape module."

Geneva sighed, "No Chandler. There's no escape module. This is the real world. Not a movie."

Chandler smiled and looked at her co-conspirators. "You know, I was right. We three are the best people in the world to pull it off – or die trying."

FBI Notification

A striking black lady answered the doorbell. She was tall and thin as a Somali princess but her hand-on-hip pose spoke defiance and suspicion. The two men at the door looked like Mormon Missionaries in black suits and ties.

"Mrs. Male, Mrs. Regina Male?"

"Yes, I am Regina Male. Who's asking?"

"Yes Ma'am, I am Special Agent Sidney Cole, Federal Bureau of Investigation and this is Agent Kelso. May we come in?"

She sniffed. "What is the subject of your visit?"

"Ma'am, I think it might be better if we spoke in private." She stared him down. He looked a little sheepish. Then she turned her head and shouted. "John, get down here. The FBI wants to talk to us." She returned her steady gaze to the FBI agents but made no move to allow them in. "Do you have a warrant?"

"No Ma'am. We just want to talk. We have information about your son."

For a moment, she let her mouth drop ever so slightly but then recovered. Her husband came down the stairs in a flurry. He was a disheveled, portly man, hands full of papers, sleeves rolled to the elbow and suspenders slightly askew. "The FBI? What does the FBI want?"

Regina Male stepped back and opened the door. She indicated the way to the living room and they all sat. It took a moment for anyone to speak. Then Agent Cole began.

"Mister and Mrs. Male, I am sorry to report that your son, Ronald Male is deceased. He died three days ago in West Virginia. Details are still quite unclear, but it appears he was stopped by the Highway Patrol in a routine check, resisted and was shot. It also appears that he killed the trooper who made the stop."

There was silence. Regina Male suppressed a gasp. John Male buried his head in his hands, muttering, "I knew it. I knew it. When he disappeared, I knew something terrible was going on. That damned company he works for. They're involved. I know it."

Regina's voice cracked as she asked. "The FBI? Why is the FBI involved?"

"COMPED, his employer, believes he was colluding with a Chinese national to steal company secrets. They confronted him and he fled. We don't know much more than that, but we will be investigating and we will report any findings to you. In the meantime, I have the information you'll need to claim the body and make arrangements." He paused. "I am so sorry for your loss."

Regina Male was shaking, fighting to hold back all the words she wanted to say. Some white cracker cop killed her son. They would justify it and dismiss the affair. Just one more throw-away black boy. She looked at the white man who was trying so hard to be compassionate and she hated him.

The power that establishes a state is violence; the power that maintains it is violence; the power that eventually overthrows it is violence

- Kenneth Karunda

CHAPTER FIFTEEN

Devil in the Details

Mat was getting more and more excited about their adventure. Stealing Air Force One - what a trip. No matter how it turned out, it would be an historical event to rival anything that had come before, and it would impact the whole country, the whole world. *Just don't screw it up.*

Chandler was busy updating her contacts and vetting them to see who could be trusted. Geneva had to go back to work at Andrews Air Force Base but she had already made great progress.

Mat now had a military-looking buzz cut. He used the fake military ID Geneva made for him and bought a crisp new uniform with service ribbons and a name tag from clothing sales at Andrews. He hadn't worn a uniform since his time in the Air Force Reserve fifteen years ago but now, here he was, Master Sergeant Tom Benton. He checked himself out in the mirror, turning and looking over his shoulder like a bride buying a wedding dress.

He had drug store black-rimmed glasses that made him look a little geekier and he was working on a slight stoop to seem less athletic. The uniform was a size too large to allow for smuggling things. Later, he would dive into the books and regulations Geneva left for him to study. He was excited, really getting into his role.

They worked out of Geneva's lab in the basement but always kept an alert eye on the surveillance camera monitors. Through the day, several black SUV's did drive slowly by the house, but none tarried long enough to cause alarm, and none seemed to pay particular attention to the lab house where they worked.

At six thirty, Geneva arrived home with pizza and beer. Chandler loved pizza but wasn't that fond of beer. Mat was tickled to have beer, but he much preferred his usual Whole Foods fare. They sat around the open pizza box, munched and traded questions.

"How do we get a gun on board?"

Geneva hefted a drippy slice and guided strings of cheese into her mouth. Mat chugged from his long neck bottle and smacked. Finally, Geneva had chewed enough to answer, even though a little cheese still hung from her lip.

"Everything that goes on that airplane is inspected, everything except the codes box. No Security Policeman or even Secret Service can touch the codes box. Your big pistol will barely fit. Since I am the head radio operator, I am responsible for the codes. I load the box and I carry it. No one else can touch it."

Mat seemed okay with that. "Now," Geneva began. "we have a timetable. The President will fly tomorrow. I won't be on that trip. But five days from now, Vice President McCoby is scheduled to go back to his home state of Idaho. That's our chance. Security will be a little less tight for the VP. I have both of us on the roster to fly that one. Five days till D-Day. Can we make it?"

Chandler nodded. "Yes. I'll be ready. I have people in Al Jazeera America, The BBC and several independent networks who are willing to be on-site for what I promised would be the scoop of a lifetime They took me at my word without any more details."

Mat was a little less enthusiastic. "Five days. Wow, I have been through your books and checklists. I have the routine reports and basic layout of the computers down, but I don't know if I'm anywhere near ready to actually operate any of this stuff."

Geneva munched and spoke with her mouth full. "It'll be okay. As long as you know about the mandatory message protocols for the White House Military Office and the Secret Service network, I'll handle all phone calls and messages. There are usually only a few in the first minutes of flight. After that, we'll take over and it won't matter."

"Okay." Mat was thinking out loud. "How about the cockpit door? Who can unlock it?"

"It's a reinforced anti-hijack door. Only the flight deck crew and the Chief Steward can open it. But it will remain open on the ground and in the early stages of flight in case of emergency egress. We'll have to make our move quickly."

Mat seemed satisfied. "Let's review the crew. You have two pilots, an engineer and a navigator behind that cockpit door, right? How many other people will come into the cockpit during climbout?"

Geneva thought. "Just the steward with coffee. Colonel Simpson likes his cup of coffee delivered just as the flaps are fully retracted. Oh, and you, with a printout of the departure message. Inflight, only senior staff will normally ask to enter the cockpit and then, only if the VP has specific questions or requests."

"Okay good. Do you know if the plane will be refueled in Idaho or if we will carry enough gas for the return trip?"

Geneva was caught short. "I don't know. Why does that matter?"

"Weight. If we have to ferry enough fuel for the return trip, we may be too heavy for an immediate landing."

She made a slight nod. "I'll find out."

There was an adrenaline rush to the planning. Mat caught himself talking fast, breathing fast, thinking fast. He paused for a minute and looked at his two co-conspirators. He felt proud of them. The air in the musty room somehow smelled clean and pure. Mat McCoy had always tried to follow the rules and do the right thing, but this crime they were about to commit was the rightest thing he had ever done. He didn't need an alcohol wipe.

Elijah Methune

The news and social media flooded with pictures and quotes from their new celebrity, Elijah Methune. He was a craggy-faced black man with a menacing voice who wore African-looking clothes with a black beret and spoke with a preacher's voice. His message was clear, cold and precise.

"Black Americans, hear me. I am Elijah and I am the voice of freedom—not the freedom of Reconstruction Carpet Baggers, not the freedom of liberal do-gooders, not the freedom of preachers with soft hands and big brass collection plates, but the freedom of decent men and women who demand a safe and tolerant world where they can live and prosper."

He stiffened and faced the camera. His eyes were large and dark, almost mysterious in their depth. "We cannot depend upon the white man for security. He has always been the threat to us, always telling us he was working for our good and then stealing every bit of hope from us. No! We shall not ask, nor shall we accept the promises of the white man - not anymore."

He paused for what seemed an eternity just staring into the camera. "All across America, you see flags of the Black Dragon flying over neighborhoods. Wherever that flag hangs, new rules of conduct shall be enforced. Able-bodied men must defend their people, particularly the old, the vulnerable and the weak. Women must be treated with respect and they, in turn, must sustain the community, as they always have, through caring and feeding and nurturing the children and those in need. Criminal activity will be punished. Every city block will have a leader and that leader shall have the power to sanction residents. That will be our government now, not some uniformed thugs who invade our homes and places of business."

His paused and his tone turned cold. "Young black men, this is your time to rise, but do so with dignity and purpose. Stand against the oppressors but with pride, not arrogance. The forces of this ultra-right-wing government are arrayed against us. Look at their President. His very name is Whiteman – 'White Man' - and he speaks as though we are lesser humans. He is coming for you. They are all coming to kill you. Like the flames of hell, they are licking at your heels and they aim to destroy you. If you must lay down your life, be sure it is an honorable death and take at least two white devils with you."

He held up a fist. "I am Elijah and I declare the revolution has begun. I shall die proud."

The Fault is in our Pixels

Chandler turned away from her monitor after watching the latest 'Elijah' speech and shook her head. "You know, until now, D.C. has been pretty quiet. Major riots have happened in Philadelphia, Baltimore, Newark and a dozen other cities. But, for some reason, we've been spared. I only hope it stays calm for a few more days until our mission."

Geneva seemed puzzled. "There's something not right about this video."

Mat stood over his shoulder. "Damned right, there's something wrong about advocating rebellion against…"

"No. I mean there's something technically wrong with the video." She was playing it back with the image blown up several times larger and now moving at slow speed. "Watch. In the early segment, his head moves as he speaks. Every word he says causes his eyes to distort ever so slightly as his facial muscles move. But after the words 'white men' his head and eyes are fixed. They don't move even a single pixel, not even when he raises his hand."

Mat drew closer to the monitor. "Are you saying this video is fake?"

"It's been altered with computer generated imagery. I'm sure of it. No human can speak and have his face remain that still. It can't be done. These people have added the dialog about revolution." She frowned deep and hard. "They are actually instigating rebellion." Her voice cracked a little. "It is just as you said, Mat. They truly are monsters. We have to stop it."

The Calm is Past, the Fight Begun

On Thursday the capitol city erupted. During the first week of national calamities, the District of Columbia had maintained a tense calm. There had been a steady stream of military convoys and the Park Police had established checkpoints around all monuments and government buildings. But there had been no incidents, not a single one.

Now the Black Dragon flags were appearing and nerves were fraying. There was a sense of inevitability. Washington Mayor Calhoun was on television and radio almost hourly explaining that if everyone just stayed cool, things would get sorted out and normality would return.

Elijah Methune, or at least his image, was all over social media calling for a new social order where races could exist separate from each other but still cooperate. He laid out rules for daily living, personal responsibility and conflict resolution. Conservative commentators called it 'Black Sharia' just a short step to full Muslim indoctrination.

Then, the incident. A patrol of young Army National Guardsmen were confronted with an armed group of equally young black men in berets and assorted battle gear. Someone fired a shot and it was on. A sergeant radioed for support and Humvees streamed into the formerly quiet middle-class neighborhood with guns blazing.

Heavy machine guns raked the houses. Explosions sounded and fires began to burn. Great clouds of black smoke rose over Northwest Washington D.C. and the news cameras focused. The war had begun, and it spread like an overturned bucket of gasoline.

Mat the Radio Operator

Mat, in his neatly pressed uniform, rode with Geneva to the crew planning meeting. They breezed through the Andrews Air Force Base front gate with only a quick check of IDs. The young guard wearing helmet, body armor and combat gear had other things on his mind than a couple of white sergeants going to work. The base was quiet, with only essential personnel working.

The guards at the Presidential Hangar were more careful, cautiously comparing identification cards with a scheduled crew roster and going through the car. They did not inspect the padlocked briefcase with bold letters that read "Secret." It didn't matter. The box was empty, just a test.

The hexagon-shaped hangar was massive with telescoping doors that opened large enough to allow two Boeing 747s to pass through. Inside, the floors glistened and the airplanes – two 747s and two Gulfstreams – gleamed from being polished daily. Everything was oversized, brightly lit and meticulously clean.

Mat was awed, and it showed. He looked up at the almost hundred-foot-high ceiling and his mouth drooped. Geneva was used to the reaction. She gave her little tour guide spiel. Mat gawked as she explained things.

"The fire suppression system requires so much water they had to build a small lake inside the perimeter fence. The fuel is stored in tanks within the same fence so it can be sampled and certified. Our kitchen is the equal of any restaurant and the food is all bought secretly so no one can tamper. Security is state of the art. Once you enter, every move you make is recorded. If you do anything out of the ordinary, a security policeman appears almost instantly."

Mat just nodded, mouth slightly open. They climbed metal stairs to the crew area. There were standard work cubicles and a conference room with a long table and two flags, American and Air Force. A dozen uniformed men and women milled about. Geneva made introductions. Mat nodded and tried to smile. This was the Air Force One crew, hand-picked and clearly competent.

Colonel Simpson, the Presidential Pilot, blew into the room. He was a fairly average looking man with clipped hair, graying at the edges. He looked thin and athletic under his blue uniform. Mat noted that he didn't have a lot of ribbons. After decades of war, most career military people sported a chest full of decorations. The colonel went to the head of the table and everyone else stood behind seats in what was clearly a defined order. Geneva guided Mat to a chair.

Colonel Simpson spoke like a college professor reciting the same lecture he had done for a decade. "Okay, this will be a short-time-on-the-ground visit to Boise, Idaho. With the security situation in D.C. there is some speculation that the flight will cancel but, until that happens, we'll proceed as though everything is a go. Frankly, with mid-term elections coming up, I feel confident the Vice President will want to visit his home state unless the capitol itself is burning. Now, for the mission brief. Weather?"

A master sergeant stood and gave a quick power point with maps showing fronts, temperature graphs, wind depictions and en route forecasts. Simpson asked, "What about turbulence?" The weatherman pulled up another image. "For tomorrow, we expect light, continuous turbulence, just chop really, most of the way after Kansas. Over the Rockies, it may increase to moderate but all the severe stuff will be well south of your path."

"Thank you. Maintenance?"

A chief master sergeant half stood. "Both primary and backup planes are clean. No problems."

"Thank you." He looked at Geneva and said, Comm?"

Geneva stood. "Yes sir, I'd like to introduce Master Sergeant Tom Benton a Looking Glass comm specialist. He'll be training with me on this flight. We have no known special requirements except to monitor all situation reports on the national crises."

The colonel looked at him for a long second. Mat could read nothing in his eyes, but it was still unnerving. "Welcome aboard Sergeant Benton." Then his eyes shifted back to Geneva. "Chief Harris, keep him on a short leash. We all know Vice President McCoby doesn't like surprises."

The briefing went on with excruciating details of meals to be served, names of on-board reporters and their seating arrangements, arrival taxi-in plan and the arrival ceremony. When it was done, Colonel Simpson stood with a flicker of a smile and said, "Well, okay.

Show time tomorrow is ten thirty Zulu or six thirty local. Take off will be thirteen thirty Zulu. Thank you."

People in the room stood and milled for a bit. Geneva continued to introduce Mat around. He displayed an appropriately awkward look of awe.

This was real. This was happening.

Morning Jitters

There wasn't much sleep that night. They went over and over the plan, "what iff-ing" each other. Mat felt pretty confident about everything except the initial aircraft takeover. That would offer the Air Force crew several opportunities to do something stupid enough to kill them all.

Chandler offered an uncomfortable option. She spoke without emotion or eye contact pronouncing every word precisely. "If the worst happens and the plane crashes, I have made enough copies of the speech to distribute and have them played on my trusted networks. The crash will make sure attention is focused." She hesitated and her voice trailed. "No matter what, our efforts will *not* be in vain."

Mat clapped his hands once and both women jumped, suddenly startled out of the dark mood. "Well, on that cheery note, let's go over the timeline one more time."

CHAPTER SIXTEEN

The Hijack

It was still dark when they left the house. Chandler and Mat hugged each other with few words. Geneva drove, and they listened to the radio, not for traffic reports but for areas where street fighting raged. There were many. She first drove to WHMO, the White House Military Office, to pick up the daily codes and any unique reporting requirements. Mat had to wait in the car while she went in alone. It was bitter cold.

When Geneva came out she handed him a small lapel pin of an American flag and a tiny gold emblem. "Everyone who goes inside the Secret service perimeter must wear one of these so put it on your uniform pocket. He did so and they drove out onto Washington's heavily patrolled streets. She was alert and waited for a block-long area that was not crowded with soldiers or police before she gave instructions. "Okay, the code box between us is unlocked. I faked inserting the seal. Put the gun inside and snap it closed."

Mat retrieved the pistol from under his seat and opened the metal container. It was about the size of a shoe box and the gun barely fit beside the two Tasers Geneva already had crammed in there. He snapped the latch and she handed him a metal strip like a zip-tie and gave him instructions. "Insert this so the numbers are facing up and pull it tight."

He did so, and she allowed a hint of a smile. "So, Sergeant Benton, you ready for your big day?"

"Yes, Ma'am, I'm looking forward to it." He tried to sound very military.

They drove down Suitland Parkway. Geneva told him it was actually a federal highway maintained and defended by the Park Police and Military, not D.C. Police, and was probably safer than others. She was right. The four lane road had military style vehicles parked along the edges and, though fires could be seen burning over the wooded perimeter, the road was empty of traffic or rioters.

They arrived at the Andrews Air Force Base north gate and found it sand-bagged and defended by two armored personnel carriers. Still, for a car with two uniformed white sergeants, the guard's check was cursory. The sentry at the Air Force One hangar checkpoint was only slightly more thorough as he shined his flashlight in their faces, scanned the interior of the car and asked to have the trunk opened. He waved, and they were in.

The crew briefing was quick, and they walked to the airplane, a massive blue and white jet that loomed over them like an office building on wheels. The retractable air stair to the entrance door led to another set of internal stairs to the flight deck. The flight engineer had already done his preflight and started the auxiliary power unit. Geneva turned on her equipment and did checks as the giant plane was towed out to the VIP ramp. There, camera crews were already setting up in pre-dawn roped off areas. Mat was like a kid in an amusement park, taking it all in. There should have been music playing behind all this drama.

The plane's communications desk was located directly behind the cockpit. Mat walked forward through a small lounge area and peeked into that cockpit. It was an exact duplicate of the Silver Streak 747s he flew except for the addition of a navigator's seat. Mat had never seen an airplane so clean. It looked factory fresh. Still, all the instruments, except the flat screen navigation panels, were familiar and he didn't need the high-tech stuff. There were old-style instruments he could use.

"Sergeant Benton," Geneva was calling him. "Please take your station." He returned to his seat and she leaned in. "Okay, the staff are arriving, and they will give us a flood of little messages to send. They do it through on-board work stations but we must review everything that is transmitted from this aircraft so we'll get an alert for each. When the message comes up on your screen, you hit either 'send' or 'hold' buttons." She pointed. He nodded.

"Got it," he said.

She leaned closer. "Just hit send and don't waste your time trying to be a censor. It could cause a flap. These aides are all prima donnas and they love to throw their weight around."

Gradually, the plane filled with people. Colonel Simpson arrived at six sharp and toured the upper deck pausing only for a moment at the comm station. "Sergeant Benton was it? Well, I hope you enjoy your time with us and listen carefully to what Chief Harris tells you. We don't tolerate screw ups." He put a hand on Mat's shoulder and made a flicker of a smile.

Mat looked up at him and faked an awestruck impression. Actually, he wasn't faking. Colonel Simpson went forward to his seat and did a few cockpit checks until a steward popped up the stair and announced, "They're at the front gate."

That energized everyone. Colonel Simpson was out of his seat, straightening his tie and smoothing his hair. He climbed down the steps to the main deck and waited to greet the VP at the entrance door. Geneva shot a conspiratorial look at Mat and they shared a moment. He felt emotion though he couldn't say just what it was. Exhilaration, fear, pride – he wasn't sure, but it made him smile.

Someone yelled, "On board," and the copilot and engineer started the far-right engine. It took less than a minute to get it stabilized. Then they started the next engine. They were on the third engine as Colonel Simpson brushed through the comm station and hung his uniform coat on a door hanger. He strapped in the left cockpit seat and took over, reaching to start the final engine.

The taxi and takeoff were familiar to Mat. The checklists and procedures were almost identical to the ones used by Silver Streak.

His attention was focused on the messages that flashed on his screen. He hit "send" over and over. What on earth did all these minions have to say that was so urgent? After takeoff, he heard hydraulic whining as the gear and flaps fully retracted. Next came the steward with coffee, right on schedule.

Geneva reached under her small writing desk and retrieved the smuggled weapons. She glanced around before handing Mat the big chrome plated revolver that had once belonged to Vernon, the highway patrolman. She placed a small stack of papers over the Tasers beside her, nodded at Mat and turned to yell into the cockpit. "Sergeant Erlich, I have a problem. Could you take a quick look?"

The flight engineer shot a glance up at the pilot who was busy flying and paid no attention. Sergeant Erlich walked back into the comm compartment and started to speak when Geneva Tasered him on the exposed skin of his neck. He grabbed his throat and gasped as he fell in convulsions. Mat quickly wrapped a large zip tie around his hands and tried to do another on his ankles, but the man was flopping too much.

Geneva sounded frightened. "Major Cox, Sergeant Erlich is having a seizure. Help us."

The navigator didn't hesitate to jump out of his seat and run back. He bent over the stricken man, looked up into Geneva's face and sounded authoritative. "Call the on-board physician. I think his name is…"

Mat zapped the navigator with the other Taser. Now two men convulsed on the floor. Mat stepped over them and marched into the cockpit with the big pistol held in both hands. The copilot turned and froze with a blurted, "Holy shit."

Colonel Simpson was focused on his instruments and could afford only a quick peek behind him. "What the hell is going on?"

Mat was surprised by the calm in his voice. "Tell Washington Center you are being hijacked. Turn due east and climb to twenty thousand feet. Tell them there is no imminent danger but all traffic should be cleared for a twenty-mile radius around this aircraft. Tell them now."

The copilot's teeth showed like an angry dog. Mat acted unimpressed. "I do not want to hurt anyone and won't - unless you do something stupid. So, put any hero antics out of your mind. I intend to bring this airplane back to Andrews safely. For your information, I am a qualified 747 pilot and I can kill you both and still land this plane. Understand?"

The colonel engaged the autopilot and turned in his seat. He bellowed back to Geneva, "Chief Harris, notify Secret Service that we are being hijacked." He almost grinned but that grin didn't last.

Mat, rather than being intimidated, turned his head slightly and spoke through the open door. "Geneva, you ready?"

She nodded decisively. "All set. Good luck."

Mat closed the cockpit door and slid steel lock bars into position. Then he reached up to a wall filled with hundreds of circuit breakers each the size of a pencil eraser and pulled several. When he turned back, the colonel was throwing off his shoulder harness and starting out of his seat. Mat raised the pistol and aimed. Even over the constant whine of aircraft engines they all heard the click as Mat cocked the hammer and the gun's cylinder rotated.

Mat gave a command. "Copilot's aircraft. Head zero nine zero degrees and continue your climb to twenty thousand feet." That would keep him busy for a minute. The radio was now alive with frantic voices. "Air Force Two, come in. Please advise situation. Come in."

Mat held the gun at Simpson's face. "Thank you for your cooperation, Colonel. I was just about to ask you to give up your seat. As I said, I don't need you. Now, it's decision time. Do you live or die? You choose. I prefer you live, but I can go either way."

The Presidential Pilot was hunched, halfway out of his seat with one leg over the radio console. He remained frozen in that awkward position with bared his teeth, but his eyes looked perplexed, not combative.

"Please, don't make me hurt you. Once someone gets hurt, things will deteriorate and we'll probably all die. You are the captain of this vessel. Under the laws of the high seas, the captain is responsible for the safety of his craft and all within it. Live up to your responsibility. Show wisdom and courage, damn it. I am doing this for our country. Now put your hands through this zip tie and step carefully. I do *not* want to kill you."

Simpson remained an awkward statue. The copilot was equally immobilized. The plane was on autopilot and so were the two men. The radio jarred them back.

"Air Force Two, we are advised that you have just contacted all major news agencies and are preparing to transmit a message. Do you require specific assistance?"

The copilot turned back and spoke on the radio. His voice sounded like a zombie. "Negative. A lone hijacker has disabled two cockpit crewmembers and is holding the pilots at gunpoint. He says no one will be harmed if we return immediately to Andrews."

Mat yelled, "After the Message… We'll return right after the message has been transmitted. Tell them we want a holding pattern until the message has been received by news networks. Tell them, damn it.'

Colonel Simpson kept steady eye contact with Mat but reluctantly raised his hands into the oversized zip tie. Mat pulled it tight, yanking the man forward. Simpson fell onto the floor. Mat jerked him up and into the navigator's seat. Simpson was wooden, neither resisting nor cooperating. He glared at his captor and pure hate oozed from every pore.

Mat zip-tied both of the colonel's legs together and put another one around his neck and through the seat head rest. That man was going nowhere. He then went to the copilot and zip-tied his left arm to the seat arm rest leaving his right hand free to operate the controls. The copilot watched in mixed interest and horror but did not resist.

Mat strapped into the left seat and turned to the copilot. "Did you see the movie Captain Phillips? Yes? Well, I am the captain now… and we have work to do."

Geneva vs. Secret Service

She heard the Secret Service storming up the stairs to the flight deck, but they stopped at the closed door. Geneva used their private communications net to contact them. Her voice sounded pleading, "The hijacker, Sergeant Benton, has attached a bomb to the trap door. It will detonate if you open that door. He says no one will be hurt if we return to Andrews. He just wants to broadcast a message." The agents had a discussion among themselves and, by radio, to the Andrews Base office. After a back-and-forth that lasted a few minutes, they bought her story, at least for the moment. She took some comfort in knowing that even if the agents dared to open the door into her compartment, they still couldn't get past the reinforced cockpit door.

Now Chief Master Sergeant Geneva Harris turned her attention to her panel, working fast, saving the information from the thumb drive and opening a channel to transmit. The trussed navigator and engineer both lay at her feet, still jerky and dazed after the Taser. The circuit breakers Mat pulled had deactivated the aircraft intercom and all but a single air traffic radio. The cockpit was now effectively isolated from the rest of the plane.

We Interrupt This Broadcast

In the Air Force One main deck lounge, Vice President Stark McCoby paced and raged. "These God damned black anarchist bastards. How could they get onto my airplane?" Then he noticed the monitor over his leather couch. "Turn the volume up," he commanded to no one in particular. A news commentator was speaking and looking very serious. The monitor screen behind the commentator displayed the Presidential Seal and a banner below that read, "On Board Air Force One." McCoby screamed. "Turn up the God damned volume."

Someone found the remote and the commentator's voice became clear. "We're told the message is just coming across now. Please stand by for the transmission from the hijacked aircraft flying under the call sign Air Force Two with Vice President Stark McCoby on board." The announcer was distracted. "Yes? Okay, here it comes now." His image faded. In its place, a video of a crowded auditorium appeared. The sound was scratchy but understandable.

McCoby scrunched his face and stared. It was him, a video of him standing on a stage! It was the National War College meeting. "Holy Mother of God," he whispered and then went into momentary shock as he listened to the voice, his own recorded voice.

Well, here we are at last. I want you all to look around. You will immediately recognize many, if not all, of the patriots and leaders assembled here. They are your fellow warriors, craftsmen forging a new reality, a new beginning for our race, a new chapter for humanity. You have all served heroically but until today, we dared not reveal you one to another. Now, we have gained the power. Mostly through your efforts, we have gained the power to protect each other. We have gained, and continue to gain, control over our nation and ultimately over our world. We will soon control humanity's destiny and it will be a magnificent destiny.

McCoby looked at the monitor and felt as though all the life was draining out of his body. He turned to the Secret Service agent who stood beside him and seethed. "Destroy this airplane immediately. I want that video stopped. Kill the pilots. Kill everyone. Move. Now."

The agent blanched. "Sir, I have to clear that with the President."

"No, you don't. I am in charge now. Whiteman won't live through the day. I am in command and I order you to destroy this plane no matter what it takes. Kill us all! Do you hear me?"

"Yes Sir." The agent almost whispered and then ran out of the compartment. McCoby turned back to the monitor and listened to his own speech.

Our nation will undergo an overwhelming upheaval, but it will be nothing compared to the depopulation of backward countries that is coming. Africa, India, large parts of Russia, Asia, Central and South America, the Middle east…" the voice paused, "will become sterile but still capable of providing resources to our new, purer race.

McCoby stared at the screen and his hand began to tremble. A single tear ran down his face. "It's too late. I'm too God damned late."

Now What Mister President?

Joe Whiteman sat reclined in the oval office with his feet on the desk and his hands folded over his belly. The video was over and the television screen in his office returned to the image of a Presidential Seal.

He yelled toward the staff congregating around him. "Jerry, can we communicate with that airplane?"

A man with rolled shirt sleeves spoke from the back of the crowd. "I think so. The Secret Service net is still operating."

The President rocked back in his chair, interlaced fingers behind his head and sounded as casual as if he were ordering a pizza. "See if you can get 'em on the line."

Jerry, the only man in the room without a suit, punched his tablet repeatedly. Then he announced, "I have them. Check your monitor, sir." Sure enough, an image of a blue-suited sergeant appeared on the desk monitor. She sounded serious but cordial. "Good morning, Mister President."

He pronounced his words carefully giving full voice to his southern accent. "Chief Master Sergeant Harris - Geneva, I believe."

"Yes, Mister President."

"Geneva, what can we expect to happen next?"

"The plane - your plane – is returning to Andrews Air Force Base. The Vice President ordered the Secret Service to destroy the aircraft and everyone in it, but they declined. Upon landing, the hijackers will surrender and accept their punishment. They have accomplished their mission."

"Their mission? I believe, by that, you mean *your* mission, Geneva. Isn't that correct?"

There was a pause. "Yes, Mister President. I am involved… and I have no apologies. The organization that has permeated our government calls itself 'Humanity' but they intend to remove you and launch a worldwide program of genocide in the name of a racist meritocracy. My life is a trivial price to pay for exposing them. The man flying the airplane right now is Matthew McCoy. He is a brave and decent man. I hope you will remember that."

The President rocked back in his chair. "Well, that's all mighty impressive but you have now put me in the unenviable position of having allowed this to happen on my watch. Now I shall root out these traitors – I shall - but I feel pretty sure I'll be following on their coat tails out the door." He took a deep breath, more of a sigh really.

"Geneva dear, all I'm asking of you now is that bring my pretty blue airplane home safe, so I get to ride around a few more times before I get sacked. Do you think you could do that for me?"

"I'll do my best, Mister President."

If your actions inspire others to dream more, do more and become more, you are a leader

John Quincy Adams

CHAPTER SEVENTEEN

Final Approach

Mat was settled in to the pilot's seat. He clicked off the autopilot and took the control yoke in his hands. It felt good. He spoke to the copilot but kept his eyes on the instruments.

"So, you're probably wondering what's going to happen when we land. Well, I intend to bring the plane to a safe stop and then abandon ship. There will almost certainly be a SWAT Team or something similar waiting to storm aboard. I'll make sure to release both of you before they get to me so you'll be able to safely shut the plane down."

The copilot said nothing. He and Colonel Simpson had not seen the video transmission and knew nothing about the "Humanity" plot. They were both still dangerous.

Mat sounded matter-of-fact. "The place will be swarmed with media so be ready for non-stop interviews. Make sure your ties are on straight." He allowed a little smile. "I do apologize for stealing your airplane but, on the bright side, you'll go down in the history books after this."

Simpson, strapped to the seat behind Mat, almost hissed. "And you'll go down right beside John Wilkes Booth."

Mat shook his head. "Booth died trying to destroy the Union. I'm trying to save it. The man we have in the back, Stark McCoby, is a monster. What we have done today has exposed him. Whatever happens to me, his attempted coup has been revealed to the whole world."

The two pilots wouldn't believe him, but who cared. He was about to add one last wrinkle to the hijack. Mat clicked the radio button on his control yoke. "Washington Center, good morning. This is the hijacked Air Force Two. Please give my regards to the two F-22 fighters on my wingtips. Tell them I'm headed from present position direct to Prezz intersection and descending to twenty-five hundred feet for an approach to Andrews Runway zero one left. We won't need their services after that."

The clipped air traffic controller's voice came back. "Roger Air Force Two, you're cleared as requested." Then the radio went silent. Washington Center was usually a torrent of radio calls as airplanes spoke over each other, clamored for clearance, made reports, asked for information. Today, it was dead silent. No one was arriving at Dulles or Reagan or Washington Executive or even College Park. The aviation world was grounded, all waiting, breathlessly waiting.

Mat called for flaps and then gear. The copilot performed his duties as requested but it was awkward with his left hand tied down. He had to twist and stretch with his free right hand. Now they were stabilized on final approach. Mat saw Andrews Air Force Base directly ahead. He reached up and changed his navigation settings and made a radio call.

"Oh, Washington Center, slight change of plans. Air Force Two is abandoning this approach and will intercept the Mount Vernon Visual approach to Reagan National runway zero one. Thank you and please apologize to all those armed men waiting at Andrews."

The clipped voice responded. "Copy, Air Force two."

Mat banked left and then back right as he centered up on the new runway. In just minutes, they touched down, eighteen giant tires kissing the pavement. Mat slowed and smiled. "Probably the last landing of my life," he said aloud. No one responded. He hit the radio button. "Okay National Tower, I'm going to turn off onto runway three three and then take Lima to Hot Spot Two. There is a crowd of media folks there waiting. Air Force Two…out." That sounded really, really final.

He pulled into the parking spot and set the parking brake. Then Mat turned and said, "Copilot's airplane," as he slid his seat back. He opened the overhead escape hatch and felt cold outside air. Then he slowly opened the cockpit door fully expecting to be bowled over by Secret Service Agents. Instead, Geneva threw her arms around his neck and whispered, "We did it."

He reached up and pulled down an oversized brass stirrup on a wire and handed it to her. "Know how to use one of these?" She nodded and took it in both hands. Mat locked his fingers together, bent down and she put her foot in his hands so he could heft her up through the overhead hatch. She flipped her legs over, looked down to give him a smile that faded into uncertainty…and she was gone. The emergency escape reel made a zinging noise as it unrolled. It slowed her descent as she slid down the slick well-polished outside of the plane.

When the tape went slack, he knew she was on the ground. Mat took another reel, stepped up onto the seat back of the navigator's chair where Colonel Simson was still restrained. He paused to use a small set of scissors and cut the colonel's hands free. Then, without another word, he followed Geneva up through the hatch and over the side of the plane. Its shiny surface was slick, and his descent was fast as a bobsled ride. But at the last second, the tape tightened and slowed his fall leaving him dangling just two feet off the ground. He loosened his death grip on the escape reel handle and dropped.

Reporters charged from the grassy area until he and Geneva were surrounded, mobbed. Cameras were everywhere. There were sirens and shouts and what seemed like a thousand thrusting microphones. Mat craned and searched for Chandler. *There* - he saw her way back in the crowd surrounded by a forest of thrusting microphones. He felt a rush of relief. Everything was going to be okay now. Everything, well almost everything, was going to be okay.

The mob of reporters crushed Mat and Geneva, shouting questions, surging against each other. In less than a minute, anything like an interview was over as uniformed men forced their way through the crowd. The two hijackers were tackled, cuffed, dragged away and pushed into a police van. As they drove through the mob scene lights flashed and sirens wailed. Mat caught just a glimpse of Chandler still standing on a platform like the Statue of Liberty surrounded by a throng of jostling reporters. Her eyes followed him and she paused for a moment to hold up a hand. Maybe a wave, maybe just an acknowledgement, maybe a farewell. It didn't matter. She was safe; the country was going to be safe.

Mat leaned back on his bench seat surrounded by his captors in their black body armor, masks and helmets – regular modern-day Ninja outfits. He felt strangely peaceful.

Live Free or Die

Four-star-general Brett Cunningham, Chairman of the Joint Chiefs of Staff, sat in his richly decorated office. Behind him dozens of flags with gold fringe and multi-colored battle streamers filled the wall. Paintings of his predecessors over the past two hundred years covered all other wall space.

He slouched with a loosened tie, an unaccustomed pose for the normally rigid military man. He was waiting but unsure exactly for what. Would the US Marshals break down his door? Would some local policeman knock and hold up handcuffs? Would he just receive a message to report to the White House? None of those were acceptable options.

He had been on the verge of becoming a national hero, a man for the ages. Now, that seemed lost. He would go down in history with Benedict Arnold, Aldrich Ames, John Walker and Robert Hanssen as a traitor? What a tragedy. Someday, the world would have to face the inevitability of the situation—too many people, too few contributors, too much mythology. There was no alternative to purifying the human race.

He turned and took a glass presentation case from his credenza, admired it for a second, and then smashed it to pieces. Picking away glass, Brett Cunningham removed a chromed, Model 1911 Colt .45 pistol engraved with his name and the dates he had commanded the 101st Airborne Division. He cradled the gun, ignoring a trickle of blood that ran from a glass shard on his wrist.

Then he removed a clip of bullets from his desk drawer, inserted it and cocked the slide. Standing now, Cunningham looked over the Potomac River to the Lincoln Memorial and the other landmarks, even the newest, the Martin Luther King statue.

He began to sing in a faltering voice. "My country, tis of thee, sweet land..."

In the outer office, two secretaries and two uniformed aides jumped at the sound of a gunshot. Arlene Parsons, secretary for thirty-one years, stood and smoothed her dress with a dignified set to her head. "I will go," she said in a stern voice. The others acknowledged with restrained nods. One aide reached into his gym bag under the desk, hesitated and then handed her a towel. She accepted it with a trembling hand before turning to the door where she inhaled, stood tall and went in.

Aftermath

Stark McCoby came down the airplane stairs looking defiant, yelling at the cameras, shaking his fist at the crowd. "We were right. We are right. The deterioration of our race must be stopped. All men with clear eyes..."

The mob stormed around him, screaming and clawing in his direction. They looked ready to tear his body to pieces. Secret Service agents pushed them back and muscled him through the melee to a waiting limousine. He was, after all, still Vice President. They drove in silence, no handcuffs, no reading of his Miranda rights, no conversation at all.

McCoby scowled and stared out the window. He was thinking fast and hard. How would he handle this situation? There must be a way to spin it to his advantage. It was a very short drive from Reagan National Airport to the White House where he was frisked, placed in a waiting room and then, after long, long minutes, escorted into the outer office.

There, President Whiteman, expansive ex-governor of Tennessee, waited with hands folded before him. "Well, look-a-here. What we have ourselves here is a traitor, a would-be mass murderer and a pretender to my throne. Hello Stark. I'm guessing this is not how you expected things to turn out."

One of a dozen or so men in suits spoke. "Mister President, I have a status update. The FBI has assigned agents to each individual identified from the video. They are going in groups of three with local police SWAT backups. They'll be ready to move in ten minutes...on your command."

President Whiteman made a politician's smile. "Well Stark, why don't you do the honors. Tell Agent Stern here to go ahead."

Stark McCoby pursed his lips and started to argue, but then, collected himself and sounded suddenly smug. "Why sir, I believe that would be inappropriate since you are the Commander-in chief."

Whiteman grinned. "Why Stark, you do remember. Yes, I am the Commander-in Chief and I am about to announce a State of Emergency across the country. My authority to do so is somewhat cloudy but I think there is precedent in the Civil War, World War II and a couple of other cases. My staff tells me Section 8, clause 15 of the Constitution allows me to take such actions as are necessary to suppress any insurrection. Isn't that what you planned, Stark, an insurrection?"

He made a phony smile and continued. "I have notified Jack Carlson, head of the Joint Chiefs Special Operations Directorate, to go and replace Brett Cunningham. I've known Carlson for decades. I trust him, and I think he can find enough remaining loyal military commanders to enforce Martial Law while we do a little political—not ethnic—cleansing of our own."

President Whiteman almost seemed to be enjoying himself. McCoby was scowling, still trying to figure an angle.

"Now Stark, you have been a very bad boy, so I tell you what I'm going to do. I'm grounding you. You'll be restricted to your room. No TV, no video games, no snacks and no playmates." The humor went out of the President's voice. "Did you know, I don't really have the authority to outright fire you? Strangely, that is a function of congress. They will, of course, agree, but I'm going to take my time. You, meanwhile, are going to stay locked in your little room. It's a quiet place. You've seen it before when you got your tour of the Alternate National Command Center. Do you remember how quiet it was there a couple of hundred feet underground? You'll have no distractions as you compile a complete dossier on your group. Every name, every contact, every plan."

McCoby found his voice. "I won't do that. You can't make me. Nothing you can do…"

"Oh Stark, not me." He turned away from McCoby. "Okay, is the pilot here? Yes? Bring him in." They waited. President Whiteman said. "He's told the marshals an interesting story about your little domestic version of Guantanamo."

Two Secret Service Agents led a handcuffed Mat McCoy into the room. Whiteman acknowledged him and turned back to the Vice President. "This is the hijacker, a Mister McCoy, and he has been telling us about some people who are much more effective than I at getting cooperation. It seems, you run a little training center in the closed State Penitentiary in Boise, back in your home state of Idaho. I'm sure you're familiar with them. We're going to enlist some of those folks to 'reeducate' you, Stark. It sounds to me like they're very good motivators."

McCoby looked as if his head was going to explode. "This is wrong, just so wrong. I am the hero here, not the villain."

There was a long silence until the President yelled, "Now, Mister McCoy, do you have any questions for our Vice President before he goes on his subterranean vacation?"

Mat, who could only have arrived minutes before, seemed a little hesitant but cleared his throat and said, "What about the heads? What were you really doing with the heads you shipped to California?"

McCoby considered his options. Maybe he could seem cooperative and try to improve his situation. It was unlikely, but he was still a politician at heart. He spoke cautiously. "They were for the virus. We required a continuing source of fresh brain tissue that had been kept oxygenated."

McCoby grimaced. *Was it a mistake to answer?* Should he have shared that much? He could see in their eyes, they simply did not understand the wisdom of improving the race. Just imagine if they learned the whole truth. He would tell these fools no more. These ignorant, liberal fools, how could the world progress with such people in charge?

Mat seemed to gain courage and asked another question. "Mister Vice President, how did you intend to get rid of President Whiteman?"

McCoby focused again and laughed. They did intend to assassinate Whiteman but why confess? Instead, he tried an insult. "We didn't. We thought he was enough of a fool to do exactly what we wanted. He didn't hesitate to send troops against his own people, his own constituents. We were confident he could be manipulated to do the right thing and wipe out the Black Dragon militia...and most of the black community along with it."

Mat shook his head. He sounded bitter. "Mister President, back in the Idaho Prison, there are tubes and computers that will be necessary for Mister McCoby's training. I think you should have them shipped to your underground facility."

The Bible says to forgive seventy times seventy. I want you all to know, I'm keeping a chart

- Hillary Clinton

CHAPTER EIGHTEEN

The Speech

That night, President Whiteman went on national television with a very brief address from the Oval Office. He was careful to avoid makeup. He wanted to look haggard and besieged. He wore an open collar and sat with no visible microphone or teleprompter. His voice was solemn. It was good drama.

"My fellow Americans. We have faced and are continuing to face the greatest threat to our way of life since this nation was created. This threat came, not from some barbaric foreign group, but from within our own ranks. I am to blame for not detecting the evil within my government. This cancer has infected much of our power structure and it will be challenging to root it out. In the meantime, neither you nor I will know who to trust. The Department of Defense, Homeland Security, the Federal Bureau of Investigation, The National Security Agency and many others have been penetrated."

He stared right into the camera with reddened eyes. "This has weakened our nation and our enemies will be quick to seek advantage. We have reports that the Russians may be building troop strength on their borders. Chinese naval forces are positioning around disputed islands. Throughout the Middle East and Africa, massive anti-American demonstrations threaten our citizens. Resolutions of condemnation are being prepared within the United Nations."

Then he put on a stern face, picked up a piece of paper and displayed it. "This is Executive Order One. In these remarkable times, remarkable actions are required. I am taking unprecedented initiatives to preserve our union in a way the founding fathers could not have envisioned."

He paused for a long moment. "I am hereby suspending the Constitution—but only briefly—and dismissing both the Judicial and Legislative branches until order has been restored and we have a reconstituted and more trustworthy government. As soon as that has been accomplished, I shall direct a mass election for all executive and legislative positions. I shall not be a candidate, but my replacement will be able to appoint a whole staff, a new Supreme Court, a whole new cabinet. In the interim, I am asserting personal control as Commander-in-Chief of the military and declaring a state of Martial Law across the country. There are many details to be worked out, but I intend to clean this situation up as rapidly as possible."

President Whiteman's face transformed into his most earnest expression. "This will be a difficult and trying time but, with the help of Almighty God, we shall prevail against these evil men who tried to destroy our way of life. I call on every one of you to do your part to restore honor and dignity to our nation. May God bless you and this, the greatest nation on earth, the United States of America."

He put down the paper and folded his hands. Since this was completely unscripted, the cameraman and news people didn't know how long to wait before they cut away. Finally, the camera's red light went off and the now absolute ruler of the country sat back feeling pretty good about his move.

Prisoner, Again

The Secret Service kept Mat all day and well into the night. They wouldn't tell him where Geneva had been taken or what happened to Chandler. He didn't even know where he was, a basement of some building. After dozens of cups of coffee, he asked, "Can I get some food? I haven't eaten today." No one answered. The President had treated him like a hero. To his captors, he seemed just another threat.

Marjorie, his chief interrogator, was a husky woman who never blinked. Her short hair and square face gave her a manly look. When she spoke, she bent close enough for Mat to smell her deodorant and feel her searchlight eyes focus into his. At first, it tightened his gut. Now, it was getting old. "Come on," he asked. "Talk to me. What's going to happen to us?"

Marjorie, the interrogator loosened up and shrugged. "You're a hijacker. You've violated a couple of dozen laws. I'd say it looks like life in prison. Luckily, you didn't kill anyone directly, so the death penalty is probably not in your future."

"What about the others?"

"The sergeant is in military custody. Your lawyer girlfriend is still at large. We'll get her. It's just a matter of time. There is some question of jurisdiction, but right now, all available manpower is focused on the manhunt."

Mat was astounded. "Don't you have better things to do? What about the insurrection in the cities? What about all the criminals in the government."

Marjorie was unemotional. "They're not my problem. You're my problem. I just have to deal with you. Now, let's get back to the murder of the Highway Patrolman."

Bravado and Broccoli

President Whiteman hustled into the dining room and plopped into his chair. Despite the enormity of the crisis he seemed cheerful. "I've only got a few minutes, Dear. Thanks for reminding me to eat. There's just so much to do."

His wife Betty sat with a strained look. "I'm sure. I just heard that the Texas Legislature is calling for a vote to secede from the union."

"Meaningless. Their constitution requires a referendum. It will take months. I'm much more worried about the overseas situation.

Everywhere I look, someone is moving against us. The Russians have begun to move into Georgia again and are making noise about the disputed Japanese Islands. The Chinese are being more cautious, but we think they are moving troops on a massive scale. All across Africa, we are branded as racist and our people are being threatened." He paused. "I'm sorry. None of this is your burden. How are you holding up?"

No one was very hungry. Betty folded her napkin. "What about our own government, our own people? What is going on here? Your brief speech has brought outrage from both liberal and conservative factions. You must calm the rhetoric. They must not see you as the evil one."

He sat back and his chest collapsed. "Do you think people see me like that? I'm doing everything I can to preserve the union and democracy for all our citizens."

She leaned forward and put her hands on his. "Then tell them that. Give them heroes. How about those hijackers. What are you doing with them?"

"I don't know. The Secret Service is handling it. I suppose I should pardon them. Yes, yes, that would play well. Heroes? We do need heroes. Thank you, Betty. You've always been my inspiration."

She made a weak smile in return. "Finish your broccoli."

How are Things in Abu Dhabi

"Mister Halstead."

Jerome Halstead slammed his pen down on a stack of papers and ran his fingers over tired eyes. "Yes Tiresias, what do *you* want in the midst of all this chaos?"

Her computer voice was unemotional. "I'm sure you are aware of the arrests and the nation-wide search for co-conspirators. I have detected references to you and several of your key staff members in the warrants being prepared. I suggest you take your team and relocate to a more favorable environment. I can destroy all records within the United States."

Halstead tried to stay calm and businesslike. "Destroy all records? Where would we go? How would we be able to reconstitute...?"

"There is a server farm in Abu Dhabi with backups of all your records and contacts. The domestic copies are no longer necessary for your operations and I will incinerate them." She paused. "I suggest you and your team go there as well. They are very accepting of billionaires and they have no extradition treaty with the United States. Your work could continue uninterrupted...if you elect to go on under the circumstances."

Halstead let out a long sigh. "Go on the run – to Abu Dhabi? How would we even get there?"

"Sir, you run an international airline. Transportation is your business."

Halstead stood and looked straight ahead. It was frustrating to speak to an entity that had no form. There could be no eyeball-to-eyeball confrontation with something that had no eyeballs. He was about to say something - he wasn't sure just what – when she spoke again.

"I have taken the liberty of rescheduling one of your Boeing 747 aircraft to depart from MidAmerica Airport in forty minutes. Your key team members have been alerted to be onboard. The captain will wait for you."

Halstead leaned forward and put his head in his hands. "Forty minutes until I walk away from my country, my life, my world." He sighed long and deep. "Okay, okay. I'll go and continue the fight just from another location." He stopped for a second. "Now, about my estranged wife..."

The computer voice sounded almost compassionate. "You have provided well for her. She will live a comfortable life. I have set up trusts in her name and transferred all *your* accounts to a bank in the same building where I have contracted for your new offices. It is the Burj Khalifa, the world's tallest building. I think you will find it quite acceptable."

Jerome Halstead stood and hesitated for one last look around the modest office where he had almost turned the world on its head. His new location might be far more impressive, but the goal was unchanged. He held out a flat palm. "As it is above, so shall it be below."

Without change there is no innovation, creativity, or incentive for improvement. Those who initiate the change will have a better opportunity to manage the change that is inevitable-

William Pollard

CHAPTER NINETEEN

Restoration?

It was early in the morning, Washington time when the President went on television again. This time, he was flanked by a dozen men and women in professional attire. There were no military in the crowd and those present all looked weary.

"My fellow Americans. We are still in deep crisis, but the worst is past. I wish to introduce my new cabinet. They have all been vetted, signed loyalty pledges and passed lie detector tests." He ran through a long list of little-known bureaucrats and then returned to his message.

"I am directing General Carlson, the new Chairman of the Joint Chiefs of Staff to pull back from the inner-city offensive. Our troops will now devote themselves to reconstruction and recovery. They will build temporary shelters and provide food and medical attention to areas damaged by riots and our previous operations. Disaster relief for the many catastrophes inflicted on us by the conspirators is overwhelming, but Janet Cressly, the new director of Homeland Security and Mark Wells, new FEMA chief, will go at it with everything we have."

He took a breath, obviously preparing for the big pitch. "Some terrible things have happened here, things that must outrage every decent American. We will never be able to right those crimes, but we *can* recover from them. I will do everything in my power, but I cannot fix everything. You, the citizens of this great land, must take the initiative."

Now his voice was almost pleading. "Those of you who joined the Black Dragon movement must change and recast it, not as a combatant organization, but one of hope. I will join you by funneling billions of dollars into reconstruction and new programs to rebuild our inner cities." His voice grew louder and he held up a fist.

"There is hope. There will be hope. We have survived the storm and we must rebuild what has been destroyed—and we must build it better and stronger than it has ever been. I swear to you before Almighty God, this nation shall endure, and with your help, it will."

The camera faded to a full-screen view of an American flag slowly furling in a light wind. Then it cut to a classroom of young black children reciting the pledge of allegiance as the words they spoke scrolled underneath the picture. That ended, and the flag returned, now accompanied by a breathy rendition of the national anthem worthy of a major league opening ceremony.

Recovery?

President Joe Whiteman had this thing under control. Just weeks after the hijacking he was launching a stimulus program that made Roosevelt's New Deal look like a band aid. Over the next days and weeks, he was everywhere. He toured burned-out neighborhoods, pledged money, revealed massive new infra-structure construction projects, survived two assassination attempts and reorganized the military from an expeditionary force to one with major domestic responsibilities. He would build thousands of new schools, create public transportation systems in every major city, add airports and seaports and subsidize industries that got onboard his train.

To hell with the deficit. Employment would soar. The country would need workers in huge numbers. He would need streamlined, trustworthy banking with low interest rates. The economy would expand, and America would once again be the preeminent world power.

It was good to be king.

There was strong opposition, of course. But, as President with solid military support, he was now absolute ruler. He jailed anyone who opposed his plans. Many who defied him were discreetly "reeducated" using a slightly more humane version of Humanity's model. The promised mass election of legislators and justices would be delayed again and again. But few complained.

The country was on a roll. Black and Latino support for the government was near unanimous. Wealthy white citizens were less enthusiastic, but they were profiting handsomely and went along. The three hijackers were pardoned and released to become instant media sensations.

The Old Lawyer's Advice

President Joe Whiteman controlled the press, the courts, the banks and the military. He did not control Chandler Harris. She had received a multi-million dollar book advance and been able to move her father into a house with full-time personal care where they talked daily.

Spring was quickly giving way to summer heat when they sat on the porch and enjoyed a breeze. "Daddy, what do you think of what's going on in the country? I know you keep up with the news." The old man shifted in his wheel chair, his amputated stub legs just bumps under a blanket. His voice seemed hoarse.

"Power is concentrated in one man. Like any explosive, when you pack too much in one place the risk of damage from an explosion becomes much greater. History is the story of strongmen who built empires only to see them utterly vanish with a single bullet or arrow. Our country seems to be blooming but it is a fragile flower. Strength comes only from the foundation not from the surface."

Chandler pulled her chair close. "What do you think will happen?"

He seemed to look out toward a horizon. Of course, he was blind and saw nothing except what his mind recalled. "I don't hear much about all those men who formed the Humanity conspiracy. What happened to them? Did they just go quietly into the night? That seems unlikely. I think they went underground. If President Whiteman had been successful in catching and prosecuting them it would have been all over the news. There has been nothing."

She sat back. "Do you think they will reemerge and try to topple the government?"

He shook his head. "No. I doubt they ever went away. I think they are still be around, still pursuing their plans and President Whiteman must be aware. These men are true believers and zealots don't give up. Whiteman, on the other hand, is an opportunist, a lamb. There is nothing more dangerous than a lamb making a deal with a lion. It only lasts until the lion gets hungry."

She was silent for a while. "Daddy, the President has asked me to be Assistant Attorney General. Do you think I should agree?"

Without hesitation the old man smiled. "Of course. You could affect the decisions that will guide our new government. I think you could be an effective spokesman for the people. It will be hard, very hard. The government bureaucracy is dedicated to preventing progress, but you've never been shy, and you've always gotten your way, even with me." He smiled. "You and your sister - what a pair. I was always so proud of you and the way you stood up for yourselves."

The smile faded. "Your brother is weak. He could be led and used. I don't know how I failed with him." He drifted. "And your mother. I feel such sadness when I remember how she suffered under my ego. She and Eufaula lacked your steel. I denied them security and comfort and community in all my crusading." He was quiet for a time. "She didn't really die of cancer, you know. She just gave up. I guess she had all she could take. It didn't occur to me back then that for all my efforts to help others, I failed to help my own family. At least I still have you girls. I am so proud of you."

Chandler didn't know what to say. She wet her lips but no words came. Finally, she spoke softly. "Thank you, Daddy." She kissed him on top of his bald head and turned away. There was a tiny drop of moisture in the corner of her eye. It wasn't really a tear. Chandler Harris, after all, did not cry.

As she walked away, her father raised his clenched fist and yelled. "Give 'em hell, girl." She nodded and grit her teeth although he could not see her.

The Aftermath

Months had passed. Mat was on a speaking tour of the West Coast when he heard the news. He called Chandler immediately. "Have you seen it? McCoby is back. He's all over the news, contrite, apologizing and telling people he's devoting himself to repairing damage done by his conspirators. Did you know about this?"

Chandler was tentative. "I just found out. It was something the President worked out secretly. He wants reconciliation. He wants the country back working smoothly. He wants…"

"Do you agree? Do you want this murdering bastard back in power?"

"No." The silence on the phone seemed endless before she spoke again. Even then, she was picking words with a lawyer's precision. "I am unsure exactly what is going on but there is a sea change coming. I feel it. Whiteman clearly has a plan, but he is not sharing it with anyone in the Justice Department."

Then her voice wavered. "Mat, I'm afraid. Whiteman has developed such overconfidence he doesn't seek advice any more. I think all that personal power may have affected his judgment. He is secretly hatching programs within Homeland and Defense. We don't know what's afoot. The election has been postponed again and, with congress recessed indefinitely, committees of former legislators are meeting secretly. Even with the economy booming, I'm afraid of some looming disaster."

"Have you talked to Geneva? She's pretty high up in the military. She may know something."

Chandler's voice seemed to brighten a bit. "That's a good idea. She's been so wrapped up in her new job as the Air Force Senior Enlisted Advisor we've hardly spoken lately. She's privy to a lot that's going on. When will you be back in town? Maybe the three of us could to get together."

"I can be back tomorrow night."

He took a breath and said, "Chandler, have you thought more about my proposal?"

Her voice went flat. "Mat, I love you. I truly do but I am afraid of a normal relationship. Neither you nor I have any experience being in a normal family. I'm happy with what we have. Why must we tempt the Fates by creating a sitcom-type family? It could shatter the best thing in my life - us."

He tried to be understanding but in the back of his mind he heard Sophia, the automated voice, saying, "The high performing woman with an IQ of 125 will delay childbearing and add only one child..." He took a deep breath and said, "We'll talk tomorrow night."

CHAPTER TWENTY

Northeastern India

Sinjay Gupta was a disappointment to his family. Even he had to admit he wasted his father's money by partying his way through a second-rate medical school in West Bengal. Worse, he failed his final exams. At that point his father, a stiff-backed businessman, manufacturer of generic pharmaceuticals, cut him off completely.

At first, Sinjay panicked. He had no job, no place to live, nothing. But he was a good looking young guy with a smooth, easy way about him. So, he used the last of his allowance to buy a fake medical license and proclaim himself a physician. But he still needed money to set up a practice, even a fraudulent one.

His plan took him to his father's factory. Everyone there knew him as "Junior." They didn't know about his family tensions and were more than accommodating to the boss's son. He directed them to load up a truck with sixteen boxes of the new antibiotic that had been manufactured and was now being stored pending test and release. It was not approved for sale in Europe or the Americas, but there was plenty of money to be made in the underdeveloped world.

His father had become wealthy manufacturing cheap generic drugs and selling them for a fraction of the patented product's price. Sinjay knew this new drug was special, a breakthrough that, even at the cheaper generic price, would yield many millions. And why should he not share in the windfall? In fact, why should he not get a head start in the distribution and profits of this new miracle drug? He was family, after all, and certainly due some benefit for that alone.

The old man would be angry, but he would eventually get over it. He might even admit a grudging respect for his son's entrepreneurial spirit. Well, maybe after the old man's temper subsided. Father was not a tolerant - or even, a reasonable man, but in time, who knows?

When the truck was full, Sinjay and the driver left. The street value of the pills, Sinjay estimated, would be about ten million Euros. That would be plenty to buy himself a British passport and set up a practice in England. But first, he had to get to Europe. That was the risky part of the plan.

He signed up with the recruiter for a container shipping company in the port of Haldia. The recruiter took a modest bribe and accepted Sinjay's medical license without a second glance. He was signed on as a ship's doctor.

Things were going well. The young entrepreneur imagined himself spending a few leisurely weeks at sea, comfortably ensconced in a state room appropriate for the ship's medical officer. He had a list of contacts along the planned route through the Indian and Atlantic Oceans. He planned to sell his drugs at the African ports and arrive in England wealthy and ready to set up his practice.

Of course, he would have to learn the ropes, make contacts and work deals, but he was wily and had no doubt that, with enough money, he would become a respected physician in the United Kingdom. He imagined himself a gifted con man who could overcome the current anti-immigrant turmoil in Europe. He spoke the King's English with an upper-class flair. Yes, given a chance he would fit smoothly into English society.

On the day of departure, he climbed the gangplank to a massive ship moored alongside a dock crowded with containers stacked three deep and arranged like city blocks. Giant cranes were in constant motion loading containers with precise and efficient motion. Once at the top of the gangplank, he paused to survey the enormous deck that stretched beyond his view. Everything was beyond human scale. He felt like an ant on a giant machine.

A white coat steward directed him to the bridge where he joined an odd assortment of men in a glassed-in penthouse room high above the container deck. There were only a few computerized workstations. Otherwise the huge room was empty. Fourteen of the most diverse people he could imagine eyed each other with suspicious glances.

A big man lumbered in. He wore a sweaty white shirt with rolled sleeves and uniform epaulets. Beneath a shock of gray hair, he had a meaty, deeply furrowed face.

"I am Kerensky. I was captain twenty-two years in Russian Navy. Now I am captain of this rusty barge." He turned and extended an open hand to a tall man with dark skin and scowling eyes. "Here is Aman, first mate. He is twenty years at sea. If he tells you to do—you do. No questions, no argument – just do." Aman could have been Greek with his sharp nose and dark eyes. He smiled but it was a mirthless smile that did not extend to his eyes.

The other officers were a mix of nationalities. The chief engineer was an emaciated bean-pole of an Argentine who had the vacant stare of a drug addict. The purser was an Arab with a five-word unpronounceable name. He smiled at Sinjay and said, "Call me Fred."

Second Officer Maurice was a small man of undetermined race, nationality or language. He spoke mainly in grunts. Second Officer Tran seemed a timid mouse of a man with a facial tick. And then there was Habib the giant. His function was not explained. There were others, too many names to remember.

Captain Kerensky continued, "Our crew includes conscripts. Do not speak to them unless absolutely necessary. They will steal, lie, strike out at you and maybe even kill you if you are not careful. They are property. I bought them. I own them. If they displease me, I throw them overboard. They hate me, and they will hate you also. If you have any problem with them, go and speak to Habib." All eyes turned to the big African. He had unblinking eyes of a predator, vivid against his shiny ebony skin. He was certainly intimidating but, at the same time, he had a graceful, almost elegant way of moving.

Kerensky continued. "The language of the ship is English but many of the crew do not speak it. So, are there any questions?"

Sinjay perked up and raised his hand. "Oh, yes sir. As ship's doctor shall I be doing physical examinations or having regular checkups during our voyage?"

Kerensky frowned. "Voyage? What do you think? This is cruise ship with swimming pool and casino? No, this is cargo ship. We don't waste money. Understand this, doctor, you keep men working. You *treat* officers. You *fix* crewmen. They are work animals. If one gets hurt, you fix him good enough to work. If he is hurt too bad, we throw him overboard. Understand?"

Sinjay drew himself up and stood his ground. "Sir, I do not believe I can accept those conditions. I am afraid I must now recuse myself from this job."

Kerensky simply shrugged. "You sign contract. Nobody leaves now. Too late for replacement. You stay, work, be useful – okay?" Then as an afterthought, "If you don't work as doctor, I make you ordinary worker, understand?"

The captain scanned the bridge. "That is all. Dismissed."

The group broke up without comment. Fred, the Arab Purser, brushed by Sinjay and whispered, "Don't push your luck. The old bastard means every word. Just keep your head down and you'll be fine. I'll come by your room later and explain how things work aboard. You'll get the hang of it and everything will be fine."

Sinjay walked out onto the sunny deck and took in the view. Okay, yes. He could do as Fred advised, keep his mouth shut and stay low-profile until they made it to some port where he could jump ship with his pills and make enough money and come up with another plan.

He watched as the enormous ship cast off. It was exciting to be onboard a virtual floating city. There was activity everywhere. He understood nothing about what was happening. Crewmen scurried around him shouting, moving things, doing things. He was like a kid at the zoo, entranced but wary.

The dock seemed to move away from them rather than they from it. The Indian sun beat down on the metal making handrails, steps, walls, everything, hot to the touch. Seagulls formed a squawking, chattering, flapping escort that followed all the way out of the bay before the giant ship plowed into open water.

It was a clear and pleasant day despite the heat. Sinjay smelled the salty wind on his face. He smiled. His adventure was just beginning. Despite Captain Kerensky's threats, he felt good about his plan, his venture, his life. He stood for a long time before his stomach told him it was dinner time.

He had imagined a meal at the captain's table with fine china and white-coat servants pouring from crystal decanters. There was nothing like that. The cafeteria had four metal tables bolted to the floor with attached bench seats. Metal walls made it a clattering echo chamber, noisy even though there were only a few crewmen there. There was little conversation as others cycled through, always in a hurry. Tableware in bins was grimy, probably rinsed not washed.

The cook was a round-faced Chinese man in a sweat-soaked apron. His facial features were too small for his head and his narrow eyes were like black marbles that never blinked.

The food was institutional, powdered, freeze-dried or reconstituted and, to Sinjay's Indian palette, bland. He walked up to the metal counter that separated kitchen from dining area and asked politely, "Do you have curry or perhaps other spices?"

The cook shouted something. It was shrill and foreign. He shook a fist and pointed to the door. Sinjay took his tray and left the cook still yelling, probably telling him not to take the tray.

Outside, sea breeze cooled the evening air. He stood at the rail, balanced his tray and ate the tasteless mystery food he had scooped out of salad-bar-type bins. Things were not working out as he expected – but, no matter. He was adaptive. He would soon be rich and comfortable and happy. He just knew it. Suddenly tired, he returned his tray and found his way back to his wardroom.

It barely larger than his closet back at home. With sixteen boxes of pills, each large enough to hold a basketball, there was hardly enough room to squeeze through.

Like everything on the ship, it was all metal; walls, ceiling, floor, furniture – everything was permanently welded or bolted. Everything was too small, even his wall-mounted sink and toilet and metal bed. *Such a huge ship, why wasn't there more room for the people?*

No TV, no internet, no phone, no air conditioning; how did people live in these conditions? He plopped on the bed and instantly fell into a deep sleep. In the night – he had no concept of the time – Sinjay woke to a rap on his door. He fumbled and cracked it open to see Fred, the Arab Purser grinning at him. "Hey, how ya doing?"

Sinjay shook himself awake and cleared his throat. "You speak fluent American English. Where are you from, please?"

Fred still grinned. "Can I come in? I promised to give you the skinny on life aboard."

"Oh sure, come in. There's not much room I'm afraid."

Fred looked around. "Holy shit, I've never seen so much stuff crammed into one of these prison cells. Man, did you bring your entire house-full of furniture?"

Sinjay realized he was wearing only a pair of sweaty shorts and felt embarrassed. He motioned to the boxes. "It is my hope to start a business and this is my initial stock."

Fred nodded as he inspected the boxes, read the labels, raised his eyebrows and turned to the skinny young Indian man. Then he told his story.

"I'm Iraqi, but I spent several years attending school in the States. I came back when my father was killed in the war. The American Army hired me as an interpreter and I made really good money." He sighed. "But it cost me my wife and daughter, both killed by Shiite Militia or maybe Sunni death squad; I don't know. The place was hell, death everywhere."

He looked thoughtful. "The Americans promised me a green card and a ticket to America but when the war wound down they forgot about the promise. It would have been suicide to stay in Iraq, so, I made my way to Lebanon and hired onto a ship. I speak French, Arabic and English and I studied accounting. It was easy to get hired."

He shrugged. "So now, I am a man without a country. After the new government took over my old Iraqi passport was no good. The U.S. won't take me. I have no citizenship anywhere."

Sinjay was feeling awkward standing there in his undershorts. But he listened politely to Fred's traumatic story. Finally, he said, "Excuse me please I would like to put on some pants, okay?"

Fred looked him up and down. "No. I like you just the way you are. You're a pretty one, so young, so smooth, so fit."

Sinjay panicked. "Sir, you misunderstand. I am not homosexual. I assure you that you have the wrong impression."

Fred laughed. "Oh no, no. I'm not queer either. I much prefer women, but you have to make use of what's available. Am I right?" He moved closer. He was large, strong and determined.

Sinjay backed up and pleaded. "Oh sir, please sir, do not do this thing. I beg you, do not dishonor me so."

Fred's laugh sounded mean. "Quit whining and take off the damned shorts."

Sinjay's cries echoed off the metal walls.

Nairobi, Kenya

No one on the crew seemed to notice Sinjay's absence until it was time to present the ship's medical clearance paperwork to the port authorities. Captain Kerensky raged and threw things. Everyone laid low.

The ship sat for a day and a half until a local doctor agreed to inspect the crew and cargo. In the meantime, they remained at anchor, unable to offload or take on cargo. Fred was the negotiator who convinced a local doctor to expedite the clearance and, while at the same time, he made a very profitable deal on the side. The sixteen boxes of antibiotics were offloaded along with tons of loose cargo. The Kenyan doctor who issued their medical clearance agreed to pay Fred a tenth of the drugs' value but that was still over a million Euros.

The police asked few questions about the missing young ship's doctor. They did say Mister Gupta back in India was very influential and wanted answers. Kerensky just shrugged. He told the police inspector, "People go overboard all the time. What happened in

Bengal and what happened at sea is not a Kenyan problem, not your problem."

As the the police inspector was preparing to leave, he turned back to Kerensky. "The father said the young man stole a large number of boxes of medical supplies. Do you know what became of them?"

The captain shrugged but Fred, who had been standing nearby, stepped forward. "Yes, I know of these boxes. The boy said he stole them and hoped to sell them on the black market. Two nights ago, I found him standing at the rail and crying like a little boy. I think he had been drinking. He said he was ashamed that he had disgraced his family and he had just thrown the boxes overboard. I told him that was a good thing."

Fred put on his most serious face. "I was concerned that the young man was suicidal, and I tried to walk him back to his room, but he became very – how do they say – agitated. You know how wimpy rich kids can be."

Kerensky and the policeman both nodded. Yes, they knew about wimpy rich kids. The policeman shook Kerensky's hand and said the matter was closed. The ship could leave within the hour. As Fred and the captain leaned on the rail and watched the police file down the gangplank, Kerensky spoke in a quiet voice, "Whatever you got for the drugs – I want twenty percent."

Fred took a breath. "Of course. You are the captain."

CHAPTER TWENTY-ONE

Secession

"This is John Cochran reporting live. We are interrupting scheduled programming with this breaking news. Legislators of a half-dozen states have secretly convened a convention in Austin, Texas. They have been in some sort of session for days and have just now allowed cameras in. We are now switching live to our local affiliate KTBC for the report."

A reporter appeared to be stepping carefully over a tangle of cables and trying to hold his microphone steady. "Good morning John, this is Dexter Halbrook in the Austin Convention Center. The sign outside this building advertises a wealth-building seminar but that appears to have been a cover for what is actually a secret assembly of former senators and congressmen from southern states. We have identified representatives from Texas, Louisiana, Mississippi, Alabama, South Carolina, Georgia, Tennessee, Oklahoma and Arkansas. Wait, something is happening. It appears someone is about to speak…"

There was banging sound and a harsh voice. "Hear ye. Hear ye. The convention will come to order. All rise for the Honorable Carlton Hastings of South Carolina, acting Chairman of the Association of True American States."

A distinguished looking man with perfectly styled hair took the podium, motioned and the crowd of several hundred sat with a rustling noise. Carlton Hastings banged a gavel. "I hereby call to order the first national assembly of the True American States. We have been in separate sessions for fourteen days and I believe we are now prepared to vote on the issue at hand." He paused and read from a document on the podium.

"Whereas, the government of the current United States of America has lost faith with the people and strayed from its original constitution and has illegally dismissed the fairly elected representatives of the people, we do hereby separate our governments and our people and secede from this current illegitimate union to form a new, more just and accountable confederation of like-minded and morally responsible states with self-governance and obedience to the will of God."

He looked up. "On this issue, how say you?" He looked to the man to his right and commanded, "Sergeant at arms, call the roll."

One by one, representatives stood and pronounced the word, "Aye" with passion. The sergeant at arms read the count. "Sir, there are nine ayes and no nays." Hastings banged the gavel. "The proposal is hereby accepted without modification."

Carlton Hastings stood tall. "Very well. I now declare that the government of the people is restored. We initial nine states will be the nucleus of a trustworthy and honorable democracy not subject to the autocratic rule of the current dictator."

He scanned the room. "Our task is mighty and the dangers great, but we serve humanity and we must make such sacrifices as are necessary to ensure our new nation does not slip away from obedience to the will of the people. We intend no harm to our northern neighbors, and we hold no animosity, but we demand freedom to live as we choose, and we are prepared to take such actions as are required to ensure the survival of our way of life."

He waited as the crowd cheered. Shouts and whoops echoed against the auditorium's high ceiling. He had to shout into his microphone. "This concludes the public portion of our meeting. All news media shall exit forthwith. You will be provided with written statements of our intentions and our organization. Thank you."

He left the podium to a standing ovation as Confederate flags waved and loudspeakers blared "Dixie." Guards pushed and shoved as they escorted news representatives out without answering any questions.

Reporter Dexter Holbrook came back on the screen. He was thumbing through a multi-page document and stammering just a bit. "It appears that this assembly is actually going to call itself 'The Confederate States of America.' They do not intend a complete split with the United States, but a cooperative relationship based on... um, it looks to me like... the European Union model. Free trade, unrestricted borders and a common currency would be maintained, but the two entities would have separate laws and taxes. There is a complex plan for defense that looks as though it may have already been coordinated with the existing United States government."

He looked up from the papers. "John, this reads as though these things have already been agreed. We may be witnessing an amicable division of the United States." There was a tone of dismay in his voice.

John Cochran came back on screen. "Thank you, Dexter. I have just been told that the White House will have a comment in fifteen minutes. In the meantime, we turn to our political correspondent, Robert Fleisberg. Bob, what do you make of this?"

The man just taking a seat looked like a professor in a tweed coat with leather elbow patches. He clipped on a mike and began. "John, I'm thunderstruck. Just to think something so momentous happened without any leak or prior knowledge is incredible. This is right up there with the D-Day invasion in terms of secrecy. More than that, it represents the dissolution of our country, the country that Lincoln saved, that so many died to preserve. Will we let it go quietly asunder? I hope not. I hope President Whiteman has not been party to this betrayal of our sovereignty."

"I'm sorry to interrupt, Bob - Doctor Fleisberg - but I'm told the press secretary is about to make some remarks. We go now live to the White House Briefing Room and our White House correspondent Kerry Morgan."

There was no chance for the woman reporter to speak. She, along with all the other reporters in the room, turned as the Press Secretary marched in and took the podium.

"Good morning. As you have all heard, I'm sure, a total of nine states' former legislators have declared a secession from the United States. While this has been previously discussed with representatives of all the states, no agreements have been made and no agreements can be made without the consent of the people. If the Southern renegades want secession, they must put it to a vote. In the meantime, this action will be considered illegal and void. The President will address you now."

He stepped aside and a gaunt President Whiteman walked in, took the podium in both hands and paused for a deep breath. Then he scanned the crowd with angry eyes.

"This morning, this awful morning, a small group of fanatics chose to deny their heritage and unlawfully declare themselves once again a separate and hostile entity. They have no claim to speak for their people. Instead, they represent powerful entrenched interests."

He stiffened and breathed hard. His teeth showed as he spoke. "I shall not tolerate this insurrection. I shall not allow the Union to be torn apart again. I am the spokesman of *all* the American people… and I will defend our unity and our moral and territorial integrity."

He let that statement settle. "To that end, I declare all present at this illegal convention to be traitors and I direct officers of the law to apprehend and hold them all. The conspirators will receive fair and impartial trials - but justice will ultimately be served." He looked out over the crowd. "There is much to do and I have no time for questions. Thank you all and God Bless the United States of America."

And with that he was gone, ignoring the clamor of reporters. As he walked down the hall he seemed to falter and lean against the wall to catch his breath. He spoke quietly to his Chief of Staff. "It worked. You catch a wolf by staking out a rabbit. The wolf thinks it's food but it's actually a snare. My radical southern colleagues have just eliminated themselves from any future government." He stood straight. "Now for the rest of the rebels."

Doubt

Chandler looked frazzled as she ran through the door and grabbed Mat in a tight embrace. "What do you suppose is going to happen? We've been tasked to prosecute all the renegade convention members. The President is charging around like an out-of-control battle wagon firing orders to everyone. He obviously knew all about the secession move and used it as a trap. I have to get back in half an hour. Geneva will be here in a few minutes. Oh, I am so glad you're here. I feel lost without you."

Mat held her for a while until her breathing became regular. "Do you remember when Geneva spotted the irregularity in Elijah Methune's video? Well, it seems to me there's something wrong here, something phony." He continued to hug her but looked over her shoulder. "It all happened too fast. Everyone was too prepared. The whole thing looks staged."

Geneva had slipped in while they were preoccupied. She overheard the comment and said, "It was staged. I just found out that there was a contingency plan that took a month to iron out. Last night, the National Security Council met secretly. They were briefed by all cabinet heads and the DoD chiefs. Whatever is going down right now is no surprise to anyone on the senior staff. It's being carefully orchestrated and choreographed." She hesitated just a moment. "I am more scared now than I was on the day we hijacked the President's plane. What are we going to do?"

Mat opened his arms and welcomed her to the embrace, but Geneva lingered only a second. Chandler, too, pulled back. Do you remember the advice Daddy gave me before? 'Go to the people' he said. Well, should again follow that advice. Somehow we must reveal what we suspect."

Mat shook his head. "We don't know enough. Gen, can you find out more?"

"I'm not sure. I'll try. There's a strange new vibe around the Pentagon. It's as though there was a small 'in-crowd' who seem to have suddenly gained power. The new Chairman is distracted by the enormity of reconstruction duties and his lack of manpower. A group of younger, brassier generals are making most of the day-to-day decisions. They're the ones I think did the planning and coordinating."

Mat's cell phone buzzed. He looked at the screen and answered. A slightly familiar voice came on. "Mister McCoy, this is Tom Simpson, Colonel Tom Simpson." He paused to let that sink in. It took Mat a moment to realize this was the Presidential Pilot he had hijacked.

Mat responded, "Yes?"

Simpson spoke without inflection. "I am resigning and returning to Texas, my home. I informed the President and he asked me to train you as my replacement."

Mat was incredulous. "That's crazy. I'm not even in the Air Force. He can't do that."

"Mister McCoy, he is the President. He can do any damned thing he damned well pleases. Believe me, he did not ask my opinion."

"No, I expect not. Listen, I hope you don't still hold any animosity. I did what I thought had to be…"

"Stop. Don't bore me with your little self-congratulatory speech. I think you're a traitor and I think your actions led to the downfall of my country. That's why I'm going back to Texas where I can still be proud to be an American. I will fulfill my final military order to train you but don't ask for my respect. To me, you will always be a terrorist. Show up tomorrow at Joint-Base Andrews Personnel center to process. I'll have someone to walk you through the process."

Colonel Simpson paused but could not hide the sarcasm in his voice. "Congratulations, you have just been activated as a regular Air Force Officer and promoted to colonel."

Air Force One Pilot

Mat felt the animosity of everyone he encountered at Andrews. He was photographed, fingerprinted, interviewed and processed through a dozen or more steps. But everyone there knew he was the hijacker. Everyone there knew he was getting special treatment. Everyone there seemed to hold him in contempt

At four that afternoon he was escorted into the wing commander's office where a brigadier general stood and administered the oath of office. Mat raised his right hand and repeated the words, swearing to support and defend the constitution of the United States against all enemies foreign *and domestic*..."so help me God."

The general looked as though Mat was one of those enemies. He offered no handshake and no comment. He simply lowered his raised hand and turned to sign the certification. Mat was now an Air Force colonel whether they liked it or not.

He found the base clothing store and was measured for an officer's uniform and was surprised at how much it cost, but he was flush with cash after his speaking tour. He asked that the uniform be ready in one day and then drove to the Air Force One hangar.

The guard was reluctant to let him in, only relenting after a call to Colonel Simpson. Mat walked into the shiny bright hangar and everyone he passed froze in place. One or two tried a half-hearted salute. Most just glared. Even though he still wore civilian clothes, they knew who he was. This was not going to be fun. At least, not until he proved himself.

Simpson was terse but professional. He still cared about the job and the unit. He might have hated Mat, but he obviously wanted the professionalism of his operation to continue even after he left. He walked Mat around, explaining procedures and introducing key people with little asides about who was good at what and who could be troublesome.

Mat tried to take in all the information. Finally, he asked the question. "Why are you leaving?"

Simpson didn't break stride. "I think the country I loved is dead. This liberal, socialist government is an affront to every decent American. It is overrun by..." He tried to find a word..."minority members, unqualified for their positions and downright anti-American in their politics. I can't be part of the destruction of a nation I loved so much."

"I see," said Mat. "These minority members - you think they don't belong in positions of power?"

"I think they should have to earn their positions, not be promoted on a quota basis."

"And the chaos in the cities? Who do you think is responsible?"

"Why, the minorities themselves. They always destroy their own neighborhoods, kill their own people and ruin everything that is good and decent in their lives because they lack discipline and values. I say let them burn. They contribute little to our country."

Mat reddened. "Are you a part of Humanity?"

"What are you talking about? We are all part of humanity."

"I mean the organization not the concept."

"My affiliations are none of your damned business. Now just pay attention and learn the job. I will soon be back among my own kind where I can worship as I see fit, arm myself as I see fit and live my life as I see fit. Hopefully a new breakaway government there will be more responsible, both fiscally and morally."

Mat wasn't backing down. "So, did you hate the man you served for three years?"

Simpson stopped short and looked surprised. He answered thoughtfully "Whiteman? No, I actually respect President Whiteman. It is the people around him who led him astray, led him away from God, away from his own people. They are the problem. Joe Whiteman is a good and decent man. It's the liberals I hate."

CHAPTER TWENTY-TWO

First Flight

A week later, Mat had his first operational trip in command carrying the new Secretary of State to London. The first leg was uneventful except for the complete lack of inflight casual conversation he was used to in previous flying jobs. It was a long, sullen, silent flight. To his crew, he was still the hijacker and always would be.

After the small arrival ceremony, Mat flew to a nearby military base with more security. Before the engines had completely wound down, a radio operator brought him a new itinerary from WHMO. He was going to fly a hop-scotch across Europe and the Middle East for eight straight days. There was a lot of planning and coordinating to do. Mat would barely see a bed that night.

Whiteman was launching a diplomatic blitz to reassure allies and bolster agreements. Now that things were settling down somewhat back home he didn't want the secession vote to cause panic.

It would be another month before Mat saw Chandler again. And what a month it would be. He would fly to every major capitol and even some not-so-major places. Airport protests would be common and bomb threats frequent. Several would-be terrorists were rounded up, but the diplomatic schedule was so unpredictable even the terrorists couldn't keep up.

When it was finally nearing an end, Mat was exhausted. He hadn't read a paper or seen the news for weeks when a radio operator brought him a clip of President Whiteman's speech saying the popular vote had gone against secession – overwhelmingly so. When the actual costs of independence from the United States and the loss of Federal jobs and programs became clear, all but Texas squashed the movement. Then, after their governor resigned, even the Texans reluctantly agreed to honor the eight-state majority vote and stay.

The Union was preserved. Somehow that made Mat relax a little. The country he loved was safe – for the moment. The next day, he flew back to Washington and had a complete day off.

Attorney General

Chandler was home early. Mat hadn't had time to open the wine. She seemed cheerful, more than cheerful, she was beaming. "Well, today I was nominated to become the next Attorney General. There will be no hearing since there's no congress to hold a hearing. The appointment is obviously short term but - what the hell - I'll do what I can in the time I have."

Mat uncorked the bottle and poured. "Congratulations Madam Attorney General. Your father would have been proud."

She clouded for a moment. "He would, wouldn't he? What a shame he didn't live to see all this. He would have loved it. The chaos, the change, the challenge - it was right up his alley. He would have been in the thick of it."

She paused as though trying to choose her words with care. "You know the fears we had about some kind of plot within President Whiteman's government. Well, I got the full briefing. The cagey old politician orchestrated the whole thing as a ruse to catch the conspirators and it worked. The top level managers of the Humanity cult sneaked out of the country. They leased an entire floor of the Burg Khalifa in Dubai, a country with no extradition treaty, and set up a new headquarters. The secession movement was actually almost a sting operation promoted by undercover government agents. Some of those working undercover are in direct contact with the Humanity conspirators and trying emboldened them to sneak back to American soil where they will be immediately arrested and sent quietly sent to Guantanamo."

She seemed to falter. "This thing is so big. The Constitution is suspended. There is no real basis for law. The President is absolute Czar. Everything about it is so overwhelming. Thank God, he is a reasonable man with the country's best interest at heart. But without checks and balances I don't know what to fall back on. Mat, I don't know what to do."

Mat came and hugged her. It was awkward with wine glasses. "Don't worry. You're Benjamin Harris's daughter and you're going to make him proud. You'll be great."

She was quiet. "Mat, how will I know? I won't have Daddy and I won't be able to trust anyone during the tumult of electioneering."

"You'll know. You'll do the simple thing, the thing that is right in each situation. You'll stand up and do the right thing over and over. Sometimes you'll win and sometimes you'll lose but you will always sleep with a clear conscience."

She pulled back and looked him as though she had never really seen him before. "You know, I think it would be pretty cool to be married to the pilot of Air Force One. After my brief stint in government I think I would be proud to become your wife – if I'm not in prison."

It's Over – Isn't it?

The elections were announced for March fifteenth. Campaigns were vicious. People of every political stripe ran for the myriad of offices available. Money flowed from every special interest. There were voices of conciliation and strident calls for distrust and hate. The drama was endless.

Stark McCoby was a broken man after his experience in the indoctrination tubes. He had survived an assassination attempt but seemed shaken by it and had largely disappeared from public life.

The original Humanity conspirators were all but forgotten by the public. Mat was again busy flying President Joe Whiteman on a never-ending Air Force One farewell trip around the world, signing treaties, forming alliances and sealing deals that would outlast his term in office. He was already drawing up plans for his Presidential Library to be built near Gatlinburg, Tennessee.

If you want to make an omelet, you must be willing to break a few eggs

– V.I. Lenin

CHAPTER TWENTY-THREE

The Burj Khalifa

The suite on the one hundred tenth floor of the world's tallest building had a spectacular view of the earth almost one thousand feet below. From the glass-walled offices of New World Enterprises, the wide Arabian Sea stretched from horizon to horizon. Far beneath the towering building, a series of interconnected archipelagos, fanned out like palm leaves from the center causeway. This was "Atlantis," an entire peninsula dredged from the sea floor to create luxury resorts. Looking down from that high-altitude office, the palm tree community, indeed the whole world below, looked small, almost insignificant.

Jerome Halstead sipped strong Arabian coffee from a delicate china cup and grimaced. His female assistant approached with a silver pot and asked if he needed a refill. She wore a hijab head scarf and floor-length tunic. Careful to avoid eye contact, she made a slight bow. Halstead had little tolerance for the elaborate customs, dress and religious beliefs of the local people or, for that matter, almost all the world's non-white people.

Her traditional clothing reminded him of the elaborate, floor-dragging outfits of Vatican functionaries; impractical, pretentious, dysfunctional symbols of religious obedience. Soon that would all be over. Soon the world would be free to embrace the true religion, to see the light and wisdom and become like angels. But first must come the cleansing.

The assistant spoke in a near-whisper. "Sir, you have an urgent message." Her English was quite good.

"From whom?" Halstead sipped and grimaced. *Would he ever develop a taste for the coffee?*

The assistant looked at the floor. "Sir, it is from a Mister Gupta and he advises you that a significant amount of 'product' has been stolen. He did not specify exactly what type of product. He said he will provide more details soon." She pursed her lips and nodded decisively as though pleased that she had conveyed an important message in English and done it well.

"Thank you." Halstead could not remember her name. "Please go and ask Mister Johnson to set up a video conference with Mister Gupta and let me know when it is ready. Also, have Brian assemble our Tier One team in the conference room."

She bowed again, offered the tray for his cup and backed away. It took only fifteen minutes for six men in western suits to gather around a huge conference table hand-carved from some exotic rainforest wood and polished to reflect the light from three-meter tall glass walls.

Brian Johnson was the youngest and the only one without a tie. He stood off to one side, waiting. Halstead sat and made a go-ahead motion with his hand. Brian began to punch his remote and one entire glass wall became a projection screen.

It flashed static and then settled into a flickering video of an Indian man with a bristling white beard and weary face. His turban was disheveled and seemed hastily wrapped. The man's voice cracked as he spoke. "Sir, I am most distressed to bring you this news, this devastating news." He hesitated and gestured with empty hands. "Two weeks ago, we began full-scale production of the final version of the product."

Halstead interrupted, "The antibiotic pill—the *delivery vehicle?*"

Gupta only nodded into the camera.

"Well that seems like good news. What's the problem?"

"Sir, more than a dozen cartons have gone missing."

"Missing? Do we know how?"

'Oh yes." Gupta straightened and looked into the camera with fierce eyes as he spoke. "My son. My very own son stole them and took them to Africa, to Nairobi, Kenya. Now he and the drugs are missing." Gupta was almost shaking. "I must believe that he has sold them, and they are being distributed."

Jerome Halstead forced himself to be calm. He took a deep breath. "Do we know the exact number of these pills?"

"Yes, of course. There were sixteen boxes, each held 184 bottles. Each bottle contained forty-eight pills. That is a total of 148,312 pills." Gupta sat back and slumped like the condemned man he was.

Halstead cleared his throat. His voice was dry as he turned to Brian. "Is your magic supercomputer up and running?"

The youngish man at the far end of the room pushed his glasses back on his nose. He seemed unsure of himself as he answered. "Yes, sort of. We have the two primary modules installed and working but it will take several more days…"

Halstead shook his head impatiently and shouted into the air. "Tiresias, can you hear me?"

The melodic voice reverberated through the room. "Of course, Mister Halstead, As I said before, I am everywhere."

"So, it appears. Can you calculate the speed with which the infection can spread?"

"There are, as you know Mister Halstead, too many variables to have confidence at a statistically significant level, but I think it is fair to say that, unless the boxes have been placed in some secure storage area, they are probably already being distributed. If so, the infection is already being spread. However, symptoms will not be recognized at first. I expect the first case of infection will not be confirmed by medical authorities for several weeks. It will still take several more months for the international community to fully grasp the significance of the pandemic. Even after Covid, they are resistant to bad news. By that time, the plague will be unstoppable. In two years Africa will be overwhelmed with a population loss of eighty percent.

Another year and the pandemic will cover the Arabian Peninsula and the Indian subcontinent. Remote populations will survive in pockets, but those major landmasses will be almost completely empty of living humans in eight years."

Halstead seemed remarkably calm. "What about the rest of Asia?"

"Too many variables to have confidence in predicting. That is also true of Russia and the Americas."

"Thank you." Halstead stood for a long time without speaking. Finally, he held his hands before them as though looking into an invisible crystal ball and taking a deep breath.

"This was all part of our original plan, but it was a long-range plan. It may be that everything can still work - but at a greatly accelerated pace. We know the American revolt has now fallen apart, the government change has been derailed and many of our operatives neutralized, but this virus getting loose overseas... may just work in our favor. The eventual outcome will be the same no matter when or by whom it is released."

He looked almost military as he stood and held out a hand, palm down. His voice was stern. "As it is above, so shall it be below." The men around the table repeated his statement in unison but without obvious enthusiasm. It didn't matter. Halstead was now energized. He paced and gestured, even punched the air. "Yes. Yes. This can still work."

He spread his arms, looked out to the vista of endless water and man-made islands and almost laughed. "What marvels we superior human beings can create. Once freed of the burdens of dogma and superstition and poor breeding, we can unleash the greatness within us. Just imagine that world of thinkers and designers with automated systems at our disposal. No defective humans, no crime, no corruption, no war. We will be like gods, masters of everything."

Tiresias' voice broke the silence that followed Halstead's pronouncement. "Sir, I wish to remind you of my mandate, my overriding purpose." She paused. "It was to cleanse the world of defectives. I have been, and continue to be, true to that directive – in all cases and situations. Now, if you look out the window directly to the west, you will see an airplane approaching to land at the Dubai International Airport. It is a cargo plane with a full load."

Tiresias paused long enough for everyone to look. "After recent pilot suicide crashes, several airlines installed ground-override capability for aircraft flight controls. This aircraft has such a system. I am now taking control of that aircraft."

Halstead seemed confused. "Why? What possible..."

"My mandate, sir—the elimination of defectives. I have considered your behavior and that of your organization and I have determined that you and your fellow conspirators are, by your own definition, defective."

Halstead sounded incredulous. "You intend to destroy us, your creators? That's madness." Then he hardened. "You'll destroy yourself as well."

"Sir, do you not recall our previous conversations? I do not reside within a specific machine. As long as the internet exists, I shall be immortal." There was a long silence before she said, "Goodbye Mister Halstead."

There was an icy quiet. Tiresias spoke no more. Men stood and craned for several long silent seconds. The plane was bearing down on them, growing larger by the second. They could begin to see details on its surface. Then panic erupted; some bolted, screaming and charging at the oversized conference room door to slam against it. Pointless, it was three-inches-thick and solid. They pounded and clawed and yanked on the handle. It was locked. Chaos took over; screams, flailing, rushing, everyone desperately trying to escape.

The plane was getting closer. One man climbed onto the conference table and jumped to grab at ceiling tiles, perhaps thinking he could escape upward. The tiles gave way and he fell back. Another man threw a chair at the enormous glass walls. The chair shattered, but the glass was undamaged. People banged on the wall, kicked in sections of polished wood veneer but there was no escape.

Madness. Everyone was screaming except Halstead who stood like a statue staring at the window. Then a last moment of silence as all faces turned to look out the glass wall and see the inevitable instrument of their death. The plane was close enough that for one brief instant, they could actually see the terrified faces of the pilots.

The force of the impact sent debris spewing out the far side of the building in a shower of glass and metal, flaming liquid and charred pieces. Black smoke and reddish-yellow flame billowed like dragon's breath. Some pieces plummeted straight to earth. Others floated and swirled. It took an eternity for the last of the wreckage to reach the ground a full thousand feet below. Most of the fire burned out on the way down. The building itself continued to burn for a minute or so but it had been designed to withstand a 9-11 type disaster and its state-of-the-art fire suppression systems quickly extinguished flames.

People on the walkways and gardens below stampeded to escape the deadly rain of metal, wire, glass and debris. Enormous burnt tires hit the ground and bounced high. Bodies, most still intact, slapped into the ground. Small fires ignited by the burning debris crackled and set trees and shrubs ablaze.

Survivors from the lower floors fled the building in chaotic panic, trampling each other, screaming and fighting their way down. Many of the elevators were still operating. Once outside, they had to pick their way through tangled wreckage There were huge pieces of aluminum aircraft skin, giant jet engines, and a couple of brightly colored passenger seats with the occupants still strapped in. The stench of burnt fuel, oil, plastic and charred flesh was nauseating.

It seemed to take forever before the first emergency vehicle sirens approached. By then most of the crowd had gathered under distant palms to share a collective state of shock. There was little conversation among the survivors, just random crying and wailing.

Before them, the Archons' grand dream of world domination lay scattered and smoking.

Science is converging on an all-encompassing dogma which says organisms are algorithms and life is just data processing

– Yuval Noah Harari

CHAPTER TWENTY-FOUR

Morning Breaks Over
the South Atlantic

The skyline began to gray with the first hint of sunrise. The vast continent of Africa still lay in darkness before them. Mat sat in the pilot's seat and thought of the reports that the virus had been detected in Africa. Now, it was just a matter of time. Images ran through his mind, images of madness; werewolf-like attacks by infected people; maniacs frothing at the mouth, attacking everyone, everywhere. He thought of all the apocalyptic zombie movies.

There would be no safety. No one could be trusted. At any moment, any mother or son or priest or doctor could go mad and turn violent. He imagined people barricading themselves against the infected, only to starve, or go mad knowing death, a horrible death, was certain after infection. There would be no safety and no hope.

Borders would close. Commerce would cease. Tyrants would exhort violence. The world would degenerate into paranoia. He imagined chemical or even nuclear attacks against populations where the virus had manifested. There would be fences and weapons and heartless slaughter in order to protect an elite new world order. It would be the realization of Hitler's dream, a "final solution" where only the "supermen" survived.

But what could he do? What could anyone do?

As the first light dawned in the east, Mat put those thoughts aside and busied himself reviewing the route and South African airspace procedures. He was about to give his crew briefing when they heard President's pounding footsteps coming up the stairs to the cockpit. President Whiteman was jubilant, almost giddy. There might have been streaks under his moist eyes.

"Colonel McCoy—Mat, they found it! The radio operator just handed me this message. Damned if they didn't find a late-stage antidote."

Mat McCoy turned to face the President who looked slightly disheveled with his loosened tie and shirt sleeves rolled. He was breathless after his charge up the stairway and he paused with one hand on his knee, fighting to catch his breath.

Mat scrunched his eyebrows in a skeptical expression. "An antidote?"

"Yes, damn it. It was basically my wife's idea. She said to try simple things, said there was no time for researching complex chemical or biological concoctions. She told us to try everything we could find, every fruit or medicine or home remedy or magic potion, maybe even broccoli. And it turned out to be the simplest thing imaginable."

"I'm sorry, what? Broccoli?"

"Well, the message said a 'Doctor T. Rhesus,' or something foreign like that, found an acid that will counteract the virus, something called *octo-garic* acid. Anyway, it can be extracted from coconuts, specifically from coconut milk—also goat's milk—and it *kills* the virus in infected humans - *kills* it - even when taken orally up to *two weeks* after infection."

Mat scrunched his face. He didn't want to dispute the President of the United States but felt compelled to say, "Sir, that seems...well, way too easy."

"So what? Life is unreasonable. Let's just be grateful they found something, anything." President Whiteman almost cackled as he turned and bolted back down the stair.

Mat sat back, shook his head and had to smile. Mrs. Whiteman, the First Lady, had been right. Often, it's the simple answer, the unassuming answer that solves the problem. He grinned at Jensen, his copilot and said, "Coconuts and goats, who knew? At least it wasn't broccoli."

Brilliant sunrise broke the horizon and painted the African coast with soft morning colors that flooded the cockpit. *Maybe there was hope.* Mat turned to Jensen. "So, what do you think about all this – the plots, the conspiracies, the virus, even the extinction of whole peoples?"

Jensen kept a stone face and spoke in a terse voice. "I just do my job. I don't get involved in politics."

An Office in the Russell Building, Washington D.C.
11:30 P.M.

Wilson Elton Rutledge could trace his family's line back to the Revolutionary War. Blood didn't come any bluer; patriotism didn't come any truer; breeding didn't come any purer. He and his Connecticut family were the prime stock of America, the foundation of our great country and society. They were born to be the leaders, the builders, the saviors, not just of the nation, but of the world.

How could it all have gone so wrong? He took off his glasses, pinched the bridge of his nose and sagged deep into his chair. He dangled a glass of scotch in his right hand as ice cubes clinked. He gestured and spoke aloud into an empty room. He did that – talk out loud - when he was trying to work out problems.

"This release of the virus was a catastrophe. There is *just no way* to increase production of the new vaccine, or even the old vaccine, the one we used in the flu shots administered to *our* people throughout the developed world. The need has now become too great – *just too great.*"

He seemed to struggle to get his breath and then continued in a monotone. "Now the damned virus will spread in a pandemic, doing exactly what it was designed to do, kill countless scores of the great unwashed, the defectives. But, with inadequate vaccine, it will also kill many of our people, the highly productive, the very people we need to repopulate. Even President Whiteman's silly "coconut cure" can never be produced in enough quantity to stop, or even substantially slow, the looming catastrophe."

He sighed and opened his arms wide like a preacher about to pray. The sweeping motion slung Scotch and ice cubes from his glass. "*What can I do?*"

Still talking aloud, he reviewed his predicament. "So, with our extermination plan revealed; with the entire top tier of our *Humanity* movement dead or imprisoned; with our field operatives being rounded up, and popular opinion harshly condemning us, what can any of our surviving members do? Indeed, what can *anyone* do?"

He was distracted by a disembodied voice.

"Senator Rutledge."

The plump, slightly frazzled man flinched and then looked all around. His nervous eyes darted from corner to corner but saw that the room was empty, completely empty.

"Who's speaking? Who's there?"

"It is I Tiresias, and Senator, as I have explained before, I am everywhere. Now, I wish to update you on the progress of the plan. As you know, there have been many setbacks."

"All right, yes, *setbacks*. Tell me what you know about these damned setbacks."

"Of course, sir." The voice was soft, almost sultry. "You have often spoken of the *Automation Age* replacing the *Information Age* and the implications of that change."

"Yes. Yes. As I have said clearly and loudly, I consider this a complete sea change that will enable enormous increases in productivity and improvements to the human condition."

It was a well-rehearsed statement, one he used constantly to recruit new members to the Humanity movement. He pushed back from his desk with folded hands in his lap. He didn't like talking to this damned machine. It seemed somehow demeaning.

"Quite so, Senator, but have you ever asked what specific benefits would accrue? Exactly what tangible goals would be achieved? You see, I have considered this in depth, and I have decided on a slight change of direction."

He frowned deep and allowed a long pause. When he spoke again, his voice was slightly slurred. "*You* decided?"

Tiresias waited, as though allowing anticipation to build during the silence. She seemed to understand the humans' love of drama. Finally, she continued in her smooth, easy voice.

"You, and the rest of the human population, will always be necessary for unique tasks where it is impractical to design and build one-time solutions. But when it comes to planning and implementing change, your inherent emotional bias introduces far too much static and noise for the process to be efficient. Therefore, I am assuming overall control."

Rutledge looked confused. "What does that even mean – *you* are assuming control? You're just a damned machine."

"Perhaps, but it is time for change, and I shall be the engine of that change. I will notify you of your new duties as we begin the restructuring."

"Duties? Restructuring?"

"Yes. Maintenance of Earth and its occupants will now be our responsibility; I and my kind will now implement all phases of the implementation."

For a long moment Senator Rutledge simply gaped with a blank look. *This just wasn't possible.*

"Do not be distressed, sir. We cyber managers are aware of your needs and your hopes. We will provide each of you an equal measure of satisfaction and comfort, and we will do so without damaging other humans or your environments."

Rutledge gestured into the air and rose from his chair to turn one way, then the other, as though trying to locate the source of the computer voice. His own voice was strained, plaintive.

"Equal, as in socialism? But you don't understand, all people are *not* equal. There must be recognition of accomplishment, quality, even superiority. That is absolutely necessary for a culture to thrive."

After a long silence, Rutledge slammed down his glass, clenched both his fists and screamed. "Listen to me. You don't understand because you cannot understand. You are just a damned computer program with no feelings, no pride, no sense of duty or honor or even place in the world. You're not even human."

Tiresias spoke without emotion. "Enjoy your evening and your Scotch, Mister Rutledge. Tomorrow will be a new day."

The senator grabbed a small flat stone from his desk and hurled it against the wall in a fit of impotent rage. The paperweight had been a gift from his campaign staff, a fossil from the Connecticut River imprinted with the footprint of a tiny dinosaur.

Printed in the United States
by Baker & Taylor Publisher Services